PRAISE F

"Shirley not only brings Africa to life but immerses you in a world of both beauty and peril. A gripping story about justice, truth, and the cost of standing up for what you believe in."

— USA TODAY'S BEST-SELLING AUTHOR
SUSAN MAY WARREN

"Loved this book! Such a great, clean romantic novel and suspenseful too. I couldn't put it down. I love the spiritual side of it too. Can't wait till her next book comes out."

— JEANNE TAKENAKA MBT AUTHOR,
WINNER OF THE FRAISER AWARD

"Do you enjoy books that are set outside of the U.S. and getting to see a new part of the world through as author's words? If you answered yes, then I have a book for you. The Sahar of Zanzibar by Shirley Gould takes readers to the island of Zanzibar off the coast of Tanzania.

Gould gives readers a taste of what both the missionary life and the vacationer's life are like including the sights, struggles, and resorts. There were moments of suspense, but this novel leans heavier on the romance side of romantic suspense. It's a unique location with a look at the beauty and struggles of life in Zanzibar."

— SUZIE WALTNER, AUTHOR OF MIDNIGHT
BLUE

"With the current world climate, I'm in no hurry to travel abroad. The Sahar of Zanzibar allowed me to experience adventure on an exotic island from the safety of my cozy chair.

This story is a delightful romantic suspense, an exciting tale of trusting our best-laid plans to the only One who can give us hope and a future. What's not to love?"

— DONNA YARBOROUGH, ASPIRING
AUTHOR

"This is a 'must read' if you like good, clean romance novels with a twist of suspense. The unusual setting also makes this a fun read! This is one of my favorite books to date and I have been a reader for 40+ years. The author did a great job of being descriptive without making me want to skip over the details as I do in some books. Fantastic book!!"

— SMITTY, AN AVID READER OF CHRISTIAN FICTION

ESCAPE
from
TIMBUKTU

THE AFRICAN SKIES SERIES

SHIRLEY GOULD

Scrivenings
PRESS
Quench your thirst for story.
www.ScriveningsPress.com

Copyright © 2023 by Shirley Gould

Published by Scrivenings Press LLC
15 Lucky Lane
Morrilton, Arkansas 72110
https://ScriveningsPress.com

Printed in the United States of America

Paperback ISBN 978-1-64917-311-9

eBook ISBN 978-1-64917-312-6

Editors: Shannon Taylor Vannatter and Linda Fulkerson

Cover by Linda Fulkerson - www.bookmarketinggraphics.com

This is a work of fiction. Unless otherwise indicated, all names, characters, businesses, events, and incidents are either the product of the author's imagination or used in a fictitious manner. Any resemblance to actual persons, living or dead, or actual events is purely coincidental.

All other scriptures are taken from the KING JAMES VERSION (KJV): KING JAMES VERSION, public domain.

To JR

I'm so blessed to have been loved by you.
You treated me like a queen and called me your lady.
You believed in me
and encouraged me to reach for the stars.
You supported my dreams
of being a published author.
Writing suspense takes me back
to the adventures we shared.
Now as I launch my second novel,
writing romance is easy to pen.
I just let my thoughts wander down memory lane to the amazing
love story we shared.

1

I f Ellie wanted to be boxed in, she'd have taken the CEO position at Bendale Enterprises. *Claustrophobic incorporated.* Flight attendant Elliana Bendale hurried around an African man who stood way too close and brushed against a woman's sweaty body, saturating her arm. *I want to be among the people—but not all of them at once.*

Deboarding from the late-landing flight, minutes behind two others, the mass of travelers resembled a herd of cattle being driven down Main Street in an old west town, stirring dust in their wake. With those surrounding her lacking appreciation for personal space, Ellie inched forward in the customs line as a woman with mismatched clothes and a ratty wig molded her body to Ellie's.

"Hey guys, I want to be your friend, but we Americans like our space." Talking to herself again. A bad habit.

I'd suffocate in an office. Four walls would close in, just like a trap from the Indiana Jones movies. All the more reason to land this job with *Above & Beyond Magazine.* At twenty-seven, it was time to prove herself—to make it as a photojournalist, to meet the challenges, and get the job of her dreams. Flying the African

skies opened her eyes to other options for her future—
presenting exciting opportunities—such as the one that put her
in this perspiring mob of travelers.

Ellie took the concrete stairs toward baggage claim, where a
sea of passengers moved en mass, crowding for a spot next to
the conveyor belt delivering their luggage at a snail's pace.

And I thought the airlines packed the cheap seats like sardines.
She shook her head and joined the mayhem, the chaos of
languages from several African tribes swirled through the Mali
West Africa Bamako Airport baggage claim area. With high
temperatures creating a stifling sauna effect, Ellie wished for
air-conditioning as sweat rolled down her back.

Her blonde hair, western attire, and fair skin set her apart
from the mass of curious dark-skinned passengers. Ceiling fans
stirred the heat, humidity, and odors, making breathing
difficult. Spotting her American Tourister piece between a
spray-painted metal suitcase and a dilapidated box tied with
twine, she moved closer to the luggage belt to grab it before it
disappeared in this throng of people. She couldn't lose it—her
research for this project was inside.

Squeezing through two sweaty men, Ellie attempted to
retrieve her shiny blue suitcase, but a hulk of a man with
earbuds in his ears and a phone in his hand barged through the
crowd to grab his duffle bag.

"Sir, yes, sir. My plane landed late. I'll be there before the
Embassy closes. I'm moving as fast as I can." Engrossed in his
loud phone conversation, competing with the noise of the
crowd, the swoon-worthy Frenchman reached for his bag.

His physique caught Ellie's attention. He looked to be about
thirty, with dark brown hair and steely grey eyes, the build of a
man who spent time in a gym, and a French accent that would
make a teenager drool.

When the Frenchman grabbed his duffle, Ellie's carry-on
toppled. She reached for it, colliding with him. He glanced at

her, paused, nodded his head, and gave a hint of a smile. With a small salute, he righted the piece, and trudged forward, his combat boot smashing her toes as he rushed past her.

Searing heat pierced her foot. Air whooshed from her lungs as she slapped her hand over her mouth, smothering a scream. *He. Broke. My. Toe!* With tear-filled eyes, she sat on her carry-on. While she lingered in excruciating agony, her suitcase traveled around the large block-walled, warehouse-style building. On the bag's fourth trip around, Ellie managed to stand and pull it off the belt.

She limped to the customs desk, gave the officer her passport and VISA, and waited as the steady throb worsened. Seeing the handsome toe-breaker detained in a glass-walled office for further screening by the officials, Ellie smiled. A customs officer had unloaded his duffle bag and was inspecting every pocket. *Ha!* The elephant in the room had met his match.

Stepping out of the baggage claim building, Ellie was greeted by a group of drivers holding signs with names on them. Glad to see a line of cabs filling the area with exhaust, she made her way to the curb, motioned for one, and reached for her luggage. While her back was turned, the cab door slammed. She spun around. The hunky Frenchman had stolen her cab.

"You're kidding me!" She stomped her foot and gritted her teeth as sharp throbs screamed a reminder of her injury. "Hey, that's my taxi! Who do you think you are?" Ellie raised her hands in disgust. But it was too late. A mixture of exhaust and dust from the fleeing cab burned her eyes. She wiped her eyes and hailed another taxi.

Something cold and hard pressed into her back.

"The gun is loaded. Don't make me use it." A man's harsh whisper sent a chill up her sweaty spine as he barged into her personal space and jerked her away from the curb.

Ellie stood frozen in one-hundred-degree sunshine.

"English, *monsieur*?" Beau de La Croix asked the driver.

"Yes."

"French Embassy—and hurry!" Beau looked back to make sure no one was following and saw the blonde tourist he'd passed at the luggage belt. Her eyes were wide under raised eyebrows. Was she upset?

Not every beautiful woman needs my assistance. Losing Jezelle has tainted my thinking. He ran his hand through his hair. *Keep your head in the game, de la Croix. You're on a tight schedule.* Beau lost sight of the blonde as dust rose behind the taxi.

Pulling his button-down shirt away from his skin, he tried to cool himself from the African heat. He lowered his window and tolerated the dust blowing in for a little relief.

"Looks like traffic ahead." The driver caught Beau's eyes in the rearview mirror.

"I must be there before the Embassy closes at five. Get me to the gate, and I'll double your fare." Beau wiped the sweat off his brow and hoped this bumpy road wasn't a precursor to the week ahead. His assignment, if successful, could benefit this region of the world, but if he failed, the situation could turn dangerous.

"We will arrive on time." The Malian cab driver took a detour through the crooked, rutted back streets lined with old kiosks and shanty dwellings. Motorcycles raced around them. The driver dodged children as squawking chickens took flight above the pot-holed road. An ibis cried overhead, competing with horns blaring as the smell of fresh cow dung fragranced the air.

After fifteen minutes of rough riding, avoiding donkeys and scrawny dogs, the driver jerked to a halt in front of the Embassy so fast a cloud of dirt blew toward them. Turning to his passenger, he smiled, displaying a jagged row of brown teeth.

Beau reached forward and grabbed the driver's shoulder. "You did it. Thanks." He gave him a stack of francs and slipped out of the cab.

"What?" Ellie's eyes widened as she scanned the mass of people hurrying around her, oblivious to what was happening. *I'm invisible. Someone is holding a gun to my back in broad daylight, for crying out loud!* "I'm a visitor here—a photojournalist on assignment. I don't know what you want, but—" Her hands slicked with sweat as icy dread clenched her gut. She willed herself not to throw up on the gritty sidewalk.

The man leaned forward and muttered close to her ear. "Don't say a word! Take a step back." He jabbed his weapon into her ribs with bruising force.

Ellie sucked in a breath—then stepped back as she turned her head slightly. *Where's a guard when you need one?* Getting a glimpse of his clothing, the man had to be foreign military since his camo was unlike American military uniforms. He spoke down to her, so she guessed his height to be at least six-foot. But gathering info like a reporter would not get her out of this predicament. Hypervigilant to his threats, Ellie let out the breath she'd been holding.

"Was that man Dubois?" His breath smelled of masala and strong tobacco as his scruffy beard brushed her cheek. His clothes reeked of sweat and motor oil, and the toes of his boots were worn and sandy.

Biting the inside of her mouth, she tried not to panic as her body trembled. The hubbub of taxis honking and backfiring added to her angst. "I don't know him." She paused, wanting to run, but afraid he'd shoot her. "He wasn't on my flight."

"I saw you with him. You watched him as if you knew him. Where is he going?" He pressed his gun deeper into her back.

"*Ow*." She sucked in a breath. "Since I don't know his name, I didn't ask him where he was going." Her eyes filled with tears. *Lord, help me!*

"What destination did he give the driver?" Spit flew from his mouth as he spouted his question.

"He took my taxi. I was yelling at him, so I didn't hear a word he said." She felt the press of the gun decrease slightly. The tightness of his grip on her arm lessened. "Is this how you treat all tourists who come to Mali? No wonder tourism in West Africa has dwindled. I was sent to write an article enticing tourists to visit this country." She waited—amid the airport chaos—no more questions came. She took a risk, braced herself, and turned slowly—he'd vanished.

The tall decorative iron gates guarding the ornate building opened as Beau approached the stately French Embassy. "Good to see you again, de La Croix." The uniformed guard saluted Beau. "Deputy Chief Auguste is waiting for you in his office. You can leave your bags with me and go right in." He waited for Beau to return the salute, then locked the gate.

"Great to see you too, John Paul." Beau left his duffle and backpack and entered the distinguished compound housing the Embassy.

Unaccustomed to being dressed in civilian clothes, he followed the pristine sidewalk leading to the building. Taking the steps two at a time, he entered the lobby. Its decor, with its long drapes on tall windows and elaborate paintings of Ambassadors who had served Mali in years past, looked out of place in this dusty West African country.

Beau took a right and hurried to the office of Dax Auguste, the Deputy Chief of Mission, his liaison on this assignment. In the waiting area, he stood at attention among uniformed soldiers until he was summoned.

"de La Croix, come in. I was glad when your name came up on my roster. It's been a while since our paths have crossed." Chief Dax Auguste stood and approached Beau.

"I'm glad to be back in Mali, sir." Beau saluted his superior.

The Deputy Chief returned the salute. "Your shipment has arrived. I think I have what you need." Dax Auguste, austere in his military uniform, carried himself with utmost confidence. He went back to his desk, a magnificent piece of furniture that perfectly matched the bookcases lining the room. Definitely imported from France. "Get that door for me."

After shutting the door, Beau stepped farther into the office.

The Deputy Chief opened a drawer and pressed a button unlocking a hidden compartment in the paneled wall. He ambled over and moved the panel revealing Beau's weapons before returning to his desk.

"Your orders arrived yesterday from Philippe Leroux. Keeping this photojournalist safe while completing your mission will be a juggling act. But if anyone can accomplish it, I believe you can." Auguste looked at the photo attached to Beau's orders.

"I needed a ruse, a cover story to get me into Timbuktu to carry out my assignment. It's imperative we know if terrorists are still active in the area. For Timbuktu to rebuild tourism, we must end their reign in this country. Several men were available for this mission, but I drew the short straw." Beau smirked and moved to the display of his weapons.

"You've been spending too much time in America. That sounds like one of their sayings." Auguste took a seat in his tufted leather desk chair and steepled his fingers in front of his mouth.

"Yes, a cynical cliché meaning I'm the unlucky guy who was given this grand opportunity—but if Hussein is involved, I'd volunteer for this task just to settle a score with the man." Beau smiled as he hid the armory on his person. "Besides, since I've been undercover on my last assignment, I had the look of a civilian with this long hair."

"You'd think as long as Saddam has been dead, we wouldn't still be haunted by his distant relatives," Auguste said.

The Glock fit perfectly in Beau's palm before he slid it into his boot. He looked at his Smith & Wesson pistol, then holstered it in the waist at the back of his pants. Beau opened and closed his spring-loaded pocketknife and slipped it into his other pants pocket. In his shirt pocket, he stashed a SOG flashlight. Once the panel was empty, he closed it and stood at attention.

"Allow me to recap your assignment. Tourism in Timbuktu has dwindled since terrorists invaded several years back. I've received intel of a cell working undercover in the city." He paused. "I requested for someone to be sent in to 'spy out the land,' so to speak. This is a tentative situation. In January, the Festival of the Desert will take place on the outskirts of Timbuktu. The Tuareg band Tinariwen is scheduled to perform. Make sure it's safe. I wish you success, but this can turn dangerous, so don't get yourself killed. Understood?"

"Yes, sir. I'll take that as an order."

The Chief leaned forward with his elbows on his desk and handed Beau a folder holding his assignment details with a picture of the photojournalist paper-clipped inside the folder.

Beau accepted the folder, put it under his arm to look at later, and saluted Dax Auguste.

"For this job, try not to act so military—it could blow your cover. Watch your back." Auguste extended his hand.

"I will, sir." Beau shook his hand.

"Reneé said to tell you hello." Auguste smiled.

"Please greet her for me and ask if I could get some of her baklavas when I get back to Bamako." Beau smiled, then pivoted on his steel-toed boots and left the office. The sound of his footsteps reverberated in the deserted halls. Leaving through the front gates, he found his taxi idling outside.

The driver threw his cigarette butt out the window and waved.

Opening the back door, Beau slung his bag and backpack into the back seat and slid inside. The smell of cheap cigarettes filled the vehicle. "You waited?" Beau unzipped his backpack and shoved the folder inside, then tossed it on top of his duffle.

The cabbie grinned. "Yes, I knew you would not be here long and would need a ride—and you tip well. I need the francs." He laughed.

"Thanks. Azalai Hotel, *Monsieur*." Beau leaned into the vinyl of the cab's bench seat and blew out a breath. He'd barely made it before they locked the gates.

The spunky driver plunged them into evening traffic as Beau relaxed for the first time since his arrival. Being armed, he felt whole—ready for action.

Terrorist leader, Dhakir Hussein rubbed the jagged scar on the side of his scruffy jaw—a constant reminder of Dubois. The scar added to his rugged look that attracted the ladies, but the pain Dubois had inflicted fueled the fire that kept Hussein fighting—pursuing all enemies of their agenda.

He released a hot breath and ran his mill file down the rough edge of his tactical knife, the Frenchman on his mind. Sweat ran down his back as the African sunshine baked his skin. He tossed the knife and file into the passenger seat and moved his Hummer to a petrol station across the street. Scanning the area in front of the station, he searched for the American woman or Dubois.

The scent of burning garbage drifted toward him. He

punched a number into his phone. "Emir, I got a glimpse of Dubois at the Bamako airport after I loaded our shipment."

"Dubois? Are you sure it was him? I didn't think he would ever return to Mali." Emir said. "He's either really stupid or extremely brave."

"Or following orders," Hussein said as fuel poured into both tanks. "It was him. I have his face memorized. Rage drives his actions. He's been waging war with us since I blew up a restaurant in Paris, killing his woman. He was livid, as he left the remains of the restaurant with her blood on his military getup. I carry a scar from our last meeting, where he stabbed me before I shot him. I look forward to facing off again. We have a score to settle."

"You will enjoy the challenge. I have no doubt. Are you on your way back, Dhakir, sir?" Emir asked.

"No. I'm waiting for Conan. He is buying provisions. The flight into Mali was delayed, and since it is so late, we'll return to Timbuktu tomorrow. Have a man watch the airport. If Dubois flies in, stay hidden, but follow his movements until I arrive. No slip-ups. Understand?" Hussein reached for his knife and sliced the file down the knife's edge one last time.

"I understand. It will be as you have said." Emir ended the call.

Hussein checked the sharp edge of his knife and shoved it into its sheath. He finished a bottle of water, crushed it, then chucked it into a pile of trash accumulating along the road. With his tanks full, he paid for the petrol and started the Hummer.

Conan tossed several packages into the back seat of the SUV and jumped in, just as Hussein plunged them into the mayhem of Bamako's traffic, daring anyone to pull in front of him. Road rage took on a whole new meaning to an angry military man driving a bulletproof all-terrain vehicle.

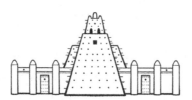

Ellie endured a teeth-jarring taxi ride into the city. Of course, she would get the only un-air-conditioned cab in the line of exhaust-emitting jalopies. When the driver finally jerked the vehicle to a stop, Ellie limped into the five-star Azalai Hotel, stopping at the hotel's shiny reception desk. The thick carpet and soft music were a welcome treat, a level of quality she was surprised to see in this poor West African country.

Lifting her foot, she stood in a flamingo pose to take the pressure off her toes. "Hello, I'm Elliana Bendale. I have a reservation." She set her bag on the desk and pulled out her passport for the registrar.

The Malian woman with glowing skin looked up from her desk and smiled. The headdress covering her hair matched her African print dress.

"Hello, *mademoiselle*. Welcome to Bamako and the Azalai Hotel. My name is Grace, and I have your reservation. Your employer wanted us to see to your needs while you are with us." She noted Ellie's passport number in her ledger and gave a key to the bellman, who had Ellie's luggage. "Suite 107 for

Mademoiselle Bendale." She handed Ellie an envelope. "This came for you."

Above & Beyond Magazine was imprinted on the stationary. Ellie opened the note and read the message, then looked up and said, "Grace, could you reserve a table for two in the hotel restaurant for seven o'clock? I'm meeting my interpreter for dinner." She pocketed the note.

"Absolutely. I will see to it. Anything else?" Grace made a note on a tablet.

Ellie shouldered her camera case and paused. "Do you have a lockup area for my large piece of luggage? The weight of it would be too much for our small plane tomorrow to Timbuktu."

"Yes. We have a closet that stays locked. We can put it there. Would you like something refreshing from the bar, a soft drink maybe?" She smiled at Ellie.

"A cold Coke would be great. Thanks." Ellie noticed the man with her luggage was leaving her behind.

"I will have it sent to your room. Have a nice evening." Grace picked up the phone to place her order.

"Thank you. I think I will." Ellie followed the bellman as closely as she could with her throbbing toes, anxious to finally remove her shoe—if the swelling would allow it.

If bumper-to-bumper traffic didn't slow their progress to Azalai Hotel, Beau could get checked in and have time for a shower before meeting the photojournalist. He hoped he wasn't irritating, whiney, or demanding. The success of his mission depended upon this trip to Timbuktu.

The receptionist was efficient. She recorded his passport number and gave him a key. His room wasn't a suite but was nice enough, and his shower was hot—both rare in third-world countries.

Two minutes before seven, early by his watch, he stepped into the hotel restaurant and took a deep breath. The place was high-class for West Africa with its service, exquisite cuisine, and ambiance.

"Good evening, *Monsieur*. May I show you to a table? Are you dining alone?" The restaurant manager wore a three-piece suit—out of style long ago but prestigious attire in Mali.

Beau gave a slight bow. "I'm meeting an American for a dinner meeting. Has L.E. Bendale arrived?" Beau scanned the restaurant but didn't see a gentleman sitting alone. The floors were clay tiles, and the tables were covered with pricey blue linen tablecloths and napkins that added a *pop of color* to the room, as his sister-in-law would say.

"Follow me." The man walked to a table overlooking the outdoor pool. "I hope you enjoy our territorial cosmopolitan entrees."

"Thank you, *Monsieur*. I'm sure I will. The buffet looks amazing. I'll start with a cold bottle of water." Beau shook his napkin out of its fancy fold and put it across his lap.

"I will send it right away." He bowed slightly before returning to the restaurant's entrance to seat more guests.

Beau got comfortable and watched through the window as a swimmer took the high dive into the pristine pool. Beau often jumped into the deep end, but not usually into water. He took in a breath and blew it out.

The waiter poured water into a goblet. Knowing he wouldn't have this finery in Timbuktu, Beau lifted the glass and took a long drink. Over the rim of his glass, he saw a tall blonde in a blue flowing sundress headed to his table with a plate of food. *Oh, no. The tourist from the airport.*

Stopping, she stared, shook her head, and limped to the

table. "Really? Wow! What are the chances?" She set her plate on the table.

As he stood to pull out her chair, he questioned her reaction. Women didn't usually frown when they saw him. They would normally capture his gaze, wink, and smile. But not this lady. *And—who is she?* He pulled a business card from his pocket.

"You're a pretty woman whom I would love to invite to dinner, however, this is a business meeting. I'm waiting for a gentleman named L. E. Bendale." He showed her the card.

She scanned it and turned away when a waiter arrived with a bag of ice. She propped her swollen foot in the chair on her left and carefully placed the ice on her toes, sucking in a breath.

Beau took a seat that put his back to the window, giving him a complete view of the restaurant and the attractive female.

"Thank you," she said to the waiter, then sat back. "So, since I am Elliana Bendale, I'm assuming you're the interpreter who will accompany me to Timbuktu." She slung her linen napkin across her lap and met his gaze.

He hesitated, sucked in a breath, and shook his head. "I assumed I was working with a man on this assignment. My mistake." He smiled and tipped a pretend hat on his head. "I'm Beau de La Croix."

She shook his extended hand, then released his fingers.

"Is something wrong? What happened to your foot?"

An uncomfortable silence hung between them. Beau endured the intense glare from her stunning deep blue eyes for several beats.

Ms Bendale sat up straighter. "I think we've already met, Mr. de La Croix. Today at the airport, you plowed through the crowd to retrieve your duffle bag before stepping on my foot, breaking two of my toes. Then—you stole my taxi and left me on the sidewalk with an angry Iraqi soldier, holding a gun to my back!"

His body stiffened, and his hands formed fists under the table. "Did he hurt you?"

"Only a few bruises while he grilled me with questions about *you*. But he called you *Dubois*. Is that your nickname? At that moment, I could have called you a lot of names. But they've slipped my mind. So, yes, I think we've met."

Beau's shoulders fell. "I am so sorry." He sat back in his chair. Waited. Then got up, put his napkin on the table, and left the restaurant. It was time to stop this conversation and start over if this was going to work. And he didn't have a choice—it had to work.

———

Ellie couldn't believe her luck. Stuck with a bull in a china shop. Yeah, he was ruggedly handsome but heavy on his feet—no, heavy on *her* foot. Would they return to Bamako in one piece—that is, *if* he returned to the table? Stabbing the meat on her plate, she cut it with force and tasted a bite of tender beef. A mix of savory spices. *Yum.* She took a deep breath and tried to relax and regain her composure. After all, she was a professional.

As she sipped her Coke, she played this interpreter's scenario in her mind. He didn't mean any harm and wasn't aware he'd broken her toes. He was in too big of a hurry to notice how he'd wounded her physically. Yep, she'd been pretty rough on him. *I hope he comes back.*

She focused on her food. The potatoes had a special seasoning that put her taste buds on alert. Or maybe the handsome Frenchman had her senses pinging at the thought of spending a week with such a fine specimen of masculinity.

The manager of the restaurant approached her table with a flower bouquet. "These are from the French gentleman awaiting your approval to join you for dinner." He held the flowers toward Ellie and smiled.

Accepting the bouquet, she turned to face de La Croix, who stood sentry, watching for her answer. "Okay, tell him he can join me for dinner." She smelled the blooms and laid the bouquet on the table in front of an empty chair.

The manager bowed and hurried to relay her message.

Beau de La Croix joined her. "Thank you for the invitation. I come bearing my deepest regrets for my actions that have caused you pain. Please forgive me."

"I'm sorry for overreacting. You didn't mean to hurt me. I know that. So—" She paused. "Since you gave me flowers, I'll consider forgiving you. Go visit the buffet, and we'll start over." She took another drink of Coke, hoping it would stop the sizzle between them. He was one fine-looking man. Go figure.

Moments later, with his plate full of steaming meats, vegetables, and a scrumptious dessert assortment, Beau took his seat. "I'm so sorry I broke your toes. Have you taped them together?" He dropped his napkin into his lap.

"Not yet. They were too swollen." She took a bite of vegetables.

"Are they straight?" He seemed genuinely concerned.

"Yes, thank the Lord. They don't need to be reset. I'll tape them when I return to my suite." She buttered a roll.

They ate in amenable silence for a few moments amid the sounds of other guests, speaking a mixture of languages, French being prominent. Strong curry smells mingled with a fragrant coffee aroma. A mixture of onion and garlic rose from Ellie's entrée. She'd chosen a pasta dish, thinking it would be fully cooked and safe to eat. She would follow her interpreter's lead on food choices to stay healthy during the trip.

As soft strands of Kenny G's saxophone played from mounted speakers around the restaurant, Beau scanned their surroundings. His gaze stopped on her and stayed.

"I have to say you're not what I expected as an interpreter."
She took a bite.

"What were you expecting?" Beau watched her with his
fork in mid-air, holding a stack of sauteed vegetables.

"Shorter, bald on top with a greasy comb-over, thick glasses,
and a potbelly." She laughed.

"I'm sorry to disappoint." He ate his veggies and hid a smile
as he cut into his meat. "I may not be who you expected, but
despite our rough beginning, I can get you to Timbuktu, help
you capture your story, and get you back safely. I'm good at
what I do." One side of his lip hitched in a smile.

"So, you do this interpreter gig a lot?" She ate her last bite of
pasta.

"No, there aren't many beautiful blondes needing my
language skills, but I work freelance on various assignments,
usually on security assignments. I'm familiar with the territory
... and I'm all you've got."

She smirked. "Then I guess you'll have to do."

He offered his dessert assortment. "Please have one of these
bite-size desserts as we plan our trek to the ancient city of
Timbuktu."

"They smell like fruit with a buttery crust." She bit into an
African tart. "Very good. Thanks." She savored the dessert.
"About our time in Timbuktu, this is what my magazine
expects for this assignment." She recited the request and goals
sent to her by the editor of the magazine. "Can you create a
schedule to meet my needs?"

"I can do that." Beau's lip lifted in a half-smile.

"As for starting over, nice to meet you, Beau de La Croix. I'm
Elliana Bendale, a soon-to-be world-renown photojournalist in
high demand around the globe. You can call me Ellie." She
attempted a cordial smile.

"It's nice to meet you." He offered her another dessert.
"Elliana is long, and Ellie is too common, May I call you E?"

"Okay." She paused. "So, how many languages do you speak?" She took another bite of dessert. "I know you speak French, since you're my interpreter while I'm in Mali."

He swallowed. "Yes, I speak French, English, and some area tribal languages. What about you?" He finished his water.

"English, Swahili, and a whole lot of sarcasm." She put her fork into another dessert on his plate. "*Capiche*?"

He laughed.

———

Beau walked her to the elevator guarding her foot when they passed other guests. "What time should we leave for the airport?" The inky darkness of nightfall could be seen through the windows as they made their way through the plush hotel lobby.

"We fly at 11:54. We can't be late." She limped along as gracefully as she could.

The bouquet he'd given her fanned a pleasant fragrance as they walked, or maybe it was her perfume stealing his breath. She was stunning. Tall, shapely, with long blonde silky hair, and a sprinkling of freckles on a perfect nose.

Beau pressed the UP button. "Enjoy the breakfast buffet in the morning—you won't taste anything like it for a while. Let's leave at ten. That will give us plenty of time to make our flight." He held the elevator door as other guests stepped off.

"I want to shop at the market across the street. Will you go with me and help me bargain for the best prices? I've been told Malian jewelry and leather goods are amazing." She looked up at him. "When I'm on assignment, I like to shop before I work so I can focus on the project without interruptions, and this project, being critical to my future employment, has forced me to plan well."

Beau motioned for Ellie to precede him into the elevator.

"Okay. Let's do breakfast at eight, then go to the market." Once the elevator doors closed, Beau turned toward her. "You said the man at the airport was asking about me. Can you remember his exact words?"

"That was scary." She hesitated, and her eyes widened. "When you took off in my cab, he held a gun at my back and asked if you were Dubois and what destination you gave your driver. I insisted I didn't know you or where you were staying." She gulped a breath.

"I'm so sorry." Beau stood rigid, fists clenched.

"No harm." She paused. "But I was terrified."

Beau paused. "Are you okay now?"

"I think so, but when he left me standing on the sidewalk, I was afraid to move at first." She fidgeted before continuing. "I took a deep breath and decided, after dealing with the sweaty masses, a handsome Frenchman, two broken toes, and being held at gunpoint—what more could happen? Right?"

"Oh, I agree. After all, now you have a tour guide slash interpreter."

"Right. And we're off on an adventure. Timbuktu has a reputation and centuries of history. I hope to do it justice. This assignment is my chance to land a permanent place with the magazine."

The elevator doors *dinged* and opened. He stepped out, checked the hallway, then walked Ellie to her suite.

She used her key and turned toward him. "Good night, Beau."

"You sure you don't need help with those broken toes?" He held the door slightly open.

"No, but thanks for the offer. I can tape them, and I'll elevate my foot to keep the swelling down." She eyed him. "You didn't mean to hurt me. It was an accident. Don't feel bad." She put her hand on his arm—but didn't let it linger. "Thanks for the flowers."

"You're welcome. Rest well." He released her door and left as soon as he heard the lock click.

Beau ran his hand through his hair as he paced the hardwood floors of his hotel room. *Hussein called me Dubois.* If he was the leader of this invasion, things could get ugly. *This could be what the intel was about.* More challenging than he'd originally thought. Elliana Bendale was passionate about her work, feisty, beautiful. And blonde—which would bring attention to her presence in the city.

He stopped pacing and scanned the activity on the street from his window. He could be leading her into trouble—giving her a bigger story than she ever expected—if she lived to tell it. Keeping his orders a secret from the photojournalist was a great plan. It would keep her safe, like she'd been at the airport. He'd go with that *what-she-didn't-know-wouldn't-hurt-her* adage.

After dropping the curtain, he tied the mosquito net to the post on the headboard. He threw his pillow to the side, slipped the Smith & Wesson from the holster at his lower back, and set it on the bed. Reaching inside his ankle holster, he removed his Glock and laid it on the sheet. In the side pocket of his cargo pants, he retrieved magazines for both guns and the SOG flashlight. His spring-loaded pocket knife was in his other pocket. He breathed a sigh of relief.

Having possession of his weapons felt good—it settled him. With his armory on the bed, he covered it with his pillow and stretched out, knowing he needed to rest. Once they reached Timbuktu, he'd sleep with one eye open.

3

Ellie bowed her head and said a prayer over her food and their trip to Timbuktu ... "and Lord, help me. This is an amazing opportunity, and I need to prove I can do this so they'll hire me for the magazine. Please, Lord, don't let me blow this. Thanks. Amen."

As she raised her head, she spied her interpreter from his boots up past his cargo pants and his tight shirt over his muscled torso to his gray eyes. "I'm sorry to keep you waiting. The Lord and I have this arrangement. I talk to Him and—" She realized she was rambling. "Never mind. Get yourself some breakfast."

"I think I will." Beau strode to the buffet, ordered his eggs, and filled a plate with fruit, and rolls. "Café' please." He told the waiter on his way to their table. Joining her, he asked, "Did you sleep well, Ellie?"

"Yes, after my toes quit throbbing and until the Islam call to prayer pierced the air before daybreak." She cut her watermelon into small bites and sprinkled salt on it.

"Salt ruins the taste." Beau pointed to her plate. He reached for the black pepper for his eggs and doused his breakfast.

"The salt accents the sweetness of the melon bringing out its true flavor. To each their own." She smiled and pointed to his plate. "You want a little egg with your pepper there, Macho Man?"

He shook the pepper twice more. "What I need is some hot sauce."

"On your eggs? Then don't mention the salt on my watermelon." She bit into her juicy melon. "You ready to help me shop?"

"Sure, what are you looking for?" He smeared orange marmalade on his toast.

"Gifts for my family and friends and something to hang on my wall from Mali. Someday I'll decorate a place of my own, but for now, I'm living with my two friends, Olivia and Jocelyn, in a condo. Olivia is engaged. I want to find something special for her as a wedding gift." She took another bite.

The waiter served his café' in a bowl. Beau lifted it and carefully took a sip.

Watching him, she asked, "What is that you're drinking?"

"It's café—half coffee, half chocolate. You should try it." He took another sip.

"Maybe tomorrow morning." She drank her coffee.

"So, you only have two friends? I thought you would have an entourage." He scanned the restaurant, his gaze landing on her.

"I've learned to choose my friends wisely. Some people are like stray dogs—they'll bite you when you quit petting them. And two true friends are enough for me." She peeled a tiny banana. "But I could add a friend or two if he or she proved to be a person of integrity. Which is rare." She took a small bite of the banana. "Do you have a plethora of friends? You strike me as a loner."

"A plethora?" He furrowed his brow, the indentions on his forehead were vertical just above his eyebrows.

"A fancy word for a variety." She smirked.

"Nope. I work with some great men who have my respect. We hang out sometimes. I have a brother I spend time with when I'm in France, but true friends are scarce with my vagabond lifestyle. Providing security and being an interpreter for people like you, I like working solo with no strings attached. There's too much pain when you lose someone you care about, so I keep moving—making my way alone." He forked a piece of bacon into his mouth.

Ellie read between the lines. Maybe it was the writer part of her brain honing in on the heart of the story. But that was for another time. She finished her coffee as he pushed his plate away. "Well, one-man show, are you ready to shop?"

Beau stood as he drank the rest of his brew. "Let's do this." He followed her from the restaurant to the hotel's front doors. His job as her protector had started. Under a cloudless sky, Bamako had a slight breeze cooling its inhabitants, but that didn't mean an enemy wouldn't be hot on his trail.

With a light grip on her shoulder, he paused Ellie at the doors and surveyed the area for any signs of Hussein or his men. "The Taureg market has the best variety in Bamako. It's the one across the street. How are your toes?"

"Better today. The swelling went down, and I taped them together. This shoe keeps them secure, which is good since they hurt when I bend them."

"Sounds like a good choice." When he didn't see anything suspicious, he led her to the entrance of the large market that boasted concrete floors and a large A-frame building with a tin roof and walls. As she stepped inside the market, a loud bang sounded. He pivoted and scanned for the origin of the noise. A puff of gray smoke behind an old backfiring truck. He relaxed.

She stopped short. "Wow. I love it, de La Croix. So vibrant and colorful." She pulled her phone out of her bag and took a couple of photographs.

"It's almost overwhelming, the bold mixture of color, the staticky African music. But it all adds to the experience of *Africa*." She took a deep breath. "Scenes like this are so alive. I wish I could portray it with my photography. People need to see this, to experience this." She pocketed her phone and commenced shopping, limping from one kiosk to another until she found some brass carved bracelets. Studying the quality, she made her selections.

He tried to view the chaos through her eyes. The fragrance of flowers was strong as they passed a massive display of blooms. Citrus smells competed for prominence in the fruit section of the market. Ebony-skinned nationals dressed in bright mismatched attire conversed in friendly banter.

At the back of the market, the smell of leather was overly strong. Several shops had engraved pieces. She purchased a computer case for her laptop. Beau bargained for her, acquiring a good price. With each purchase, Beau helped her get a lower price, counted her unfamiliar currency, and carried her packages.

"Great choice on this laptop case." Beau put the wrapped purchase under his arm.

"Thanks." She smiled. "It's one of a kind. The workmanship is superb. I'll enjoy using it to protect my laptop, research, writing guidelines, and photography."

"When you sell this article, you'll become famous?" He asked.

"This opportunity could change my life. It would open the field of photojournalism. Have you ever been passionate about an assignment?"

"Yes, I have." Beau stood to her left when people passed—

patiently protecting her foot. "I'll help you get your pictures, but writing the article is up to you."

"I write better than I use my cameras." She limped from booth to booth. "I see you scanning the market. Are you looking for unwanted guests?"

"One can't be too careful when in the company of a famous photojournalist." Beau masked his real concerns with a smile and moved her aside as a man carried a load of leather goods down the aisle toward them.

"Thanks."

"At your service, *mademoiselle*." Beau tipped his imaginary hat again, then followed her up and down a few rows of kiosks.

Ellie stopped and faced Beau. "What are those wooden pieces on the wall behind me?" She kept her voice down as she breathed in his masculine scent, a pleasing mix of soap and toughness.

He scrutinized the display. "Those are antique tent stakes. Bedouins used them to secure their tents in the desert sand, especially during *haboobs*."

"What are *haboobs*?"

"Blinding sandstorms."

"Okay, I want those three that are grouped together on that far wall. Can you get me a good price? They would be a perfect muse for my article." She gave him her best pleading look.

With a slight shake of his head, he stepped around her and spoke in French. The shop owner responded.

"What did he say?" She leaned closer, touched his arm, and kept her voice down.

Beau leaned toward her. "He wants a hundred dollars for the three tent stakes," Beau whispered.

"That's too much. Tell him the wood looks very old and

dirty. I'll give him twenty dollars." With her hand still on Beau's arm, she pushed him toward the man to make another offer.

Speaking to the shop owner again, Beau reported his response. "He thinks you'll pay one hundred dollars."

"No, let's walk away." She shook her head and moved to the next shop.

The African man yelled out.

"He's down to ninety dollars." Beau interpreted for her.

Looking at other shops with Beau's hand on her back, she kept limping along. His protection was nice. Being with him was growing on her. *Be still my beating heart.*

"Do you want the tent stakes?" Beau whispered.

"Yes, but don't let him know that." She walked further and chose a scarf. "This is perfect for my mother to wear with her winter coat." As she paid for her purchase, an elderly gentleman rushed toward her with the tent stakes wrapped in newsprint. He held them out and spoke rapidly in French.

"He's saying twenty dollars."

Ellie grabbed the tent stakes, piled them in Beau's arms, clapped her hands, and gave the gentleman the money, adding a tip. "This is a great find."

Adding the tent stakes to his load, Beau shook his head and followed her again. "I don't think these will fit in your suitcase."

"I'm a flight attendant. I don't have to worry about that." She limped a little farther. "I think I've finished shopping. Are you ready to go back to the hotel?" She pivoted to ask him while eyeing his dark hair and stunning eyes.

"Sure, you're fast. I'm surprised." Beau smiled.

"When it comes to shopping, I don't lollygag." She limped toward the exit.

"What?" He stopped her and looked out the doors before leading her into the street.

"I don't waste time."

"So, tell me, if you're a flight attendant, is writing just a hobby?" His eyes darted across the area and watched the traffic as they crossed the busy road being patient with her injury slowing their pace.

"My domineering mother has my life planned for me. When I got my degree, she gave me a professionally decorated office at my dad's company as my graduation present. I thought she was going to croak when I turned it down to fly the African skies as a flight attendant. Me earning big bucks is foremost in her mind. She wants me to do something prestigious."

Dodging a stray donkey, they stepped onto the curb. "I don't want to fly the skies forever—I love traveling but would like it to be on a schedule I could control. Being hired by *Above & Beyond Magazine* would open that door for me. That's where you come in, de La Croix." She poked him in the chest with one of the tent stakes.

"*Ow!*" He jerked away.

"We've got a plane to catch." She stepped into the hotel lobby with Beau on her trail.

"Your writing must be exceptional. They don't invest in newbies to get a story like this." Beau sounded surprised. He pressed the button on the elevator.

"After winning a few contests with my work, this was the next step." Once in the elevator, her phone *dinged* with a message. She checked it. "Seven missed calls from my mom. No pressure there." She blew out a breath and pocketed the phone, regretting she'd added the international plan.

As they approached the door of her suite, Ellie reached for her room key, turned to Beau, and took the tent stakes from his arms. She sucked in a breath as her skin touched his. "I—I will meet you in the lobby at ten."

He took her key and unlocked the door. "See you there."

———

When the door clicked, Beau ran his hand through his hair and scratched his beard, scruffy now as a disguise. *She's a beauty, but keep your guard up, de La Croix. In one week, she'll be gone. Remember the gut-wrenching pain of loss. The heartache.* He hurried to his room and packed in ten minutes, determined to shake off the effects of that blonde hair and those blue eyes framed by a long set of lashes.

Using the extra time, he checked in with two men, his bosses, Philippe Leroux in Paris, and Axel McCabe in Washington D.C. He got McCabe on the phone.

"I'm glad you called," Axel McCabe answered. "I was notified you'd arrive in Mali. I wasn't looking forward to sending this info. Our intel reports that seven men have set themselves up in Timbuktu." McCabe paused. The sound of papers came over the line. "I'm looking at the file now. From drone photos, it looks like they come and go from a building at the opposite end of town from the school."

"The church school the missionaries built?" Beau paced the room.

"Yes. And they've been visiting the mosque regularly. Which is odd. Confirm their location, their numbers, and their plans if possible. We can't allow them to get another stronghold in the area. Once your job is complete, we'll move in and eliminate the threat."

"Yes, sir. I'll send messages to Dax in Bamako when possible, if not, I'll report in as soon as I return to Bamako." He watched the busy street out his hotel window, searching for any enemy activity. Always on the lookout. "Is Hussein leading this battalion?"

"That info hasn't been confirmed, but I suspect he is." He paused.

Beau blew out a breath. "Give me a week, and I'll have this mission complete."

"And we'll be ready to finish this task—removing all enemy forces from the ancient city. Thanks, de La Croix."

"It's what I do, sir." Beau ended the call and reminded himself he needed to keep his military manners at bay on this trip. He was an interpreter and a tour guide for a savvy blonde. Piece of cake. *Not.*

4

Ellie was first to reach the lobby as a cool morning breeze floated through the front doors. Her flowery print dress with cap sleeves was cool in this hot, dry climate and was modest among the Malian ladies, who didn't wear slacks. A few minutes alone helped her get her bearings.

The sizzle she'd felt when she touched Beau's arm served as a neon sign blinking WARNING: HEARTACHE AHEAD! Time to focus, get this job, and seal her future occupation.

Once she secured her large piece of luggage and the tent stakes in the locked luggage area, she sat on the comfy couch and dialed her mother's cell. It was best to get it behind her before she flew to Timbuktu.

"Hi, Mom."

Anne Bendale let out a breath. "Oh, Ellie. I'm glad you called. Are you in Mali yet?"

"Yes, I arrived safely and met with my interpreter yesterday. We fly again in two hours." Ellie saw Beau coming toward her. "You threatened to send me to Timbuktu when I disobeyed as a kid. Now I get to go there." Ellie laughed. "Do you think it's too late for me?"

"Well, I wasn't sure it existed—but my threat worked. And you turned out great, Elliana."

"Thanks, Mom. I'll let you know when I'm back in Bamako." Ellie checked her watch.

"Please be careful, Elliana. And give some consideration to working at the company. It can't be safe for a beautiful young woman to be traveling alone to such dangerous places."

Her mother sounded concerned. "I'll be careful, Mom, but I have to go where the story is. It's time to leave for the airport. Love you. Tell Dad I love him too."

"I will. I love you too. Bye, Elliana."

"Bye, Mom." She ended the call and stood.

After scanning the area, de la Croix turned toward her. "Our ride is here. You ready to go?"

"If you're waiting for me, you're backing up." She smiled, limped to the taxi, and slid into the backseat. She fastened her seatbelt and took her small Sony camera out of her bag.

Beau loaded their small bags, slid into the cab, and shut his door. "Modibo Keita International, *Monsieur.*"

The driver, a Malian wearing a Dallas Cowboys cap backward on his head, wasted no time getting them into the throes of traffic.

Bamako was a cacophony of noise. Hawkers selling their wares tried to find buyers in every vehicle. Donkeys brayed in protest of pulling tanks of water, and ugly marabou storks circled in the treetops. Laughing children rolled their homemade trucks in the dirt beside the road. Ellie captured the images with her Sony.

"Don't you use one of those big expensive cameras? Your case had Nikon on it." Beau asked.

"Yes. I love my big camera and my lenses. I'll use them in Timbuktu. But for quick shots while on the move, this Sony is perfect." She put it to the window and captured pics of the market, the potholes, and the raw meat hanging in the butcher shop. "I'll use these frames to add culture and local dynamics to the scenes when I'm writing," she said as she took another shot.

"You sure sound professional!" Beau glanced behind them.

"That's encouraging." The flowering trees in the middle of a garbage dump caught her eye. She took the picture as ibis flew from the trees. "Mali, a land of beauty amid total devastation."

"A land of mystery, intrigue, and peril," Beau added.

In no time, Beau and Ellie were at the airport. It was less active than when they flew in. With only carry-ons, they checked in, then waited for their plane for fifteen minutes.

"I want one of those badges you flashed at the security. I'd wait a lot less in airports." Ellie sat in the waiting area with her foot propped on her carry-on and checked the shots she'd just taken.

"Well, apply at Global Entry when you get back to the States." He didn't want her to know his military badge got him through security without an issue since Dax had notified the authorities—a necessity, since he was traveling heavily armed. He scanned the area and took a seat across from Ellie with his back to the glass.

He checked a message on his phone and then looked at her. "I kept wondering all night, why the tent stakes?"

"There's a scripture in Isaiah that says enlarge the place of your tent, stretch the curtains, strengthen your stakes. It challenges me to broaden my horizons, try new things, and take a chance."

She could tell he didn't get it. "Things were going great for me in high school, then my life fell apart. In college, I had a stalker, who made my life difficult. Sometimes it's hard to keep moving when you get the wind knocked out of your sails. So, I can use the extra motivation from the tent stakes metaphor to reach for my dreams."

The terminal filled with travelers going to various destinations.

"I could use the tent stakes metaphor in my article when talking about Timbuktu resurrecting their tourism after going through some difficult years."

"That makes sense. You had to get rid of the bad guys to move forward." He watched the people arriving for their flight. "Do you still have a stalker problem?"

"Not anymore. He's been quiet while serving time in prison." She smiled. "The tent stake concept could also be a great teaching for Christians to reach out, to witness more, so people will accept the Lord as their Savior."

Beau thought about her words. He'd floundered in his faith since God hadn't answered his prayer. Maybe the faith thing worked for some people more than others. He had begged God to save Jezelle in Paris.

She stared at the camera screen. "I love the colors and the handiwork of these people. It's so bright and cheery." She showed Beau a frame.

Hiking his backpack onto his shoulder, he looked at the screen and stood. "You'll have to work your magic to make Timbuktu colorful. It's very brown." He gestured for her to walk in front of him. "It's time to board our plane."

Their arms brushed against each other in the smaller plane's tight space as they made the short trek to Timbuktu. Beau attempted to lean away, but the large passenger across the aisle didn't appreciate him invading his space. He counted his blessings that it was a short flight.

"Welcome to Timbuktu." Beau released his seatbelt before landing. Ready to get this done.

"You weren't kidding. It's brown, beige, cinnamon, taupe, and bronze. And that's just around the airport." Ellie looked out her window as they came in for a landing. "I think sepia tones might work. I'll try that as I photograph the scene."

Following Ellie off the plane, Beau took a deep breath at the top of the stairs rolled up for them to disembark. They walked together through heat waves radiating off the black tarmac. Now his work began. Game on.

With only carry-ons in tow, they strolled through the airport, past customs officers, and entered one of three old cabs that filled the area with a cloud of exhaust.

"Hotel Bouctou, Monsieur." Beau instructed the driver, then sat back beside Ellie.

The old taxi back-fired and stalled, jerking its passengers.

Ellie laughed.

"He's getting us ready for the potholes," Beau said. "Hang on."

Using her Sony, she took pictures of some light-brown-skinned boys playing soccer in the street, a young lady balancing a yellow five-gallon bucket on her head, and a skinny boy following a donkey loaded with firewood. A handful of pretty flowers grew in the middle of a pile of garbage. She snapped a picture and looked at her screen.

The taxi stopped in front of a reddish-brown stucco building, probably six stories high. A rickety fence bordered the front yard of the hotel. The entrance had two wooden doors that stood open, allowing chickens, dogs, and sand to enter at will.

Beau got out, looked around, and walked to the back of the cab to retrieve their belongings.

Their driver opened Ellie's door. "*Merci.*" She offered him a smile.

"I thought you didn't know French?" Beau said when she exited the cab.

Grabbing her carry-on, she raised the handle. "Why, Mr. de La Croix, I have a vast knowledge of the language. I can say *merci, monsieur, mademoiselle, oui, croissant, bonjour,* and French fries." She laughed when he shook his head.

After paying their driver, Beau led the way into the hotel. The security scan beeped when they stepped onto the terrazzo floors, but the manager wasn't alarmed. The man's face lit up when he saw Beau.

"Good to see you, my friend," Beau said in English, then repeated the phrase in French.

The interior walls were as brown as the exterior ones. A wooden reception desk and three straight-back chairs gave the semblance of a hotel lobby to the sparse area. A sorry excuse for a palm tree in a clay pot blew in the breeze that wafted through the door.

While Beau checked them in, Ellie pulled out her water bottle and emptied it on the thirsty plant.

"I'm glad you are well, Zamir." He addressed the hotel manager in a mixture of French and English, confirmed their reservations, and made sure they were expected for lunch. With skeleton keys in hand, Beau turned to Ellie.

"Antique skeleton keys?" She watched him swinging them around his finger. "I haven't seen those in years."

"They're a bit behind the times here in Timbuktu." He gave her one of the keys. "We're on the first floor, up those stairs." He pointed to a winding staircase.

"But this is the first floor." She palmed the skeleton key.

"In Timbuktu, the first floor is up one level. The restaurant is on the fifth floor, which is the roof. They serve lunch in one hour, and dinner is at seven."

Swinging the key on her finger, she mocked him. "Okay. Mr. Tour Guide, can we take a walk before lunch? I'd like to get the feel of the city and try different camera settings before I start my work."

"Sure. Wait for me right here. Don't go out on your own.

Your fair skin and blonde hair will attract attention." He waited for her to acknowledge his directive.

She gave him a thumbs-up and went to her room, still limping. Beau followed and entered her room to be sure it was adequate. The accommodations were plain, but clean, with a hard bed and a mosquito net, a flashlight, and a candle, but it was self-contained with a private bath. A warm breeze caused the mosquito net to sway. Beau left her there and went in search of his room.

Not wanting to offend the locals, she chose a flowy dress. It would be the coolest thing to wear today. She put her hair up in a messy bun. After she donned sunscreen and lip protection, she grabbed her trusty sunvisor.

With her camera in hand, Ellie returned to the lobby and waited for her interpreter. Watching everyday life in Timbuktu from the open hotel door, she took a picture, adjusted the camera settings, then took another shot and examined her screen.

Beau looked like Indiana Jones in his rugged khaki outfit with a hat and shades as he took the stairs two at a time.

"I like your shades, McGarrett. I would wear mine, but they get in the way of my camera. Thus, the visor." She pointed to her headgear.

"Who's McGarrett?" His brow furrowed.

"The tough guy on Hawaii Five-O. You favor him." She watched his reaction.

"So, he's really good-looking?" Beau grinned.

"Yep, in a non-arrogant, charming kind of way. Looks are where your resemblance stops." She smirked.

"Are you going to abuse me for the whole week?" He motioned for her to exit the lobby.

"Yep. That's the plan." She took another photo and checked her screen. "You're a tough guy. You can take it."

He shook his head. "Ready for our walk?"

"Yeah. I've been experimenting with my camera settings. As we stroll, I'll try several options and review them during lunch." She adjusted her Nikon again.

"Sounds good. Let's go to the right. This is the main street through the city, and there are many smaller roads off of this one. The airport is south of town, between Timbuktu and the Niger River." He began his tour guide act as he surveyed the city.

As they ambled down the street, Ellie soaked in her surroundings. The dry air was hot without a hint of the breeze that blew through the hotel lobby. An infant's cry pierced the air, dogs barked in the distance, and people conversed in a mixture of French and other languages.

The landscape had a few trees and some shrubs here and there, but it was mostly sand, sand, and more sand. Strong aromas of spicy food and grilled meat would have been pleasing if not mixed with the acrid smoke of burning trash and the stench of camel dung on the road. The good came with the bad. It was both mysterious and smelly.

———

Beau's eyes scoped their surroundings for a different reason. If rebels were in the city, he'd not seen a hint of their existence at the airport or around their hotel. They were well hidden. Camouflaged.

Ellie stopped and looked up at a building. "Why do they leave these boards protruding out of their structures, especially their mosques? In America, we would cut those off." She took a picture.

"These buildings have to be re-mudded every year. The

boards make it easier for the masons to do their job." Beau grabbed her arm and pulled her to the right to keep her from being trampled.

After taking a picture, she started walking, trying to keep his pace. "Thanks. I got a great shot of that runaway donkey."

"Let's take a right, and you can see how the poor people live in Timbuktu. Their meager domed huts will make you thankful for your home in the States." Beau watched her as she interacted with the nationals in the area.

Carefully putting her Nikon into her cloth shoulder bag, she took out the Sony. With the screen on, she took photos without putting the camera to her eye. Children trailed them, watching the screen on her camera. She took their picture, then showed it to them. The giggling group followed them to their hotel. Ellie waved goodbye and walked to the restaurant, guarding her toes as they ascended the stairs to the roof.

"I think you've made some friends."

"They're adorable children. I love their laugh. Kids everywhere love to see their pictures on my screen."

"Just hold the camera tight. They could grab it and run."

"But that's why you're here, de La Croix. To keep me safe— and that includes my cameras." She smiled.

Once they reached the roof, he chose a table near the edge under a canvas. The restaurant had twelve tables, some in the sunlight and others under canvas pieces stretched overhead. A half-wall surrounded the roof's perimeter.

"I think this canvas will keep your skin from burning. Come to the wall and look down. You'll love getting photos from this perch above the action." He pointed to the left.

"Thanks. This is perfect." She scanned the scene from their elevated position, then took a seat and propped her left foot in the extra chair.

"In this restaurant, they bring you whatever they have cooked. It's usually skinny chicken, bread, and rice, with fruit for dessert." He took a drink of warm bottled water from the table. "You don't realize how dehydrated you can get in this dry heat. You need to drink a lot of water." He handed her a bottle.

She opened it and took a sip. "The magazine sent money for the expenses on this trip. We need to settle up."

"If I run short, I'll let you know. I was also given funds for our expenses."

"Okay." She put a sepia tone on a photo and showed it to Beau.

"You caught the subject at the exact moment he drank milk from that gourd. His surroundings show a glimpse of life and the heart of Timbuktu. This shot would be amazing if it was enlarged and put on a canvas. I like the camera setting you used." Beau wiped his brow.

"I do too. I think I'll do full color and include some sepia shots for the article." She leaned back as her food was served. "It smells good." She bowed her head and prayed.

Waiting, Beau refused to feel convicted. He used to pray over his food until the Lord quit answering him.

"This one has been on a diet." She took a bite. "But it's good."

"Did the magazine assign a specific focus, or are they letting you frame the article as you want?" He picked up his chicken leg and tore off the meat with his teeth.

"They're giving me free rein, but I know they want the article to be inviting for tourists to visit the area, especially during the upcoming music festival. I have a few ideas but haven't made a decision yet. If we can ride camels, visit the dunes, eat at the restaurants, and visit the mosque, I can glean material and make a plan from those experiences." She took a drink, probably to help the dry meat go down.

"Sounds good." He pulled some meat from his chicken bone and stuffed it in his mouth.

"Since you've been here before, if you plan what we do next

—I'll follow. Along the way, a story will emerge." She looked through the lens of her camera, took his picture, and checked at the screen. "You look like a hunk of eye candy, heartache, and loads of drama."

Laughing, he shook his head. "I don't think I'm what you need for your magazine spread."

"I can't get the story by myself. And you have a job to do. So, buck up, buttercup."

"Do buttercups lollygag?" He teased her.

"No. They get the job done." She smiled.

"That's what I do."

5

"Ah, Emir. You have masala tea prepared for my arrival?" Hussein greeted his comrade in arms.

Emir poured a cup for his leader. "That drive is dusty, Dhakir. Shake the dust off before our meeting this evening."

The leader took a sip and stretched out on a couch along the small room's back wall. "Did my nemesis arrive by plane today?"

"Taking Seif with me, we hid as you instructed. No American soldier was on the flight from Bamako. An American couple did arrive, but he had long hair and civilian clothing. I didn't think he would travel with a woman if he was military. The woman spoke like an American, and she talked a lot. We waited for the later flight, but only Malians disembarked from that flight." Emir refilled Hussein's cup.

"It was Dubois. We will be diligent as we do our maneuvers. He could interfere with the mission, but ending him would be a delight." Hussein smirked. "We should have our orders sometime this week or next. Help Seif with our provisions. We will unload the guns and ammo when the men arrive."

Emir bowed and backed out of the room, leaving Hussein.

Beau finished his food and surveyed the movement of Timbuktu residents under the noonday sun. When their dishes were cleared away, Ellie took a series of photos as she leaned over the wall surrounding the restaurant. Beau used her other camera with its powerful lens to survey the land. "Great lens."

"I use that one when I'm on a safari in Kenya. It brings the animals so close."

A suspicious character was at least a kilometer away. The lens brought him into view. Dhakir Hussein—the evil man who'd killed Jezelle. Beau's temperature rose, and it wasn't from the sun simmering his skin. He took a picture and sent it to his email, thankful the hotel had Wi-Fi, then deleted the shot. Hussein was overly confident by moving about town in broad daylight as if he didn't have a care in the world. At least he stayed at that end of town.

"You ready to walk again, Mr. Tour Guide?" Ellie stood by their table.

He handed her the Sony, and she put both cameras in her tote and shouldered the bag.

"Sure. Let's ride camels in the dunes. But first, we need to run by the mall and buy you some proper attire." He led the way.

"What's wrong with what I'm wearing? I love this gauzy sundress. It's cool, and it matches these sandals that support my broken toes." She hurried to keep up with his stride.

"Nothing's wrong with your clothing, E. Just trust me." He kept walking.

"Do I have a choice?" She limped quicker.

"Nope."

In the lobby, the feel of gritty sand under her sandals made her want to grab a broom and take up housekeeping.

"We're going left this time." Beau stopped just outside the hotel entrance and spoke in French to a lady. She pointed around a corner. They followed her instructions. "Here's Walmart. You ready?"

"Sure. But you said we were going to the mall." She put her hand on her hip.

"This is the best I could do, for now." At a kiosk of fabric, he picked out a long narrow white piece of gauzy material, then another much wider piece. He bought both and thanked the woman, then stuffed his purchase into Ellie's bag, smelling her floral shampoo when he got too close. Touching her arm alerted him to the softness of her skin. *Big mistake.*

"Now, let's ride some camels." He walked with purpose toward some dromedaries sitting in the sand in the distance. Ellie limped behind him.

When they reached the end of the road, several African men waited with saddled camels. Beau greeted the men, discussed payment, then paid the amount agreed upon. He selected a camel for Ellie that had a decorated saddle of carved leather with tassels hanging from it.

"Let's get you ready. Remove your sun visor." Beau took the gauze material out of her bag and twisted the long narrow piece. He fashioned a headpiece for her, allowing the ends of the material to fall from her shoulders to her waist. Being this close increased his heart rate. He hurried his movements.

Her eyelashes fluttered as she watched him work. He adjusted the cloth on her head, enjoying the feel of her silky blonde locks. When her blue eyes caught his gaze, his breath hitched. He hadn't considered how it would affect him to be so close to the lovely photojournalist.

Stepping back, he took a deep breath. "Now, put on your sunglasses."

"Won't this cloth make me hotter in the sun?" Ellie questioned as she pulled out her sunglasses case.

"You're going to love it. When you perspire, it dampens the cloth. Then the breeze flows through the cloth. It's like an air-conditioner. I got this other piece for your arms if our ride gets long." A few freckles scattered across her nose added a youthful touch to the spunky female.

"Thanks, McGarrett." She put on her sunglasses and felt the headpiece.

"At your service, *mademoiselle*. Give me one camera, and I'll get your picture. It would make a great Christmas card photo." He took the Sony. "Have you ridden a camel before?"

"No. I've studied camel facts, but this is my first attempt to ride one." She turned her focus to the smelly cud-chewing animals.

"Approach the camel slowly so you won't startle him. When you get on, hold the horn of the saddle tight. The camel will toss you forward as he gets his back feet up, then he will throw you back when he gets his front feet up. Okay?" He waited to make sure she understood.

"Okay." She sounded nervous.

Beau helped her mount her camel and then took a series of pictures. She hung on, squealing. Her laughter was music. The camel herders smiled at her enthusiasm. Some little boys giggled at the scene. Once the camel was on all fours, Ellie posed for Beau to take her picture.

"Your turn, Beau." She took out her camera and got ready. "You're a natural, Mr. Tough Guy, showing no emotion while a camel tosses you about. You didn't laugh one time. You've done this before, haven't you?" She propped her hand on her hip.

"A few times." He smirked.

As the African men in long robes and twisted headwraps led the camels, Ellie photographed scorpions in the sand, a bird on a tall cactus, and the handsome man riding beside her. Beau on a camel in the desert near Timbuktu gave a whole new meaning to the word *hot*.

"This is called camel trekking. Did you know?" Ellie spouted information.

"No. I haven't heard that."

"Camels have a double row of long eyelashes to keep sand out of their eyes, and their bushy eyebrows work as a sun visor to keep the sun out. They live up to forty or fifty years and can run forty miles per hour." Ellie took a drink from her water bottle.

As they crossed a dune, Beau listened to her diatribe.

"Camels are called ships in the desert. They're smarter than horses and form close bonds with their owners." She paused for a few minutes. "Across the desert sands, crossed a lonely caravan. Men on camels two by two, destination Timbuktu."

"So, you're a poet too?" Beau watched her.

"I didn't write it. I found it in my research. The author's unknown. Hey, Beau, have you ever eaten camel meat?"

"No. I can't say that I have." Beau listened to Wikipedia on the camel next to him.

"You dip it in salt. It's my favorite meat. I've eaten it in Kenya." She smiled.

"Camel?"

"Yep. It is rich in protein and vitamins. Did you know that camel milk has over two hundred different proteins? Nomads can live on camel milk alone for up to a month in the desert." She rubbed her hand on the camel's neck.

"You're full of facts, E." He wiped his sweaty brow.

"Irritating, aren't I?" She grinned.

Throwing his head back, he laughed. "You are entertaining."

Riding in silence for a bit, she took photos of the camel herders, her camel's eyelashes, and Timbuktu in the distance. When the call to prayer sounded, the herders stopped the camels, took out their rugs, knelt, and prayed to Allah.

"When they do that, I pray to the Lord for the truth to come to them. There is a true and living God—they just don't know it yet." She watched the men on their rugs.

"Missionaries brought several teams here from America in 2004, and shared the gospel, making an impact. They built a church and a school where children are taught by Christian teachers, and as a result, the congregation is growing in the city."

"Can we visit the church? I haven't heard about it." She focused her Nikon on the blooms of a large cactus.

"I'll see if I can arrange that." Beau saw an old Hummer leaving Timbuktu. He lifted Ellie's camera, focused on the license plate, and snapped a picture. He turned and took a shot of the building where it had been parked, and then sent both photos to his email before erasing them from her camera.

The camels picked up speed as they returned to the corral in Timbuktu.

"E, look this way." Beau took her picture on the camel with Timbuktu in the background. "Your friends will like that shot."

"Thanks."

Before they left the camels, Ellie had Beau pose on top of a dune, holding the camel's reins as he squatted, looking into the distance. "Perfect."

He jerked around when Ellie used the word perfect.

"Thank you, Beau. That was so much fun." Ellie dusted her dress off and removed her turban. "This did make me cooler. I didn't read about that in my research."

He guided her toward the shade provided by the buildings —to keep them out of the sun and out of plain sight. "I'm glad.

Did you get any writing inspiration from that elevated viewpoint?"

"Trust me, my wheels are turning. I'm anxious to see these pictures." She turned off her camera.

"Tomorrow, we can visit a mosque, and it's market day in Timbuktu. The women will be selling their wares. It should make some colorful pictures." He handed her the Sony camera.

"That sounds good." She stored the camera. "I'll look forward to it."

Only the sounds of their footsteps were heard as they walked toward their hotel.

"You're quiet," Beau said.

"Yeah, I saw a look of anguish cross your face when I said 'perfect' after taking your picture. There's a painful story there, isn't there?" She waited.

"I guess everyone has a story." He paused. "Several years ago, terrorists attacked a concert hall, a major stadium, some restaurants, and bars simultaneously, leaving one hundred and thirty dead and hundreds in critical condition." He hesitated.

"My fiancée was waiting for me at a restaurant in *rue do la Fountaine au Roi*. I'd asked her to meet me there. Five were killed in that building. She died holding her hand over a child's wound to stop the bleeding. The child survived."

Her vision turned glossy. "I'm so sorry."

He swallowed hard. "She would call me 'perfect' when she took my picture. It was one of the few English words she knew." He sucked in a deep breath as they stepped into the hotel lobby.

Beau addressed Zamir at the desk. "Could we have two cold Cokes delivered to the sitting area on the first floor?"

The manager nodded and made a call as Beau followed Ellie upstairs. When he sat in one of the chairs, he glanced at her. "You're crying. I'm sorry. That was more information than you asked for."

Using the edge of her sundress, Ellie wiped her face. "I'm sorry for your pain. What a horrible story." She released a breath. "So now you bury yourself in your work, trying to move fast enough so the past can't catch up with the present. I understand."

The waiter from the restaurant delivered their sodas.

"It sounds like you've experienced some heartache of your own." He sipped his Coke.

She took a deep breath and blew it out, then took a drink of her cold soda. "I was engaged to my high school sweetheart. He was the star quarterback, and I was the head cheerleader. You know the type—popular, handsome, smart, with a great personality and loads of talent—he was all that and a bag of chips. You get the picture?" She took another drink.

"But two weeks before my walk down the aisle, I discovered my fiancé loved my bridal party more than he loved me, especially the Maid of Honor, my best friend. My knight in shining armor turned out to be a jerk wrapped in aluminum foil. I cried, canceled my wedding, left town, and started to work on my degree."

"During my freshman year at the university, a stalker in one of my classes made my life miserable. He wouldn't take 'no' for an answer. I was terrified." She shuddered. "After a restraining order failed to keep him away, I took a self-defense course and took him down when he attempted to kidnap me. He was sentenced to serve six years. I moved in with my two best friends in a gated community." She finished her soda and wiped the condensation off her empty Coke bottle.

He held her gaze.

"Beau, everyone experiences difficult things. We each have our war stories. It's how we process it and move on that's most important. The Lord helped me. Maybe you need some help from above too."

He ran his fingers through his hair. "I needed help from

above all right. I begged the Lord to put a sniper on the roof to take out the bomber. I prayed, but it didn't happen. So, I'm moving on with my life." He finished his soda and reached for her empty bottle.

"Bad things happen. It doesn't mean the Lord turned His back on you. Maybe God had a plan for that child and placed your fiancée' there for that exact moment. Some things we don't understand. But don't stop trusting in Him, whatever you do."

Her sincerity held him captive, but though he listened, he didn't want to dwell on the topic. It was too late for that. He was accustomed to making it on his own—and didn't plan to change.

Singing and handmade instruments could be heard in the distance. Glad for a diversion, Beau looked out a window. "Grab your Nikon. You're going to love this."

They hurried downstairs and into the street as a group of Malians came toward them, celebrating in song and dance. Ellie captured the group with her camera, but as they got closer, she scanned the area instead of taking photos.

"What's wrong?" Beau asked.

"I'm not high enough to get the shot I want."

"Then get on my shoulders." He squatted.

"I can't do that. I'm a proper girl. And I don't know you that well." She kept looking for another option.

"You have a job to do. Hurry, or you'll miss your shot."

Huffing, she grabbed the back of her skirt, pulled it between her legs, and tucked it into her belt while he waited. With Ellie on his broad shoulders, Beau put his arms around her legs, holding her steady as she snapped away, capturing happy faces, colorful costumes, and big toothless smiles.

She touched Beau's hair. "I love this, Thanks, de La Croix."

"At your service, *mademoiselle*." He worked to keep her in

front of the homemade parade. "Don't miss the faces of the onlookers."

"Great idea." When the marching throng faded into the distance, she patted Beau's head. "You can put me down now."

He eased down to his knees, took her hand, and helped her dismount. "You good?"

"Yeah. That was awesome. I'm glad you're built like a statue. Those pictures may be the shots I'll use for the article."

He dusted off his knees. "I'm glad."

"Dinner is in two hours. I'm going to my room to make some notes and look at these photos. See you at the table." She took the first step into the hotel lobby but stopped and turned.

Beau didn't follow.

"I think I'll take a walk around town." He paused.

"Watch your back. I won't be there to protect you." Ellie gave him a thumbs-up.

The sound of her laughter faded as he strolled away.

Staying in the shadows, Beau made his way toward the suspected target. He leaned against a building, hiding behind two spindly tree trunks. The breeze caused the limbs to sway while he stalked his prey.

"Do you want me to unload the truck, Hussein?" A guy in uniform stepped to the door and waited for an answer.

Using his phone to take a picture of the soldier, Beau enlarged the image of the man's face. He didn't recognize him. Must be a recent recruit.

Hussein joined him and helped unload what looked like three long boxes of rifles. "Mostafa sent these. He said we will need them. I'm expecting our orders soon."

While the men worked, Beau snapped pics until they shut the door. He hurried back to the hotel to email an update to

Dax Auguste before time to meet Ellie for dinner. These soldiers were preparing to attack—and soon.

Ellie looked up from writing in a journal. "I ordered a drink for you since it's so hot."

He paused at the door of the restaurant. "I could use a cold drink. Thanks." He took a seat. "Are you making progress?"

"Yes. My pictures are telling a great story, but the musical parade was classic. It shows what the magazine wants for the future of Timbuktu." She turned her camera screen to let him see a shot of the boisterous crowd. "I may have a winner with this one."

Taking her Nikon, he brought it close. "You have a gift. That's a wonderful shot."

"Thanks." She fiddled with her napkin and met his gaze. "I can tell you love this city. Will you tell me about Timbuktu?" She watched his facial expression.

"So, the famous reporter wants to interview me, a common laborer?" He eyed her with obvious amusement.

"Yep." She had her pen ready and her journal open.

He paused. "Okay, but don't put my name in the article."

"I promise." She smiled and waited.

"Timbuktu started when nomadic tribes made the area a summer encampment. Later, during World War II, prisoners were kept here. For a time in its rich history, Timbuktu was a city of gold with a busy trade route for ivory, salt, and slaves. Now it's a poor area of various shades of sand, where her citizens struggle to survive." He took a drink.

"Today, there are no traffic lights—a non-issue since there are few vehicles. The city is run by donkeys, except for a few old Land Rovers and three beat-up taxis. Being on the edge of extinction because of war and neglect, it's time for Timbuktu to thrive again—to be the popular tourist destination it once was."

Their entrée of roasted lamb and vegetables was served. Ellie bowed her head and offered thanks, then jumped right back into their conversation.

"That was very well said." She cut into her meat. "When I told my friends I was traveling to Timbuktu, they didn't think it existed. The definition of the word is 'in the middle of nowhere.' My mother threatened, 'I'm going to knock you all the way to Timbuktu,' when we were bad as kids. And here I am—in Timbuktu." She took a small bite of lamb and chewed for a minute. "Is this Mary had a little lamb?"

He smiled. "I'm afraid it is."

"Okay." She tried the vegetables.

"And now, you're offering a glimmer of hope for the future of Timbuktu, a forgotten spot on the globe." He held up his soda. "I thank you, E."

"You're welcome." She smiled.

"Emir, Seif, load the guns and ammo I retrieved from Bamako into the Hummer. Mostafa wants our arsenal distributed to the mosque and the south post. We will move those tomorrow, so get them loaded." The men hurried to do as instructed.

Punching a number into his phone, Hussein walked away. "Yes. Prepare lunch. We will visit the mosque on our way to you." He paused. "I don't have final orders yet. But we must be ready." He ended the call, pocketed his phone, and perched his hands on his hips. *Victory is imminent. I can feel it.*

6

The Islam call to prayer woke Ellie early. Sleep wouldn't return, so she dressed in another flowy sundress, blue with rope strands for straps, and went to the rooftop restaurant to capture the sunrise. Peach hues hinted the sun would soon rise. Ellie captured a series of shots as the day dawned and the shadows lengthened. The waiter brought her a cup of tea to enjoy as Timbuktu came to life.

"You're up early." Beau joined her at the half wall.

"The call to prayer was loud and lengthy, making sleep impossible. Look at this shot of a new day in Timbuktu. The sky is the color of orange sorbet." She held her camera screen for him to see.

"I love the way you captured the light and the silhouette of the buildings." He accepted a cup of coffee from the waiter. "The magazine should be thrilled with your work."

"Thanks." She looked at the sunrise again. "I hope you're right. My future as a photojournalist depends on it."

"If your writing is half as good as your photos, you'll get the job." He sipped his brew as she photographed the sun making its appearance. When he'd emptied his coffee cup, he held it up. "It's not café', but I need the caffeine. I'm going for a refill. Want something?"

"Yeah. Another cup of tea would be great." She gave him her cup, careful not to touch him. She could only handle so much temptation this early in the morning.

After a quiet breakfast, with Ellie working on the story between the photos and her journal entries, they walked toward the Djinguereber mosque, which stood tall in the desert's sun.

"An architect was brought here from Cairo to build it. This mosque was built from the earth it is standing on, they call it *earthen architecture*. It's maintained by the descendants of the original builders." Beau waited as Ellie photographed the building from different vantage points.

"The scalloped points remind me of a medieval castle." She checked her camera screen.

"I see what you mean." He stared at the building. "It is solidly built. In 2012, al-Qaida occupied Timbuktu. They destroyed most of the city, but the mosque only suffered a few cracks. The masons have repaired it. They're faithful to keep it in good condition."

"It casts a large shadow figuratively and literally." She took a deep breath and blew it out.

"Yes, it does." Beau touched her elbow. They started walking again. "One good thing about the shadow is every Monday, the women gather to form a farmer's market for the region. Let's go there. You'll like this."

Ellie followed Beau's lead and heard singing and laughter as they approached rows of vendors displaying their fruits, vegetables, and colorful wares.

"These ladies set up every week and stack their products in pyramids with precision. The display is a work of art, and their banter back and forth is comical to watch. Friendship is strong among these hard-working women." Beau gave his tour guide spiel.

Women were making their way to the market with huge loads balanced on their heads. Some used donkeys to haul potatoes and charcoal. Their bright clothes of mismatched prints and colorful buckets stood out in vast contrast to the brown-stuccoed Mosque behind the market. A few of the women had erected colorful tarps to shield them from the sun. Ellie looked around for a higher vantage point.

"What are you looking for?"

She didn't want to answer.

"E?"

"A higher vantage point for a panoramic shot. Have you got a ladder in your pocket?" She bit her bottom lip.

"You like sitting on my shoulders?"

"My mother would be mortified." She smiled. "I'm sorry for the imposition, but you are quite sturdy, and I need the shot. Do you mind?"

He squatted, and she secured her skirt between her legs to give her a bit of modesty and climbed on.

His hands held her legs as they walked. "Can you go to the end of the market and turn back for a slanted shot? Their smiles would be a great shot for the magazine."

"At your service, my lady."

Children of different ages gathered around Beau's legs. They waved and giggled, touched Beau's hand, then ran away. Ellie smiled at their game—many African children wanted to touch white skin. She got some amazing photos.

"Can we go toward the center of the market now?" She pointed.

"Yes. Africans don't point with their fingers. They used their chin." He demonstrated the action.

"Their chin?" She tried it and laughed. "I'm assuming pointing is offensive."

"Yes, so I would refrain." He put her front and center to photograph the action. Citizens of Timbuktu crowded in and bartered for fruits and vegetables. Having two white people visiting the market drew a crowd of admirers, creating various shots for Ellie's camera.

Beau noticed an old Hummer coming toward the market. "You ready to come down from your throne, E?" He needed to get out of sight.

"Sure. I've gotten some amazing pictures. You can let me down." She almost seemed reluctant but acquiesced.

Down on his haunches, he let Ellie slide down his back. He hurried over to one of the ladies selling wrapped candies, pulled out a large bill, and gave it to her. She smiled at him as he grabbed a handful of sweets and threw them to the children.

Squeals filled the air as they raced for the candy. Ellie was busy with her camera as Beau scanned the area.

"You okay here for a few minutes?" He stepped close to her. "I'm going to see when we can tour the mosque."

She snapped a pic of a sleeping baby tied to his mother's back. "Sure. I'll stay right here." She checked the shot on her screen, then took another picture.

Careful to stay hidden beneath the tarps, Beau wove his way through the kiosks to see the Hummer's driver. He positioned himself with a bird's-eye view and waited. The Imam opened the large carved wooden door, and Hussein stepped out of the mosque, turned, leaned close, and spoke to the leader before giving him a wad of francs. The Imam stashed the money in a pocket of his robe and nodded to Dhakir Hussein.

Capturing the culprit on his phone, Beau made sure to get the license tag in one of the pics. What was he up to? Why involve the Imam? He kept out of sight until the Hummer pulled away, going in the opposite direction from where the main headquarters was located.

After its dust had settled, he approached the mosque. With the terrorist leader gone, it would be safe for Ellie's tour. The heavy doors were still open when he knocked. The Imam stepped into the opening wearing a new robe.

Beau started with the traditional greetings, then posed his request. "Imam, I have a tourist visiting Timbuktu who would love to tour the mosque. Is that acceptable, and is this a good time?"

The old Imam looked back into the mosque and then looked at Beau again. "If you give us ten minutes, those praying will be finished."

Beau gave a slight bow. "Thank you, Imam. We will be here in ten minutes." When the Imam turned away, Beau glanced into the mosque and found it empty.

Turning, he walked away, his mind spinning. The Imam seemed nervous. What was he hiding? Was someone keeping guns here for the terrorists? The terrorists appeared to be thriving financially in a poverty-stricken area. Where was their money coming from? He shelved his questions for later contemplation as he approached Ellie.

"Get the pictures you wanted?" He set his hands on his hips, at ease.

"This has been fun."

"Knowing tourism brings wealth to Timbuktu, the nationals welcome visitors." He watched the women interacting. "They're happy with their lot in life."

"I want to get a few closeups of the women and their vegetables before we go. Is that okay?"

Lifting his wrist, he checked his watch. "We can tour the mosque in eight minutes, so go for it."

The women responded to her with smiles and perfect poses while Beau scanned the scene. This mosque was strategically located to stop an attack from the east. The house Hussein was using could serve as an armory on the west side of Timbuktu. With the desert on the north, maybe it was time to have dinner on the south side of town.

"Give me your camera, E." Beau took some fun pictures of Ellie interacting with the women and the children, then returned the camera. "It's time for your tour of the mosque."

Bidding her friends farewell, she joined Beau as he ambled to the ancient Islamic structure.

"Non-Muslims aren't allowed in parts of the mosque, and you can't use your camera in certain areas. You can ask a few questions, but not too many." Beau instructed her as they approached the mosque.

"You're taking this tour guide gig to a whole new level. You expecting a tip or something?" She smiled.

Laughing, he knocked on the mosque door. He greeted the Imam and introduced Ellie.

They followed the Muslim leader through a large, hauntingly quiet room. Going down a long hall, the walls were stucco, not unlike the outside of the building. Burning incense filled the building with an unusual scent. With few lanterns, most of the corners were eerie with shadows.

The Imam stopped by three steps and a seat that had been built into the wall. "This is the seat of honor for us." He led them to a back room, hidden from view. "This is where women stay when having blood issues." He took them to a large dim room with small rugs rolled up for later use. He didn't linger there but showed them the stairs to the roof. The Imam didn't follow.

Once on the roof, Ellie stood in the blazing sunshine and rubbed her arms as if chilled.

"You okay?" Beau watched her. "You look pale."

She faced him. "What an experience—seeing such darkness up close like this." She took a breath. "What a hopeless religion when contrasted with the Gospel and the promise of eternity in Heaven." She walked the roof, humming a song as she took pictures of the market from this vantage point.

"What's that song?" Beau waited for her.

"It's a new worship song called, 'Falling in Love With Jesus.' My pastor sings it. The song makes me feel close to the Lord no matter where I am."

"Even in such a dark building?"

"Yes, even here." She pivoted and took more shots of the desert.

"Ready to have lunch?" He hesitated. "We can go if you want."

"Yes. Let's leave the mosque behind. It won't be in my article." She moved toward the stairs and looked back to make sure he was following.

When they hurried out the front door, Ellie put her hand on Beau's arm. He paused and waited as she shook one foot and then the other.

"Can I ask what you're doing?"

"I'm shaking the dust off my feet. I don't want to take any of that place with me, but I'll be praying for these people to see the light."

"Am I stretching your religious thoughts?" Ellie watched for something interesting to photograph as they strolled to the hotel. "I know I can be a handful, but God gave you two hands for a reason." She offered a slight smile.

"I have to say, I've never met anyone like you. You wear your faith like a sweater." He stopped and held his hand up, on alert, signaling for her to wait. "E, I think something's happening at our hotel." He pivoted and surveyed the surrounding area, but she saw nothing out of the ordinary.

A group of women waited at the hotel entrance with Zamir, the hotel manager.

Stepping close to Zamir, Beau greeted him and asked if there was a problem. They conversed in French for a moment. Beau turned. "They're waiting for you."

"Me—why?" She stared at Beau, then turned and smiled at the women, recognizing one of their waitresses among the group.

"You've made an impression since you arrived in the city. People have seen you praying over your food, and they know you talk to God. Their friend is very sick, and these ladies want you to pray for her." Beau kept his voice low.

"Okay. I would be glad to pray. Which one is sick?" Ellie stepped toward the ladies, greeting them and touching them on their arms or hands in kind gestures.

The group parted to show her a frail woman sitting on a stool, bent over and holding her stomach. She was well-dressed in a matching African print dress and headpiece. One woman was holding an umbrella over her, keeping her in the shade.

"Will you interpret for me?" She waited for him to move closer.

"Sure." He reached for her camera, took a shot of Ellie with her hands on the woman's forehead and her stomach, and repeated her earnest prayer in French. Ellie made a lengthy appeal to the Lord to heal this woman, to let her touch the hem of His garment. When Ellie said 'Amen,' the women repeated it in French.

The old woman smiled, stood, and put her hand in Ellie's. With a grin on her face, she put her stool under her arm and led her followers down the street. The ladies walked beside her, talking and laughing among themselves.

She turned and met Beau's gaze. "What?"

Shaking his head, he motioned for her to proceed with him into the hotel lobby. "You want to stop by your room? We have fifteen minutes before they serve lunch." He paused by the reception desk.

"That would be great." She sang as she climbed the stairs, still limping on her broken toes. "Falling in love with Jesus is the best thing I've ever done."

When he reached the rooftop restaurant, Beau stood at the edge, watching the foot traffic below. Just three more days. Then he'd get Ellie back to Bamako, and she'd be out of his life —but her pure faith would linger in his mind, along with that vanilla fragrance she wore. But the Lord didn't answer his prayers, leaving him with an unbearable heartache. He had to get a grip and not let Ellie or her faith invade his life.

"I'll have a cold Coke and a cold bottle of water," Ellie told the waiter when she reached the table.

"Same for me, *Monsieur*." Beau joined her.

"You okay? You seem deep in thought."

Meeting her gaze, he paused. "You didn't know who that woman was, did you?" Beau leaned back for his drinks to be served.

"No. Does that matter? She was sick and needed prayer. Beau, I can't heal people, but I serve the Lord who can."

"If she gets her miracle, it will mean a lot for the Christian message in Timbuktu. She's a direct descendant of Mohamed

—*the* Mohamed." He paused. "That's a big deal in this country."

"Wow. I had no idea. I'll keep praying for her." Ellie said. "Maybe the Lord sent me here just for her." She took a drink of her Coke as if oblivious to the impact she'd made.

Eating tough chicken and vegetables again in amenable silence, they listened to the sounds of the nationals, the animals, and the Islam call to prayer. Ellie closed her eyes in prayer, leaving Beau lost in his thoughts.

Ellie leaned over the half wall, watching some children play in the streets. "I wish I could bottle the tastes and smells of Timbuktu to take home with me. As hard as I try, it's difficult to put the descriptions into my prose adequately." She took a deep breath, sighed, and returned to their table.

"I think you'll transport your readers to West Africa by the end of your first paragraph."

She sat back and smirked. "Was that a compliment, de La Croix?"

"I don't dish them out frequently, so enjoy it." He finished the last of his water.

"Let's go to a restaurant on the south side of Timbuktu for dinner tonight. I can show you a bit more about the city. Is that okay?" He finished his chicken and wiped his hands.

"Yes, I'd love that." She smiled.

He took her picture with his phone. "I'll send that pic to your phone. It catches the light perfectly, even if I do say so myself."

"So, you're complimenting yourself now too?" She joked.

"I would die of old age if I waited for you to acknowledge my many talents." He smiled at his remark.

"That was good. You're also fluent in sarcasm. Add that to your resume and make some real money someday." She gave the waiter her empty plate and reached for the fruit dish he offered.

Beau received a text, answered it then pocketed his phone.

"Bring your camera tonight. It's a different view than you've experienced so far. We'll see some of the nicer domed huts, where the more prosperous nationals live."

"All kidding aside, you've done a great job as my tour guide, McGarrett." Ellie put her hand on his arm. "I appreciate it."

He tipped his imaginary hat. They finished their fresh fruit, perfect for such a hot day.

"What do you want to do this afternoon, Ms. Bendale?"

"I think I need to elevate my foot for a while. I stepped wrong and bent my toes. Now, they're swelling and throbbing. And I'll work on the article and edit my plethora of photos." Her eyes showed excitement for the task.

"You like that word, don't you?" He finished a piece of mango.

"Yep." She put her napkin on the table. "So, I'm giving you the afternoon off. Can you find something to do?"

"Thanks. I think I can manage. I'll meet you in the lobby at six. We'll tour a bit before we go to Restaurant Poulet d'Or for dinner. You'll see a beautiful African sunset as we dine at another rooftop restaurant."

Standing, Ellie pushed her chair in. "Sounds like a plan."

"Wait, E." Beau touched her arm. He motioned for their waiter and spoke to him in French, then faced her. "He's bringing you ice in plastic to help with the swelling."

"That's great." They waited for the ice, then left the restaurant. "Is your name just Beau or is there more?" She sounded like a nosey reporter.

"I'm Beauregard Dubois de La Croix at your service, *mademoiselle*." He bowed slightly.

"Dubois?" She stopped short and faced Beau, her eyes wide. "Is that a common French name? Was the soldier at the airport looking for you? Oh, wow. Should I be worried?"

"It is possible. But you not having information keeps you safe from men like him."

"Are you sure?" She gripped his arm and squeezed.

"Limping with two broken toes, your white skin, that blonde hair, and a camera around your neck—your look screams tourist. It keeps you safe. So, relax." He patted her hand. "I'll protect you."

Wearing a nervous smile, she proceeded to her room. When she unlocked her door, she turned back. "Later, Beauregard."

7

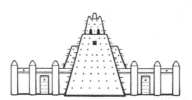

With her long hair flowing in the late afternoon breeze, Ellie descended the stairs in her gauzy sundress and sandals. Adding a touch of makeup and earrings made her feel like she was getting ready for a date. But Beau wasn't interested in a relationship of any kind, and she'd do well to remember that.

"Is our chariot ready, Beauregard?"

He turned, and his eyes widened. "You look great, Ms. Bendale." He bowed slightly.

"Thanks. You clean up pretty good yourself, Magnum." She curtsied.

"Are you ready?" Beau extended his hand toward the door.

She put her hand through his elbow. "I'm ready, sir."

When he opened the door of the old taxi, Ellie slid in. He hurried to the other side. "Restaurant Poulet d'Or Monsieur." He instructed their driver.

The Malian did a U-turn in front of the Bouctou Hotel and drove through narrow roads. Dodging children, animals, and potholes slowed their progress.

Conversing in French for a bit, Beau sounded like he was

asking a question by the inflection of his voice. He and the driver seemed to agree on something before he switched to his tour guide role again.

"These homes are made of thatched or woven mats. With their domed shape, they remind me of large haystacks. They aren't expensive, and the owners can move them if they need to. People with funds will live in one of these while they build a more permanent structure." He pointed to a domed hut beside a partially built home.

Ellie took photos and set her phone to record Beau's diatribe.

"These are difficult days for Timbuktu, but the people take it in stride." Beau scanned their surroundings as he talked. "They are proud people."

The driver stopped in front of a business closing for the day. Beau stepped out and spoke to the owner, then turned to open Ellie's door. "I think you might want to see this."

Always curious, Ellie grabbed her bag and slid out of the cab, following Beau to the quaint building, small but sturdy. As the proprietor uncovered some glass cases, Ellie saw an array of ornate knives of all sizes. "Wow. These are amazing. Are they made here in Timbuktu?"

"Yes. I thought you might want one for your father. I have a great collection displayed on my wall." He turned to the man. "Would you show the lady some knives?"

He nodded and pulled out several specimens of various sizes.

"Are these pricey?" Ellie picked up a knife and turned it in her hand. "I love the leather sheaths."

"What you see here we can buy for twenty-five dollars to a hundred and fifty for the larger knives and swords." He pointed to a specific knife in the glass case and held it out for Ellie to see.

"I like that one." It was a small ornate knife in a decorative sheath resting on a brass stand. "My dad isn't much on decorating his walls, but he would love this on his desk." She turned back to the glass case and pointed to two larger knives, one bigger than the other, with identical decorations of beads and brass and fringed leather hanging from the sheaths. She held them up.

"My brother would love these. Can you get me a good price on these three?" She offered her best smile. "You're the best. No matter what they say." She laughed.

"Ha, ha." He turned to the shop owner, pointed out a set of three knives she wanted to buy, and began the bargaining process. After several moments of sparring in French, he turned to Ellie. "I've got him down to sixty dollars for the three knives you want. Is that okay?"

"Sure, if that's the best you can do?" She grinned.

"You're enjoying this too much."

"How much does he want for your knives?"

"Fifty dollars."

"I have a dinner reservation. Tell him I'll pay him one hundred for all six, or we're leaving." She turned toward the door.

Apparently, the shop owner knew a little English. He stuck his hand out to Ellie and said 'sold,' then grinned.

Laughing, she plopped the money in his hand. "I'll see you in the cab. Can you bring the knives, please?"

"At your service, *mademoiselle*." He collected their purchases.

When he slid into the cab with the knives wrapped for transport, he told the driver to proceed to the restaurant. "You enjoy that?"

"That was fun, and I love the knives. So will the guys in my family. Thanks." She reached over and squeezed his arm. "Oh, I know what you're thinking."

"And what's that?"

"That you can't wait to get me back to Bamako." She laughed and moved her hand back to her lap. "I bet you're counting the hours."

"Yep. Counting the hours."

The driver stopped the taxi in front of a stucco-covered structure with a portico. An array of cacti filled the flower beds around the front of the building. Beau got out and held her door, paid their driver, and greeted the restaurant manager in French. He did the customary bow to the man and listened to his greeting. He turned to Ellie. "We have thirty minutes to wait. Would you like to go to the roof and watch the sunset? You could get great pics of their houses."

"Yes. I'd love that." She took her Nikon out of her bag. "I like taking photos from elevated positions." She winked and tried not to smile.

The stairs were uneven and shaky. Beau grabbed her hand to make sure she didn't fall or stump those broken toes.

The strength of his grip made Ellie want to hang on and not let go. Peace flowed through her—safe and secure in his presence.

When they reached the roof, he dropped her hand and directed her to the best place to utilize her photography skills. The area resembled an outdoor restaurant with some potted plants along the half wall. Beau perched himself on a tabletop with the package of knives at his feet. He searched the area and took a couple of pictures with his phone.

Ellie took photos from different angles, including one of Beau from behind with the sun setting in the distance. It was perfect, but she refrained from voicing her opinion—especially using that word. He was a man of strength, integrity, and amazing good looks. *Guard your heart, Ellie. Beau isn't healed from his last heartache.*

The manager sent a waiter to inform them their table was

ready. Ellie followed Beau with her hand on his shoulder for stability—from the stairs and her heart.

Their food was served right away. "I called ahead and ordered for us. I hope that's okay."

"Of course. Good idea." She opened the cold bottle of sparkling water on their table.

Her fish was very light and perfectly roasted. "This food is amazing. Great choice. Have you eaten here before? I didn't think you ate fish." She took a bite of rice.

"Yes, on another trip to the city. But it has been a while. This is the only place I order fish." He selected a piece of bread from a basket on their table.

"This is the best rice I've ever tasted." She scooped another bite onto her fork.

"They grow it near the river about ten miles from here and cook it in chicken broth with spices." He took a bite.

"Could we get more?" She held his gaze awaiting his answer while enjoying the view.

"Sure." He motioned to the waiter and ordered another serving.

When Beau finished, he sat back and watched Ellie enjoy her rice.

She took her last bite. "Can you ask them what spice they put in the rice? I'd love to try this at home."

"I will before we leave." He paused. "We have two more days in Timbuktu. What do you want to do tomorrow?"

Ellie tapped her finger on her chin as she thought. "Could we get a cab and go outside of town on all sides of Timbuktu and let me get some shots? While we were riding the camels, I took pictures of the city, but I got a view of the back of the mosque."

"I'll ask Zamir if we could borrow his truck for a while." He asked for their check.

"And could you show me where the festival will be held? I'd

like a picture of the area." She laid her napkin on the table. "You do know the place they've chosen, don't you?"

"I think I do, but I'll ask Zamir." He counted out the francs.

"That would be great."

The next morning, Beau revved the engine of Zamir's truck as he waited for Ellie, causing it to backfire, clouding the area with exhaust.

When the smoke cleared, Ellie stood at the front of the hotel, waving her hand in front of her face. She coughed a couple of times as she got into the truck. "Does this thing have any air-conditioning?"

"Only the air blowing through the windows." He made a U-turn, drove in front of the mosque, and out of Timbuktu on the east side. After parking on a hill with the morning sun rising behind them, he turned to Ellie and smiled. "Can you get some good photos from this angle?"

"It's a great place. Can I stand in the back of the truck?" She looked excited.

"Of course. I'll let the tailgate down for you." He opened his door and helped Ellie into the truck bed. Using his phone, Beau took pictures of his own that he would send to the Chief. Getting a good view from all sides of the city was a great idea.

Ellie jumped down and got into the cab. "Come on, Rambo. We have more pictures to take."

On the second attempt, Beau cranked the old truck and drove them to the south side of town. "I do have to make one stop. Zamir needs me to go to the river and pick up a bag of rice."

"That's great. I can get some pictures of activity along the river." Ellie noted the shots she'd just taken in her journal and hung on for the rough ride.

Men loading and unloading their dugout canoes kept Ellie busy with her camera while Beau bought and loaded the rice. He stepped up into the truck bed with her. "By that smile on your face, it looks like you're having fun." He leaned closer, looking at her lips.

"What's wrong? Do I have dirt on my face?"

"You've been smiling so much, I was checking for bugs in your teeth." He laughed

"There's always a comedian in the crowd." She checked her camera screen.

"That's amazing, E. Great job." He smiled at her. "Ready to go to the festival grounds?"

"Absolutely." She paused. "So, be a gentleman and help me out of this truck."

"At your service, *mademoiselle*." He winked and planted his boots in the sand.

Accepting his extended hand, He watched Ellie brace herself for the jump. "Thank you, kind sir." She climbed into the truck as Beau started it. "Is it far?"

"No. Just over a couple of hills. See those palm trees? That's the corner of the grounds." He drove over the hill, then stopped. "Those scrawny trees in the distance mark the other end of the festival area. It's the most level place for the event, and it's close to an electrical pole for the instruments."

"Do you think readers would be interested in a photo of an empty field or sandpit? I don't think so. But I'll take it just in case." She slid out of the truck, put her foot on the bumper, and hoisted herself up. After taking a few shots, she slipped back into the cab.

"Your toes doing better?"

"Yes. Thankfully, they're on the mend. We can go on to the other side of Timbuktu now."

Beau hesitated. The west side of town was not a safe place

to be. "That side of the city doesn't look very photogenic. You sure you want pics there?"

"You know what, I think you're right. Is there a watering hole where they bring the animals to drink? It would give me one more view of everyday life. I could incorporate those into my work."

Relieved at the change of plan, Beau turned the truck and took a few back roads to safely take them in the other direction. "You can never tell what animals are drinking at any given time."

"Could we watch the watering hole for a while?"

"Sure. Zamir doesn't need his truck until after lunch." He looked at his watch. "That gives us at least two hours. How many pictures can you take in two hours?"

"Mr. Tour Guide, you find me an interesting subject, and I'll count the shots." She turned the camera toward him and framed a photo, then waited for him to look in her direction.

Because of a lull in their conversation, Beau glanced at her.

Ellie got the photo she wanted to remember him by. That sexy grin, his hand resting on top of the steering wheel, his hair blowing in the wind—ruggedly handsome. She showed him his picture on her camera screen. "I'm going to entitle that one Timbuktu Tour Guide."

"Just don't put me in your article."

"Don't worry, I won't. You might want half of my big paycheck." She laughed.

Stopping the truck under the shade of a scrawny tree, he said, "Can you get some good pics from this angle?"

"The view from here is perfect, but I'm going to get in the back of the truck again. I need to be at a higher level." She opened the door to get out.

"So, you tired of riding on my shoulders?" He waited.

"I was afraid you'd give me a bill for carrying charges, Macho Man." She grinned and shut the door.

Laughing, he joined her in the truck bed.

Adjusting her lens, she took some close-ups. "Look at that little guy telling those goats what to do."

"He's the one watching the goats, E." Beau leaned against the cab of the old truck.

"That little guy? He can't be more than six years old."

"In Africa, they start them young."

"But he's not even wearing shoes. Doesn't the sand get hot on his feet? And he needs more clothes on." She let her camera hang from its strap and propped her hands on her hips.

"His family is poor. This is the best they can do. You see this all over the continent."

Tears welled in Ellie's eyes. "It's sad."

"Don't let it bother you. Look at him. He is a happy little boy. He doesn't know any different."

"I know you're right, but my American mind has a hard time processing it." She took another photo of the little boy's smile.

"Here come some donkeys. Focus on them." He pointed with his chin as per African custom.

"Are they being led by a little boy?" She didn't want to look.

"Nope. A skinny senior citizen."

"Oh, no. That's worse." Ellie hid her face behind her camera and focused on the donkey herder. He had ragged clothes, wore a pair of flip-flops that were too big for him, and an old straw hat. He tapped a stick on their hinder parts and led them to the water.

"What are you thinking?"

"He is too old to be doing this. He should be resting in the shade with a Coke in his hand." Ellie sighed.

"He has probably never tasted a Coke and would rather have tea."

"When do people here retire? Do they just work until they die?" She took a few more pictures as the old guy led the donkeys away.

"They work until they can't anymore, but they're happy. It's their way of life."

"It's a hard life." She focused her camera on a man leading a camel and took several pictures, then turned her Nikon off. "I'm ready to go to the hotel for lunch."

Beau followed her out of the truck bed and slid into the driver's seat. "You okay?" He glanced at her.

She watched the camel at the watering hole for a minute. "It's a bit of culture shock when you immerse yourself in their everyday lives and see how the other half lives." She took a deep breath and blew it out.

"Your soft heart is showing, E. You care about those less fortunate than you." He put his hand on her arm. "It shows what a wonderful person you are." He squeezed her arm, then cranked the truck and put it in gear. They rode in amenable silence.

When they stopped in front of the hotel, Ellie turned to Beau. "Thanks for the tour. I got some great pictures. I'll meet you at the lunch table." She slid out of the truck and hurried inside, leaving Beau to unload the rice and return the truck.

———

Ellie was writing in her journal when Beau joined her at the table.

She didn't look up. "I ordered you a cold Sprite and a bottle of water. I thought your life needed some variety."

"Thanks. You don't think you're adding enough spice to my boring life?" He pulled out his chair, turned it around, and straddled it. With his arms propped on the back of the chair, he stared at her. She ignored him.

After a few minutes, she looked up and met his gaze. "What?"

"You're going to have to buck it up, buttercup."

She smiled. "Using my sarcasm on me, Beauregard?"

"Yep." He laughed then his smile faded. "When you get this job, it will take you into a lot of settings like you experienced today. Take your shots and write your stories so you can share their plight with the world. Through your work, you can show what you see, feel, and experience in places like Timbuktu. You have a gift that will be difficult to share sometimes, but you must persevere."

Their drinks were served. When the waiter had gone, Ellie lifted her Coke toward Beau. "Thanks, I needed that pep talk."

He lifted his Sprite and touched her bottle, then drank the refreshing liquid. "No charge for the advice." He winked and turned his chair around as their lunch was served.

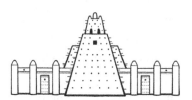

8

"What's on the agenda for the afternoon?" Beau pushed back from the table and finished off his water.

"Is there anything we've missed?" She wiped her mouth.

Beau ran his hand over his scruffy chin. "I'm all out of ideas."

"Then I think I'll spend the afternoon working on my article and going through the photos. If I have any holes in my story, we can fill them in tomorrow."

"That sounds like a plan. I'll be around if you change your mind. Zamir can find me if you think of another picture you need. If not, I'll see you at dinner."

"I appreciate all you've done for me, Beau."

"At your service, *mademoiselle*." Ellie was getting sentimental, and he didn't want to go there. Saying goodbye would be hard enough without having an intimate conversation now. "Why don't you order another drink to take back to your room? In this heat, you'll be burning up the keys with amazing prose."

"Good idea."

He squeezed her shoulder. "Have a wonderful afternoon." He left her at the table, but the feel of her skin stayed with him.

———

That evening, Beau pulled out his chair. "Didn't I leave you at this table earlier today?"

Her smile told him she was over her melancholy mood. "I left this spot for the afternoon and got a lot accomplished."

"So, did you finish it?"

"Not yet, but I'm getting close." She put her napkin on her lap. "Did you enjoy your afternoon off, interpreter?"

"I had some emails to answer and a few calls to make." He motioned to the waiter for a bottle of water. "I'm glad you had a productive afternoon."

Their entrée of roasted goat was served with vegetables. Ellie took a bite of goat and chewed and chewed and chewed. She covered her mouth and laughed.

"What's so funny?" Beau smiled.

Speaking with her hand over her mouth, she answered, "I've chewed this goat for a while, but I can't swallow it."

"Spit it out, E." He sat up in his chair.

She kept chewing and tried to swallow, then coughed.

"You're going to choke. Spit it out." He handed her his napkin.

Holding the napkin, Ellie rid her mouth of the mound of fatty goat. "Now that was lady-like." She covered her face with her hands. "I'm humiliated."

"Why? You were choking."

"Beau, a lady doesn't spit! Under any circumstance. Especially in front of a handsome gentleman."

"Forget it, E. I'd rather you spit it out than choke. I'd have to give you the Heimlich maneuver or mouth-to-mouth."

"Now that would be fun." Ellie smiled and fanned her face with her notebook. "I'm so embarrassed."

"Have you ever eaten goat before?" He cut a small piece and picked it up with his fork.

"No, and maybe I'd better not try it again."

Demonstrating, he ate a tiny bite. "When you eat goat, take it in small bites. It's not filet mignon." He lifted his fork to demonstrate. "Eat your vegetables. They're pretty good." He eyed her as he chewed.

After stabbing her carrots, she tried them. "They're good." She snuck a chunk of her goat onto his plate when she thought he wasn't looking.

"So, our plane flies at four tomorrow evening. In the morning, bring your things down to the front desk and turn in your key."

"Sure. I can do that." She took a drink of water.

"Do you need any more photos?" Beau looked around the restaurant and didn't see anyone suspicious.

She thought for a minute. "Could we take a walk tomorrow? I'd like some pictures of donkeys loaded with firewood or maybe a camel caravan on the horizon. And I'd like to visit the church the missionary built."

"No problem. Let's go right after breakfast." So much for hoping she forgot that idea. Now he could only hope it wasn't being watched by enemy forces.

"Perfect." Ellie put her fingers to her mouth. "Sorry, I didn't mean to say that word. I'll just end the evening saying it sounds like a great way to conclude our journey to Timbuktu." She stood and pushed her chair in.

After seeing Ellie to her room, Beau stepped into the darkness to make a final sweep of the house used by the suspected terrorists. Staying in the shadows, he returned to the location where he'd seen Hussein unloading a Hummer. He held his phone by the open window and recorded their Kurdish conversation, with plans to have it translated later.

When the men inside the house got quiet, Beau slipped away and headed toward the hotel. Hearing footsteps behind him, he slipped into an alley between two buildings and waited. Two of Hussein's men walked past him. After about fifteen minutes, he returned to the hotel.

There was a definite threat to the city, and Beau was anxious to report his findings to Chief Auguste and his military leaders as soon as he returned to Bamako. It was time to leave Timbuktu before he was discovered.

"Morning, Ellie. Are you packed?" He signaled to their waiter for a cup of coffee and sat across from her as a mild breeze rippled the tarp over their table.

"Yes. My suitcase is packed, locked, and ready to be taken downstairs. It is a bit heavier with the knives inside, but I think it will be under-weight." She cut into her mango, bowed her head to pray, then took a bite.

"I'll take care of it after we eat." He buttered a roll and added his favorite orange marmalade.

"Marmalade is a bit tart for me. I want something sweeter first thing in the morning." She took a bite of her roll with berry jelly.

Reaching over, Beau wiped jelly off her upper lip. He tensed, regretting the touch.

"I was saving that for later."

"You can always reapply it before we go," Beau teased.

"I'll pass." She sipped her hot tea. "Are you packed, Macho Man?"

"Yeah. I'm ready to fly." He leaned back when the waiter brought his eggs. "How much longer are you in Bamako before your flight?"

"For me, it's better to write while I'm still in the setting. I added three days to my itinerary to lay by the pool, relax, and work on the article and photos. I like to have it ready before I leave. It comes across as more authentic when I do that." She finished her tea.

"From the mouth of a professional." He saluted her with his coffee cup.

"Oh, I hope they offer me the position. I'll let you know." She paused. "If you give me your email address."

"I can do that if you won't pass it out to all your friends." He gave her a hint of a smile.

"Are you afraid a mob of beautiful women would start stalking you, McGarrett?" She smiled. "I'd never do that. I'll keep it close to my heart." She put her hand over her heart in an exaggerated move and fluttered her eyelashes.

He shook his head. "Now I'm really worried." Close to her heart? Very tempting. Counting the hours—if only she knew. Beau was getting uneasy with their friendly banter. He had to keep things in check where Ellie was concerned. Relax, and people can get hurt. It was best to finish this ruse and get her back to the capital city—and hurry.

"Ready for a walk?" He stood and left a tip on the table.

"If you can get my luggage, I'll be ready." She took the last drink of her water.

"At your service, *mademoiselle*."

Stopping at her room, he took her carryon bag to the lobby and parked it next to his duffle. He gave their room keys to Zamir. "May we leave these here at reception until we depart?"

"Yes, Monsieur. They will be safe with me." Zamir put the keys away.

As she descended the stairs, Ellie held her hair off her neck as if the warm breeze might dry the perspiration dotting her skin. When she looked up and smiled, Beau's breath caught.

"Well—" he coughed. "You look like you're ready to stroll the city."

"The question is, are you ready to finish this tour guide gig, de La Croix?" She winked as she donned her sun visor and strolled to the door.

"You're walking better." Beau hurried to catch up.

"My toes are healing." She spoke over her shoulder. "Try to keep up, Dinozzo."

"Dinozzo?"

"You know the good-looking guy on NCIS. The one who makes all the movie references."

"Guess I missed that one. I must catch up on my cop shows when I'm in the States again." He checked the street before stepping out of the building. It was a normal day in Timbuktu.

"This scrub brush reminds me of the tumbleweeds I've seen in New Mexico. I feel sorry for these scrawny chickens scratching in the sand, not finding any worms. Does the restaurant buy these chickens for our meals?" She held up her hand. "Never mind. I don't want to know. Oh, I hear donkeys. We're getting close." She pulled out her Sony, loaded a new SD card, and turned it on. "I lightened my load. My bigger camera is in my suitcase."

"Smart idea." He motioned for her to turn left. They came to a clearing where the donkeys were being loaded. "Let me hold your bag." Beau shouldered the strap, stepped back, and watched her do her thing.

She took pictures from different angles—photos of the donkey's face, the load on his back, and the handler working up a sweat in the heat of the morning. Beau laughed out loud when she stepped in donkey poop. Holding her nose, she looked at him and grinned. He took that picture with his phone.

"That pose needs to be in the article."

She rubbed her shoe in the sand and sage grass to remove the smelly dung. "Do I have it all off?" She held her foot up for Beau to inspect.

"I think you got it." He tried to hide a smirk.

"It's not funny." She walked to where he stood and socked his arm.

He rubbed his bicep. "I think we should make our way to the camel lot." He pointed in the other direction. "I'm not sure about the caravan shot, but let's go back to the ones we rode and see what we find."

After putting her Sony into her bag, she pulled out two bottles of water.

"Thanks." He took a long drink. "I needed that."

Camels were being saddled for some waiting riders.

"You may be in luck if you don't mind waiting until they travel into the distance." Beau slowed their pace.

"Can you find us some shade?" She looked around for a tree. "These plants look dehydrated—in need of an IV for sure."

"Let's back up next to the brown stucco building and sit on that bench."

"Good idea." She paused. "But they're all brown stucco. Lead the way." Once seated, Ellie took her camera out. "Camels are emotional animals."

He stared at her. "I've never seen a camel get emotional."

"Are you making fun of me?"

"No, do continue. You keep things from getting boring." He finished his water and started tearing the label from the bottle.

"All camels are social creatures. They greet one another by blowing in each other's faces. But with people, they spit on them, so don't get too close. You don't do that, do you, Beau?"

"No, I'm not a blower or a spitter." He smiled.

"That's good to know." She took some pictures of the camel

preparation. After fifteen minutes, the caravan was loaded and trekking across the dunes. Ellie walked closer and lay on the ground to get the exact shot for the magazine spread, serious about her work.

Beau took her picture sprawled out on the sand with the camera to her face. She didn't seem to mind that her long blonde hair was on the ground, not to mention her clothes were getting filthy.

She stood, dusted herself off, and hurried toward him. "I got it. It's a great shot." She hugged him and then lifted her camera screen so he could see the photo.

"It—it is a good shot, Ellie." He caught her gaze. "It's perfect." His gaze caught hers on that last word. "You're going to get that job. I'm sure of it."

"Thanks." She kissed his cheek. "I couldn't have done this without your help." She put her camera away, took a deep breath and blew it out in a huff. "I'm going to have that photo put on a canvas. It would look great over the fireplace in the condo. You ready to visit the church?"

He stilled.

"Beau?"

"Yeah, sure. It's down this main street and on the right after the curve." He led the way. "The pastor's name is Yatarah. He speaks English and French. You'll like him, if he is there. He has taken new converts into his home after their families disowned them when they became Christ-followers."

Ellie's hand flew to her mouth. "They really do that—disown their family members?"

"Sometimes they beat them, demanding they renounce their new faith. It's a hard life, E." He put his hand on her shoulder, stopping their movement. "Your job is to get the pictures and tell their stories to the world. You should be happy there's a strong Christian witness in Timbuktu."

She held his gaze for a long moment. "Thanks." She

grabbed his hand and squeezed it. "I needed to hear that." She linked her hand through the crook of his elbow. "Now, show me the church."

He strolled to the entrance and held the gate open. "This church and school offer free education for Muslim children. They're taught to read using the Bible as their textbook." He opened the door and flipped on the light.

"That's awesome. What a great ministry. The Bible says if we train a child, showing them the right way to go, when they're older they will remember it and not depart."

After showing her the classrooms, he led her into the church.

A holy silence permeated the sanctuary. Ellie put her arms straight out from her sides and pivoted, spinning in circles in the center aisle. "Don't you love the peace you feel in this place?" She spun again. "I'm glad we ended our tour here. It's like a story with a happily ever after ending, because when they find Jesus, they get their happy ending. They get eternal life."

"You're glowing, E."

"I think that's the sunlight coming through the high windows."

"Maybe." He paused, his gaze riveted on her. "Um—it doesn't look like the pastor is here right now." He scanned the area as they returned to the gate.

"By the time we walk to the Bouctou, lunch will be served, so step it up, Rambo."

Her exuberance brought him back to the task at hand, to the hard reality. Lost in his thoughts, he walked toward the hotel. The feel of her arms around him—she fit perfectly in his embrace. Her kiss on his cheek stole his breath. *She was just saying thank you. It wasn't personal.* But it was getting personal for him. He needed to get her to Bamako—soon!

9

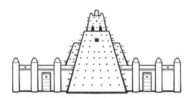

To get to the hotel quicker, Beau led Ellie between two stuccoed buildings toward the main street. Some chickens squawked and ran in the other direction.

"What's the hurry? My toe is better, but racing might be out of the question."

He slowed his stride. "Sorry, but I'm hungry."

"Well, I wouldn't want you to starve." She tried to catch up.

"Hello, Dubois! I knew that was you at the airport." Hussein took a military stance in the sand.

Beau froze.

That voice grated on her last nerve.

Beau grabbed her hand, shoved her behind him, and jerked around to face the enemy. "Well, if it isn't Dhakir Hussein, well-known murderer, and terrorist leader. I thought you left Timbuktu when the military ran your cohorts out of town." Beau sized him up, seeing a pistol and a Glauca tactical knife.

"You wish, military hero. What are you doing here? Spying again?" He spat as he hissed his words—standing poised, like the snake he was, ready to strike.

Moving closer to Beau, Ellie hung on.

"This is a mistake. We're just tourists taking in the sites. I'm of no consequence to you, Hussein." Beau began to back up, putting distance between them and the threat. Ellie kept in step. "We've got a plane to catch."

"That's out of the question. I can't let you leave Timbuktu, Dubois. You know too much. You'll report our presence in this city. I should have killed you last time we crossed paths—when your knife sliced my face." He touched the jagged scar. "I'm afraid you and your lying friend will be missing that flight." The soldier stepped closer.

"Another soldier is closing in behind me," Ellie whispered.

Squeezing her hand, Beau let her know he heard her.

"I'm working as Ms. Bendale's interpreter while she writes for a magazine featuring Timbuktu. I'm at the end of my military career. But you know that." Beau tried to reason with him—to buy them some time.

"Um, he's getting closer," Ellie whispered.

With a pistol in his hand, Hussein stepped forward and aimed. "Dubois, you have cost our cause too much through the years. Mostafa Al-aziz wants you dead. I have my orders and must obey." He cocked the gun.

Beau tapped on Ellie's arm getting her attention. "*Moja, Mbili—*"

Swahili. Ellie knew the words—one, two, three. She stiffened.

"*Tatu!*" Beau said.

As Ellie made a jerky movement behind him, the soldier he couldn't see, yelled.

Beau filled Hussein's eyes with sand as he knocked the gun from his hand in one lightning-fast move. A stiff kick to the gut and Hussein went down. But he bounced up on swift feet and landed a blow on Beau's jaw. Beau punched him hard, knocking him out, then grabbed Ellie's hand.

"Can you run?" He yelled as they darted down the street.

"Hurry, or you'll be eating my dust." She kept up with him.

"Let's get to the hotel. They'll be right behind us." Beau tightened his grip on her hand.

"I hope you have a plan, Rambo." She matched his stride. "I think we've seized the wrong day."

"Oh, I'll think of something." He looked back, checking to see if they were being followed.

"Well, think fast." Ellie breathed hard.

They rushed past people, dogs, and donkeys. Taking another shortcut, they made good time. When they rushed into the lobby, the manager was at the desk.

"*Monsieur* Zamir, I need your help. Soldiers are chasing us." Beau huffed, trying to catch his breath. "Can you send our luggage on today's plane to Bamako and have them taken to the French Embassy to the attention of Chief Dax Auguste?" Beau unzipped his suitcase and put his flashlight into his pocket.

The manager wrote the details on a piece of paper. "Are you taking the flight?"

"No, we must escape another way." He looked out the door before he transferred some things from his luggage to his person.

Bent over at the waist, Ellie took some deep breaths. "My side—hurts."

"Give it a minute," Beau wiped the sweat beading off his brow.

Ellie grabbed pants, a top, and tennis shoes from her suitcase. She pulled out the gauze material and stuck it in her bag along with her snacks before hurrying to the lady's room.

A few minutes later, she joined Beau in the lobby and removed the band that only held a third of her bun after their run. She pulled out some francs. "How much do we owe him?"

He asked in French then told her the amount. She paid Zamir.

"*Monsieur*, water bottles?"

She stashed six bottles in her bag and offered additional francs, but he refused the money.

"*Monsieur* Beau. I will get my truck and drive you to the river. Will that help?" Zamir hurried around the counter with keys in his hand.

"Yes. Do you know a man with a canoe who can take us down the river? We need to travel as far as Mopti on the Niger." Beau tugged on his vest and loaded the pockets with a compass, a Swiss Army knife, and a few things from a first-aid kit.

Zamir rushed back to the phone on the desk and made a call. "I will arrange." Sand scattered around his feet as he hurried.

"I'm so sorry, Ellie." Beau turned toward her.

Ellie saw a different side of her tour guide. He exuded focused strength with each movement. Bravery. Fortitude. In his luggage, he retrieved a phone from the inside pocket. She spotted a gun in a holster at his waistband, and the noonday sun shining through the front door glinted off a knife in his boot. *Who is this guy?*

"It is arranged, *Monsieur* Beau. I will bring my truck to the back of the hotel. We must make haste." Zamir rushed away.

Beau stepped away and returned wearing cargo pants. He stuffed his satellite phone and other items in the pockets, then motioned for Ellie to join him at the back exit. "Let's wait here until we hear Zamir's truck. You ready for some adventure?" He kept his voice down.

"Are you giving me a choice?" Ellie whispered. She pulled her hair into a messy bun using a band she had around her wrist.

"No. I was just being nice." He eyed the hotel's front entrance.

As the sound of an engine approached, Beau eased the door open and dodged a right hook. *Hussein.* Beau tossed his backpack toward Ellie's feet and went into fight mode behind the hotel, matching the enemy blow for blow. With a leg lock, Beau threw him to the ground. The angry Iraqi twisted and escaped Beau's grip.

Dust stirred as Beau kicked Hussein in the stomach. Hussein stumbled back, trying to catch his breath.

Zamir said something in French, then motioned for Ellie to get in the truck. She dove into the bed, and he cranked the vehicle.

With her bag and Beau's backpack, Ellie lay on a sand-covered canvas that lined the truck bed while listening to the battle raging. Risking a look, she leaned up to see Beau take a hard hit in his ribs. Hussein moved in as Beau strained to catch his breath. Taking advantage of his closeness, Beau socked him in the jaw, then caught him in a chokehold and held tight until Hussein passed out.

Zamir yelled to Beau in French. Ellie could only guess the meaning of his words.

After dropping Hussein in the dirt, Beau jumped in beside Ellie. Zamir sped out of the alley. Beau held her shoulder in an attempt to stabilize her body on the rough ride. With dust billowing in their wake, they left the city behind.

Ellie raised her head enough to watch the building, people, and memories growing smaller in the distance. "I thought I'd be sad to leave Timbuktu, but I think I changed my mind." She stared at Beau. "Are those guys friends of yours?"

Either he didn't hear her or didn't have time for humor as he placed a call. He reported the attack to someone named Dax Auguste at the French Embassy on a satellite phone, then paused. "Our luggage will be delivered to you sometime this evening. And I have the proof you needed. One attack can remove this threat." He listened. "Yes, and I will get her back to Bamako." He signed off and pocketed the phone.

Ellie stared at Beau.

"What?"

Eager to get out of the truck as Zamir slowed down, she shook her head and grabbed her bag.

"Wait. Let me make sure it's safe." Beau put his hand on her arm.

Rising slowly on his knees, he checked the area. "A Hummer is coming in this direction! He knows we've left Timbuktu." He held his hand up in front of Ellie. "Wait here."

Ellie recognized his stealth mode as he cased their situation. It was like watching Rambo in action. But the movie was her life, and she was the one running from terrorists. Her heart hammered. A chill crept up her spine, as she peeked over the truck bed.

Zamir spoke to Beau in French.

Several canoes loaded and unloaded fish, bags of salt, and rice as Beau scanned the river. "The soldiers are closing in fast. Ellie, get out of the truck and go lay down in the first canoe to the right of the pier. The man in the boat has a round, pointed hat. Hurry. Stay there no matter what happens." Beau helped her out of the truck.

She bolted for the river. Once in the canoe, she peered over the rim and caught his eye.

Following his instructions, she hunkered down in the hand-carved vessel. It dipped and swayed with the water but didn't make too many waves in the slow-moving river. After putting her bag where her head would rest when they fled, she took another peek under the blazing sun and watched, listening as the action thriller played out in front of her. Sweat beaded on her brow, and moisture rolled down her back.

"Zamir, take off *monsieur*. This could get dangerous. Thank you for your help." Beau waved at Zamir.

Shaking his head, as if hating to leave, he put his hand on Beau's arm. "I Christian. I pray." He spoke in broken English and waved goodbye as he drove away.

Beau hid behind a stack of canoes. He waited as their pursuer drew closer.

Hussein was standing in the Hummer with his gun drawn. His driver nursed a bleeding, broken nose, making Ellie proud of her quick moves that deterred the soldier. The Hummer came to a screeching halt, sending dirt and pebbles airborne. Ellie guarded her eyes against the dust that momentarily clouded her sight. Hussein leaped from the truck before it came to a halt. Stomping toward the river, he scanned the area.

"DeBois, I owe you for this scar. Don't hide like a frightened child. We have a score to settle." He shouted. Dirt dusted his camouflaged uniform.

From his hidden position, Beau slung something shiny— hitting Hussein in the left arm. A knife. When he grabbed his arm, Beau ran for him and spun around kicking him in the stomach with his boot.

Hussein howled from the hit.

In a flash, Beau had him on the ground in a leg lock, sending sand air-born.

Hussein threw Beau off and bounced to his feet, hitting him in the chest. Beau gasped for breath and jerked away. When Hussein rushed Beau again, he blocked the Iraqi's punches and got him in a chokehold. Hussein struggled to suck in air several times before he flipped Beau over his back and slammed him into the desert sand. Beau sprung to his feet, pivoted in a circle, and slammed his boot into the side of Dhakir's head, taking him to the ground again.

"Give it up, Hussein. You're bleeding and need to get that stitched up." Beau stood over him.

When Hussein reached for his gun, Beau stomped his arm. He jerked free and stood. Beau pummeled Hussein, keeping him off guard. When he had the upper hand, he planted a final blow, knocking him down into a spray of sand.

Beau bolted for the canoe and dove in beside Ellie. His large body weighted the canoe deeper into the river. Waves rocked the vessel. Beau asked the rowman to cast off and hurry. Beau pulled Ellie down into the smelly canoe beside him. As they left the river's edge, he peeked over the side and drew the gun out of the holster at his waist like a gunslinger in the old West. He aimed and fired.

Hussein yelled and fell, grabbing his thigh. Ellie saw blood staining his pant leg.

"You got him. Good shot, Dead Eye."

"I kept him from shooting one of us or the canoe. But that bullet won't stop him—it will only slow him down and increase his rage. My superiors want him alive and taken into custody." Beau breathed in and out, catching his breath. He felt his side, probably checking for a cracked rib, then laid down in the dugout canoe, his body touching Ellie's as they lay face to face.

Oh, this is great! We're being chased by terrorists, that's pretty scary, but now I'm skin-to-skin with a hunky hero—in more danger in a smelly canoe than I was in Timbuktu. The threat just escalated big time!

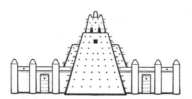

10

Beau stared into Ellie's blue eyes and saw red flags waving in his mind.

Breaking their gaze, Ellie lifted her head and looked around in the canoe.

"What are you looking for?"

"A bag of chips." She kept searching, causing the canoe to rock.

"What?"

"You know—all that, and a bag of chips. You're a regular one-man army! Do you dream up those tactical moves in your sleep, Bruce Lee?"

Her smile disappeared as all teasing slipped away when she inched closer to his face. "Who are you? Why did *you* come to Timbuktu? You owe me an explanation! And don't sugarcoat it. I want the truth. Did you use me to get info on those terrorists? How much trouble are we in?"

"If I tell you, then I'll have to kill you." He smiled.

"This is serious, Beau." Her gaze was piercing, angry.

Taking a deep breath, he paused and blew it out. "You might be safer if you don't know the answer to those questions." He wiped the perspiration off his face, then grabbed his aching side, bracing his ribs, and groaned.

"I'll take my chances." She wasn't backing down.

"This is classified information." He paused. "I'm a double-agent working for the U.S. and France, trying to secure Timbuktu before the Festival. With the info I've obtained, the terrorists will be taken out, making the city safe. I was on assignment, following orders to accomplish my task, while I helped you complete your job for the magazine. I'm sorry it put you in danger. That wasn't part of the plan. I'll get you to Bamako safely. I promise, E." He held her gaze.

"Can you keep that promise? These are terrorists we're talking about."

"I finish my assignments. I'll see you through this." He infused his tone with confidence.

They rode without conversation for a while, with only the sound of the paddle slicing through the water, birds cawing above them, and passing canoe owners greeting their guide. Ellie was depending on him to get her to Bamako. He'd always considered himself capable. But their attackers were the number one enemy of the world, and this was one assignment he couldn't fail.

"Are you with me?" He asked.

"With our perspiration blending as we travel skin-to-skin, under the blazing African sun, in a fishy-smelling canoe, I'm with you." She paused. "I'm not happy about the secrets you've kept or this turn of events, but I trust you to keep me safe."

Ellie pulled the gauze material from her bag and covered them. "For UV protection." A small breeze cooled them, as did the shade of trees that lined the river's edge. She pulled out a package of cheese crackers and handed Beau half of them. "Keep your strength up, Hulk Hogan. There are three types of crocodiles in this river, and I may need rescuing." Her sarcasm was more matter-of-fact than humorous. She put a whole cracker into her mouth.

Attempting a smile, he took the crackers. "Thanks. I didn't think about food."

She grabbed two bottles of water and gave him one.

"Resourceful, aren't you, Ms. Bendale?" He drank it without taking a breath.

"I try." She sipped her water, making it last. "So, do you have more bullets for your gun in those pockets?"

"Yeah. I have enough ammunition."

"But you left your knife in that guy's arm. That only leaves the knife in your boot." Ellie waited for an answer.

"Observant too. Ever thought about being an agent? You broke that guy's nose. You know that, right?"

"Yep. With my elbow. I told you I took a self-defense course when I was being stalked. I can hold my own, in a pinch." She finished another cracker.

"You did today. Hidden talent. You've got grit. I admire that."

Raising up on her elbow, Ellie moved the gauze.

Beau followed her gaze to the owner of the canoe. "His hat tells me he's from the Bozo tribe. They're the main fishermen on this part of the Niger." Beau surveyed the area and then relaxed again. The canoe rocked with the movement of the river while the man rhythmically paddled them downriver. He was a quiet man, a friend of Zamir, and their means of escape, for the moment.

Ellie peeked over the lip of the canoe. "Are there hippos in this river?"

"Yes, but I haven't seen any in this area. They are usually found farther down the river." He hesitated. "We're leaving the river before we reach the hippos."

"I'm glad. They don't like people in their water." She checked the river again. "How long is this river ride?"

"Several hours. Why don't you take a nap? It will be a while." He wiped his sweaty brow with the back of his hand.

"If I take a nap, you're my pillow. I can't exactly move to another canoe."

"It's fine. Let's rest while we have the chance." He moved around a bit to ease his aching ribs and multiple bruises.

Ellie laid her head on Beau's shoulder. "Thanks."

Soon the canoe rocked her to sleep.

If he allowed it to happen, he could get used to this. Holding Ellie as she slept made it impossible for Beau to relax. She smelled so good compared to the fishy scent of the canoe. Ellie was pure sunshine in a beautiful package. Being with her had softened the hard walls he'd built around his heart. It would be difficult to say goodbye, but there was no way he could risk a relationship. It hurt too much.

Beau used the time to devise and strategize and considered their options to get from Mopti to Segou, where he could secure camel rides for them to Bamako. They would be sitting ducks on the camels, but it wasn't Hussein's style to kill with witnesses who could identify him. He would wait until he could make a surprise attack. Beau knew vigilance was crucial —he had to keep his guard up.

As his aches and pains subsided, Beau dozed off—but deep sleep transported him to the past. Sirens blared as Beau ran the streets of Paris. Bombs exploded behind him and off to the left. He kept running as another bomb exploded near the restaurant.

"Jezelle! No!" He plowed through a crowd, some wounded and bloody, screaming as they ran. Flames reached for the sky. Glass windows blew out. "Jezelle!" he screamed as he approached the restaurant.

A haughty laugh spun Beau to his right. Dhakir Hussein aimed his gun. Beau threw his spring-loaded knife with lightning-fast speed, grazing Hussein's face and leaving, a jagged gash. Hussein got off a shot before Beau darted out of his sites.

Grabbing his arm with two wounds from a through-and-through, Beau rushed into the restaurant and found Jezelle as her life slipped away. Ignoring his pain, he held his fiancée in his arms.

She kept one hand on a child beside her but reached for Beau's face. "*Jet'ame*, Beau." She rubbed her finger down his cheek. "Perfect—" Her body went limp ...

A loud crash jerked Beau from sleep. The canoe moved to the left. The man had it righted with a few strokes.

"Wow!" Ellie woke and reached for the edge of the canoe. "What was that?"

The man rowing the canoe said something in French.

"Crocodile." Beau interpreted. Grabbing her hand, he pulled it to his chest. "Don't give him something to eat."

"I don't think he wants us using his part of the river." Sitting up straight, she eyed the crocs in the water, sucked in a breath, and grabbed Beau's arm, her fingernails digging into the flesh. "Can they tip the canoe over?" Her eyes grew wide under raised brows.

"I think they've made their point, and our guide is taking us into deeper water." Beau eyed the man with the paddle. "He doesn't look worried to me."

Ellie blew out a breath. "I've never had a croc wake me before." She drank some of her water, then handed it to Beau and let him finish the rest of it as she scanned the river's edge. "They say crocodiles cry tears when they are devouring their prey. I don't want them crying over me."

Several crocs were sunning themselves on the bank. A few trees and some tall grasses thrived with access to the water. The area was an untouched oasis in the wild desert.

"I told you there would be adventures on this journey." Beau tried to change positions in their cramped space.

"So, you scheduled the crocodiles, Tarzan? What's next, a herd of charging elephants?"

"Not exactly."

"Did you sleep?" She straightened the gauze again to guard her skin against being sunburned. "You were moaning, and your body jerked a couple of times."

"Sorry. Nightmares haunt me when I've been in battle."

"Under that cool demeanor, Hussein has you on edge?"

"Until you're safely in Bamako, I'll be on alert. Keeping you safe is a full-time job." He shifted again in their tight quarters in an attempt to relieve his aching body from the blows he'd taken. "I'll come up with a plan for our escape from Timbuktu."

"Do you think they'll send a helicopter to drop down and scoop us into the sky, 007?"

"I'm afraid not. We don't have the budget for that."

"A girl can dream. You'll figure it out. I have faith in you." Ellie put her head on his shoulder again.

The swaying of the canoe had Ellie relaxed in no time. Beau could tell she was asleep by the heaviness of her head. She didn't know the weight she was putting on his heart. But he had to keep his walls up. Love hurt too much, and getting close to him put Ellie in extreme danger. As the afternoon wore on, he tried to relax as he worked on a plan to get her back to Bamako.

The owner of the canoe tapped on Beau's boot and spoke in French. "We will be at the pier soon. We are reaching Mopti. I was hired to get you to this place."

Tendrils of Ellie's hair had escaped her messy bun. Beau moved them out of her face. "E, we're at the end of our canoe ride."

"Are we in Bamako?" She looked into his smokey grey eyes. "Is it safe for me to sit up?"

"This is Mopti. We have a ways to go yet. Let me look around before you sit up." Beau scanned the pier and riverbank. "I don't see them. It's okay to get out."

"Wow, I'm stiff." She stretched and looked around. "Look. Those birds are Mali firefinch." The bank had some bushes and a few trees lining the water. A rickety pier whitened by the sun's rays protruded six feet into the Niger. A quaint village bustling with Malians was fifty feet up a rocky path. Some children were pushing a tin can with a stick. A donkey brayed in protest of carrying the heavy load strapped to his back.

At the pier, Beau tied off the canoe.

"Are we getting in another canoe?" Ellie grabbed her bag but stayed seated until Beau was standing on the pier.

He extended his hand and pulled her up beside him, then held her until she was steady on her feet. "No, we're traveling overland from here." Beau motioned for the canoe owner to paddle toward him.

"You need money to pay for our canoe ride?" Ellie reached into her bag.

"I have enough." He paid the guide, who smiled at the size of the tip Beau included.

After thanking the man, Beau led Ellie toward the hubbub of town so they could get lost in the crowd. He needed to secure a ride to Segou, their next stop. Surveying the area, he got his bearings as Ellie bought some bananas from a fruit vendor.

After peeling one, she took a bite, then handed one to Beau. "Here, you need the potassium."

He downed the fruit and took a water bottle she offered him. "Thanks."

"Let's go to that small café over by where the trucks are being loaded. Can you order for us, and I'll get us a ride to Segou?" Beau waited for her to answer as he scoped the area again.

"Okay. I am hungry. I offer soft drinks and meals when passengers fly with me." She fussed.

"Then you should have booked first class, Ms. Bendale." He laughed.

They played the tourist card among the Malians, and Ellie bought another gauze scarf. A blue one this time. After purchasing a loaf of bread from a lady on the sidewalk, she wrapped it in the blue gauze and stuck it into her canvas bag.

The afternoon was leaning toward dusk as she approached a small café. Ellie took out her French phrasebook and ordered rice with vegetable soup over it, two Cokes, and four bottles of water for their trip. While she waited, she took down her messy bun and attempted to rid her hair of its tangles with her fingers. Just as their food was being served, Beau joined her.

"We have thirty minutes before our truck departs." He sat and drank some of his Coke. "They like to travel at night because it isn't as hot for the animals they're transporting."

"Are we riding in one of those trucks?" She sipped her soda and motioned toward some rough-looking lorries in severe need of a coat of paint.

"Yeah." He tasted the soup.

Holding up one finger as if saying, 'wait a minute,' she bowed her head and prayed over their food and their safety.

Beau waited till she finished, then continued to eat. "This is good."

"Ordering food is a talent of mine." She swallowed a bite. "Do you think the bad guys know where we are?" She scanned the people milling about outside the café.

"They know we're going to Bamako, but I don't think they know how we're getting there. And Hussein is wounded. They'll get medical help for him. But we need to be careful every step of the way. Be on guard."

"Well, that's on you, my friend. I'll do what you say, and you be the hero. Okay?" She pulled her hair up into another messy bun, allowing a breeze off the river to cool her neck.

"At your service, *mademoiselle*."

They finished their meal in silence, with Ellie taking photos of the small village and its inhabitants while Beau scoped high and low for signs of danger.

The outhouse had an odor Ellie couldn't describe with words in the English language. "Pungent, filthy, disgusting, noxious, rank—"

"Trying to describe the outhouse?"

"Yep. But I'm at a loss."

"Time to go." He led the way, quiet as they walked to the truck for their long ride on potholed roads across the desert.

Beau turned to her. "Uh, Ellie. There's one thing I failed to mention. We're riding in the back with the animals. It's the best way to be camouflaged in case they're following us, and the single seat in the cab has four men and a dog as its occupants." He paused for her response.

She stared at him.

"Don't you have anything to say?" He waited.

"Nope."

"I can't believe you're speechless. You're a journalist with a stream of words rolling around in your pretty little head."

"None there. Just help me into the truck, Beauregard." She hitched her bag onto her shoulder and lifted her foot.

"It makes me nervous when you don't spew sarcasm." He bent over and cupped his hands together for her to use as a step.

Ellie placed her hand on Beau's shoulder, her foot in his hands, and let him lift her into the truck.

"Say something."

She took a deep breath and blew it out. "For this—I have no words."

Once in the truck, he motioned to the bales of hay by the cab. "Let's sit for a minute before the animals are loaded."

Choosing a bale, she took a seat and pulled out a piece of hay. "In case you're wondering, where I come from, 'hide and seek' doesn't involve fighting, knives, guns, crocodiles, or smelly animals." She rubbed hay off her pants.

"Saying I'm sorry doesn't change where we are." He ran his hand through his hair. "I never meant to put you through this. When I let someone get close to me—their life is put in jeopardy. Being in my world could cost you."

"What happened to your fiancée wasn't your fault. Terrorists took her life along with the lives of many other people that horrible night. *You're* not the problem. I'll prove it to you. When we get to Bamako safely, you'll see." She threw the piece of straw into the bed of the truck.

Before Beau could respond, the men started to load the goats.

Ellie's eyes widened at the sight and smell invading their space.

Beau looked around. "I have an idea. Help me move this hay forward a bit. We can get behind it and not be among the livestock." He pulled her to her feet and got busy. They worked in tandem and climbed into a little square of space they'd cleared.

"Good idea. It's compact but fairly clean. Let's put some hay on the truck bed so we're not sitting on a hard surface." Ellie arranged the hay and tried to get comfortable.

Bleating goat noises became a cacophony as the truck was loaded. Beau laughed. "Can you listen to that for five or six hours?"

She faked sign language to add to the comedy of their situation. "Did you say something? I see your lips moving." She yelled.

"That's not sign language." He laughed.

When the truck started moving, the engine noise competed with the goats. Ellie grinned. "Man, you know how to show a girl a good time. Do you always ride around in the back of trucks full of goats?" She eyed him. "Classy, real classy, de La Croix."

"If you must know, I drive a black Hummer in the States and a dark blue Ram truck in France. And they are spotless."

"So, you wow the ladies with your tough truck and good looks."

"No. I travel too much to take time for socializing. I'm pretty much a loner. And I'm okay with that." Beau twirled a piece of hay between his fingers.

"We both have our backstories, our gaping wounds. You can continue being a solitary guy, risking your life while saving others as you lick your wounds and feel sorry for yourself—or you can let the Lord soften your pain and take a chance on love again. Is this how you want to live the rest of your life? It's your choice."

He flinched but remained speechless.

She'd obviously hit a nerve. "Okay. Let's change the subject."

"Let's turn the tables, E. What about you? What's your story?"

She pushed some stray hairs out of her face. "Well, I have a domineering mother who is pressuring me to take a position at my father's company and eventually take his place as head of their successful business. But you already know that. The four walls would be confining. Smothering. I don't fit there. She refuses to see it. But I know it in my heart." Ellie hesitated.

"Do you have another sibling who could step in and take that position?" He asked.

"My sister Marissa is too flighty to be considered for the job. She's the artsy one of the bunch, who bounces from one job to another and loves each challenge for a while. My brother Austin would be perfect, but a career in the military is his focus. With a chest full of ribbons and medals, he may be a career man like you." She shook her head.

"I want to be a photojournalist and travel—to choose my own career. If I get this job with the magazine, I can travel on a schedule of my choosing." Ellie sighed.

"Then, why not have a heart-to-heart with your mother? This pressure she puts on you isn't fair. I bet you hear her voice in your head, and it holds you back. You're a beautiful woman, E, with a plethora of talents." He smiled at the use of her favorite word. "Your future holds so many possibilities, and you get to decide your career."

"But I'm trying to respect her as my mother. I know she loves me and wants what's best for me."

"But there has to be a balance. Is she trying to live her dreams through you? Is the company her baby that she doesn't want to let go of? With you in charge, she could still have her hands in it, making your life miserable." He hesitated. "I don't know your family, and I'm probably speaking out of turn, but you need to feel free to accept the position with the magazine when they make you an offer. She should want that for you." He held on for a pothole.

"You've made some good points. I need to talk with her when I get home. It would set me free to pursue my dreams, wherever they take me." She tapped her chin as if in thought.

A bumpy spot in the road jostled them. Ellie's head smacked the back of the truck.

"*Ouch.*" Ellie rubbed the side of her head.

"You'd better move toward me. You could have a concussion before we end this part of our trip." Beau tried to move the bales a bit to give them more room, but the goats protested.

She scooted closer to Beau in their tiny cubicle of hay. He put his arm up on the hay to guard her head against any more bumps and bruises. Always the gentleman. Too bad he gave his heart away a long time ago.

"Tell me about Paris. Is it as amazing as I've heard?"

Beau's eyebrows lifted. "You're a flight attendant, and you've never been to Paris?" Beau was glad for the change of subject. She had a way of getting to the heart of the matter—bringing his heartache to the surface.

"I've been to Paris, but only inside the airport. I'm saving it as my honeymoon destination someday. The sidewalk cafés look so romantic in movies, and the music is unlike any I've heard in other countries." She wore a soft smile.

"It is a great city. I love the Eiffel Tower, the Seine River, and the Louvre. The art displayed on its walls is the best in the world. It is a city of love for so many." Beau's tour guide spiel seemed to please Ellie.

"I want that photo in front of the Eiffel Tower as I kiss the man I love behind a red heart-shaped umbrella. Have you seen that picture?" Ellie had a dreamy look on her face.

"Yeah, I've seen it, and it's a popular thing to do. They sell red umbrellas on the sidewalk for tourists." He suddenly had a desire to be that guy behind the umbrella.

"I didn't know that. I'll wait and buy one there." She smiled.

"Do you plan everything?" Beau teased her.

"Not everything. I like to be surprised sometimes. As you've probably already figured out, I wear my heart on my sleeve and have a passion for life. But I hide it behind sarcasm to keep from getting hurt. My sarcasm and planning ahead protect me. So, it's a win-win." She dusted hay off her pants again.

"You're doing the same thing I'm doing. Guarding your heart?" Beau asked.

"Yes, but there's a big difference between you and me. I'm open to falling in love. I'm asking the Lord to send the one across my path as He orchestrates my life. I feel peaceful about it. And a little excited."

The goats got loud when the truck turned, sending them

stumbling to the right. Their smell floated toward the cab each time the truck stopped and started again.

"It's going to be a long night." Ellie dug into her bag and pulled out the bread wrapped in the blue gauze material. "Want some?"

"Sure."

Breaking the small loaf, she gave half to Beau along with another water bottle.

"Did you finish your article for the magazine?" He wanted to talk about something else—being so close together for hours on end led their conversation into uncomfortable areas.

"Almost. I like to write something and then let it rest for a few days, then read it with fresh eyes. I'll tweak it again, polishing it for publication." Her countenance brightened when she spoke of her work.

"You're great with that camera. If you get the job with the magazine, will you quit your flight attendant job?" He ate another piece of bread.

"I enjoy flying the African skies, but projects like the Timbuktu assignment are what I'd love to do with my life. So, yes, when and if the magazine becomes a regular job, I would leave my flight attendant position." She drank some water. "What about your family? How do they feel about your one-man-show to save the world with one hand tied behind your back attitude?"

He laughed. "In one week, you have me pegged pretty well." He paused. "There's not much to tell. My dad left when I was three, and my mom died in a car accident when I was nine. All my brother and I knew were foster homes. We had one family, Amos and Hazel Henderson, who were great to us while we were in high school. They're Christians and tried to show us God's love." He took a drink of water to wash down the dry bread.

"My brother Alexandre talks to the Hendersons more than I

do. He and his wife Vivienne live in Paris and see them regularly. I contact our foster parents on birthdays when I'm in Paris and call them on Christmas day—a phone call from wherever I am in the world. I think Hazel has kept a list of where I've called from. She prays for my safety every day. So, you're blessed to have a real family, no matter how annoying they can be."

"You're right. I'm hoping things will get easier when my mom gives up her quest to control my life and the lives of my siblings. What does your brother do? Is he a stud-muffin like you?" She nudged him in the ribs.

"*Ouch.*"

"I'm sorry. For a moment there I forgot you single-handedly battled a terrorist leader today."

He laughed. "Very funny. I haven't been called a stud-muffin before." He cleared his throat. "Alex is tall and slim, but we do favor. Our foster parents sent him to culinary school after I joined the military. He owns a restaurant in the heart of Paris. Vivienne works in a dress shop on Rue Desaix Street, not far from the Eiffel Tower. They've been married for almost a year. Alex is my best friend—my family. We've walked a long road together."

They bounced along in silence for a while. Ellie pulled out another pack of cheese crackers and shared them with Beau.

"I think the foster system has made your solitary nomadic life easy for you. But you're missing out on so much. I hope you find some peace and happiness along the way." She put her hand on his and squeezed before releasing it.

"Thanks, E." Beau moved around, trying to find a comfortable position in their smelly, rough-riding cubicle. His ribs ached. "If you lean on the back of the truck, you'll bang your head with every bump. Use my shoulder again and get some sleep while you can. We still have a long trek ahead of us." He stretched his legs out in the cramped space.

"If you don't mind, I'll do that since the sun's going down." She shifted her position and leaned on his shoulder. "You smell like muscles and mayhem, Rambo."

"I'm glad you didn't say goat urine and fish scales." He gave her a partial smile.

Leaning his head over on a bale of hay Beau tried to drift off. He needed to be clear thinking on tomorrow's journey into Bamako. Thankfully, the goats got the same idea and hunkered down to rest making the trip a bit more pleasant. *For now.*

A jostle woke Beau. Ellie's arm was wrapped around him with her head on his chest. Traveling in such close quarters was weakening his resolve to guard his heart. At least on the last leg of this journey, they would ride camels. Not skin-to-skin, giving opportunities for poignant heart-to-heart chats.

He eased his phone out of his shirt pocket and checked in with Philippe Leroux in France by text, then sent the same update to Axel McCabe, the Secretary of the Navy in Washington. He sent them up-to-date information on his findings, just in case, God forbid, things got crazy in Bamako.

He received immediate confirmation that his message had been received by both offices, followed by all the intel they had about terrorist hideouts and activities in Bamako, thanks to his government-issued phone. While they covered several kilometers on this bumpy road, he studied the info. When the rank goat odor got too pungent, Beau leaned closer to Ellie to inhale the scent of her shampoo. What a contrast.

11

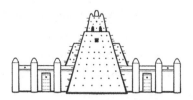

Ellie stretched and felt Beau's beard on her forehead. Still half asleep, she nuzzled his neck and dozed a while longer until the truck hit a pothole, jerking her awake. In her drowsy state, she pushed herself up, putting her face to face with Beau. Blinking her sleepy eyes, she focused on his handsome face.

In his embrace, their closeness would tempt any woman to kiss his perfectly shaped lips, run her hand down his handsome face, and let herself fall in love. Caught in his gaze, she wished for mind-reading capabilities to give her a hint of what he was thinking. No such luck. She took a risk and gave him a quick kiss on his lips.

"Did you know that kissing burns up six-point-four calories a minute? But you don't look like you're ready to exercise right now. So, I'll just say I appreciate you being my pillow. I slept well. Thank you for asking." Her face warmed.

When she started to move away, Beau slipped his hand behind her neck, pulled her close, and kissed her tenderly. Ellie froze at first then relaxed in his arms, enjoying the feel of his lips on hers. When he ended the kiss, he stared into her eyes.

"You're welcome. Ellie, you've been brave during our escape, you've kept up every step of the way. I'm glad you're not a weakling or a crybaby."

Not wanting the moment to end, she didn't move. He was a man of integrity. A man's man. A great catch—if he would let his walls down and allow himself to love again. Reluctantly, she pushed herself away.

"I'm getting concerned you won't be able to resist my charms. We need a mode of transportation that doesn't put us in such close quarters for hours. I'm not complaining. Don't get me wrong. You've been great, but being as good-looking as you are, showing your superpowers by saving my life—a girl could let it go to her head. And a damsel in distress is usually beautiful and pretty tempting for the knight in shining armor."

The rickety truck hit a pot-hole jostling them into each other again. "See what I mean?" She tried to move away again. "I'm just too tempting for you."

"You temptress, you!" He smiled. "I'm kidding. You will be a successful travel writer for any magazine you choose. You're an amazing woman and quite brave for a girl."

Punching his shoulder, she repeated his words, "For a girl?"

He laughed, throwing his head back.

Parched, Ellie got out another bottle of water for each of them. Her mouth felt as dry as the desert they were crossing. Maybe it was the temperature heating up between them, making her thirsty for more. She downed the liquid and tossed her empty bottle into the hay at their feet, then undid her messy bun and finger-combed hay from the strands. "Will they be waiting for us, Beau?"

"They know our destination is Bamako. I think Hussein will be waiting and is plotting my demise as we travel. But I plan to get you to the hotel for a well-deserved shower, and some great food, and then on your plane to Nairobi. We can get lost in the crowd once we reach the city, and I'll keep you safe until your plane takes off. Try not to worry."

"That sounds great, but I think you're trying to get my mind off the danger we're walking into. Can't you use those two phones and call for help?"

"You don't miss a thing, do you?" He pulled a piece of hay out of Ellie's hair and gave it to her.

"I should be upset that you used my visit to Mali for military purposes, but you've kept me safe. So, you're forgiven." She hung on as they hit another bump on the road.

Struggling to stand, Beau, pulled her up beside him. "It feels good to stand and stretch your legs. See those lights in the distance? That's Segou, the end of this joyride. It will be dawn by the time we get there."

"Your hospitality has been over the top, but I could use some food and a lady's room. How about we stop at Pizza Hut for a meat-lovers pizza or drive through at Taco Bell? I'd love a couple of their bean burritos and a cold Pepsi."

"It's too early for those options to be open, so don't get demanding on me now." He teased.

"Okay. I'll stand in the corner and put myself in time-out until I can act better. This may take a while." She shuddered and took in a deep breath.

He put his arm around her shoulders to keep her from bouncing around too much. "I know you're nervous. Be brave, okay? We're going to make it. Trust me."

"What choice do I have?" She sighed and laid her head on his shoulder.

The rickety lorry stopped in an area of town to deliver the goats to market. Several wooden corrals held animals. The rank odor of manure baking in the morning sun made it hard to breathe.

"Breathe through your mouth. It's easier. We will get out of here as soon as they unload the goats." Beau gave Ellie her bag and shouldered his backpack.

She leaned over the stack of hay bales. "Will they hose it out after they unload?"

"Probably not, I may have to carry you. I'd hate to see goat droppings on your white tennis shoes." He winked. "But you did well with the donkey dung."

Holding her nose, she turned away from the bleating goats to scan the town. "When we get away from this odor, do you think I'll get my appetite back?"

"Yep. When you pass the women making bread, you'll be ready to eat."

The goats got excited when the men opened the back of the truck. It didn't take long to unload their cargo since the goats jumped to freedom, landing in the dirt as they were herded into a pen awaiting their sale.

"Should I have warned the goats they were being taken to market? This isn't going to end well for them."

"With your language limitations, I don't think you can speak goat. They wouldn't understand your English with that southern twang." He smiled.

"I do not have a twang." She watched the last of the goats jump from the truck.

"Okay, mount up." Beau took his backpack off and leaned over at the waist.

"You mean it?" Ellie grinned.

"You either ride or walk. Make your choice quickly. The offer will expire in five seconds."

After putting his backpack on, Ellie shouldered her bag, stepped onto a bale of hay, and got on Beau's back, wrapping her arms around his neck. "I'm ready. Let's do this."

Beau grabbed her legs and made his way through the truck bed littered with animal dung. When he got to the back of the old lorry, he turned and let Ellie ease off his back to the bumper.

"Thank you, kind sir. I appreciate the ride." She held on to his hand and jumped to solid ground.

"At your service, *mademoiselle*." He paid the driver, who offered a toothless smile. "Ready?" Beau grabbed her hand and led her toward the little town that was slowly waking up. Roosters crowing at different areas served as an alarm clock to the sleepy village. Mamas cooked sausage and bread while shop owners opened for another day of business as the sun made its appearance. The smell of coffee was refreshing.

"We're riding camels to Bamako. I need to hire some. Can you find us some food and meet me over there in the town square?" He pointed to the center of town.

"Sure. Do you want McDonald's or Arby's?" She teased.

"How about Arby's with curly fries?"

"You've got it. Coming right up." She released his hand.

Beau watched her perfect form take off as if on a mission, making her first stop at an outhouse. Then reminded himself to keep his feelings in check. She would disappear from his life soon. He ran his hand through his hair and went in search of a camel caravan, following his nose to the rank odor coming from the stables.

Ellie held her breath and used the disgusting outhouse with her canvas bag hanging around her neck. While in search of nourishment, her fair skin drew stares from the nationals, but their expressions softened when she smiled and tried to communicate. She bought two well-cooked sausages, four boiled eggs, and toast, and packaged them separately. Bottles of water and two warm Sprites rounded out their breakfast fare and snacks for their onward journey to Bamako.

Sitting on a felled log in the center of the square, she took pictures while waiting for Beau. Within hours they would be in Bamako, in the sites of soldiers holding AK-47s. An icy dread washed over her. She rubbed her arms to soothe the goosebumps. Prayer was her only weapon, so she kept an earnest petition on her lips.

She used the screen instead of putting the camera to her eye, capturing shots of babies riding in a cloth tied to their mothers' backs. Scrawny dogs scavenged through the garbage for scraps of food while a cripple begged for alms from passing shoppers. Colorful clothes on the women added a pop of color to the drab setting of aged boards and rusting tin roofs.

Smoldering garbage sent smoke toward her, burning her eyes. She turned just in time to see a butcher gutting a sheep he'd killed. *Ew!* She pivoted from the gory sight. Chickens scratched in the dirt to catch insects before the heat of the African sun dried them to a crisp.

An old woman walked past, struggling under a stack of wood tied to her back. Ellie reached into her bag and got the equivalent of ten dollars of their currency and walked toward the woman. She put her hand out to greet her. Clasping her calloused hand brought tears to Ellie's eyes. She placed the money in the old lady's sweaty palm, making her cry. Ellie caught one of her tears on her finger and then watched her trudge toward her home.

Beau witnessed Ellie's interaction with the local. He stood mesmerized at her kindness. Ellie turned and saw him with one foot on the felled log as he leaned forward with his elbow on his knee. After a pause, she took his picture and strolled toward him.

"You'll forever be her hero. You know that, don't you?" Beau stepped forward and took one of the bags she was carrying.

"Did you see the load she had on her back? It had to weigh a hundred pounds. Bless her heart." Ellie took a bottle of water out of her tote and gave it to Beau. "Did you rent some dromedaries, de La Croix?"

He shook his head.

"What?" Ellie put her free hand on her hip.

"Great segue, lady. Yeah, I got you a camel, Elliana. We depart in an hour."

"Then let's go eat some samosas. They should be ready. How about a warm Sprite?" She pulled a green bottle from her bag and smiled about her find. Seeking familiar sodas and snacks in third-world countries resembled a scavenger hunt in the States.

"Sounds great to me. Lead the way." Beau extended his hand, motioning for her to go ahead of him.

The aroma made her mouth water. "Can you order for us? Your French is much better than mine."

"Sure." Beau stood, stepped on a huge spider, probably deadly, and ordered their food.

They found a bench and enjoyed their breakfast while watching the villagers go about their day. People watching took on a whole new meaning in Africa. Every moment proved different.

"We're blessed, aren't we?" Ellie spoke as the hard-working people, scratching out a living.

"Yes, we are." Beau enjoyed his meal of eggs and samosas as they watched the nationals. "You ready to go?"

"Yes. I have sausages and bread for each of us, bottles of water, and some bananas for our journey. I put them in separate sacks since we won't be riding the same camel." She gave him one of the sacks.

"Good thinking." He put it in his backpack.

"Thanks. I have my moments." With her toes healing, she matched Beau's stride, unhindered, toward the camels sitting at the end of the pot-holed dirt road. "How long is the trip to Bamako?"

"Probably at least six hours. We'll be there by early afternoon. Use the gauze cloth to protect your skin. We'll stop halfway at a village to water the camels." Beau scanned the area for anything suspicious.

"I guess I'll have to stay awake since I don't have a shoulder to lean on. Don't miss me too much. Which camel is mine?" She looked from camel to camel.

It took a moment for Beau to digest her words. *Does she have any idea how she affects me? It's all I can do to keep her safe. Guarding my heart takes more strength than I can muster—*

"Beau?"

"It's the one on the left. Let me ask when we need to mount up." Beau approached the main guy and conversed with him in French. He checked his watch, then joined Ellie under a piece of canvas added to a kiosk, the only shade from one hundred degrees this early in the morning.

"It will be at least an hour before they want to leave. You want to go back to the village? Walking now will help us later." He faced Ellie, allowing her to make the decision.

"I've got an idea. I want to buy some water and wash my hair. You can help me." She took off toward a row of kiosks and fruit stands.

"But I'm not much on washing women's hair. Maybe there's someone here who does that." He followed, expressing his concerns but Ellie was undeterred.

"Can you carry some of these?" She paid for six bottles of water and loaded his arms. "Let's go over to that rickety bench under the sorry excuse for a tree." She led the way.

"How are we supposed to do this? Can I dump the water on

your head? That would be fun." He held one of the bottles over her head as if practicing his mischief.

"No. Hang on a minute." She fumbled through her bag for something. "I have some shampoo samples in here somewhere."

"Oh, that makes perfect sense. What was I thinking? I always carry shampoo when I ride camels." He opened a bottle of water and smiled.

"You're so funny, Rambo." She pulled out two small bottles. "Okay." She put her bag down beside their food bags and took the rubber hairband out of her blonde locks. "Will you slowly pour a bottle of water over my hair? Try to get it completely wet if you can."

Ellie shook out her hair and leaned back as she looked to the sky. "Okay. I'm ready."

Opening one bottle, he hesitated.

"Don't get any big ideas, Rocky. Just get my hair wet." She looked up again.

Stepping behind her, he poured the cool water on her hair. Suddenly aware of how intimate this was, his stomach knotted. Ellie's eyes were closed. He was glad.

"Can you get the water close to my hairline? Dust and sand have accumulated there." She pointed to the edge of her hair.

He finished one bottle and opened another. "Your hair is so long I may get your clothes wet."

"It's okay. It will cool me off as we travel the desert." She slapped at a fly that landed on her face.

"It's wet now." He stepped back.

Ellie opened a bottle of shampoo and attempted to pour it on her head.

"Hey, you're missing your hair. Give it to me." Beau took the bottle and poured its contents on her gorgeous strands. "You need more shampoo."

Opening another bottle, she said, "Use half of this one. It should be enough."

Following her instructions, he tried not to let this experience get to him as he worked his fingers, massaging her scalp.

"If you'll add a little more water, it will help."

Adding water, he worked it through her hair. Ellie helped him by scrubbing the front.

"Thanks for doing this, Beau. When I thought about the fish scales or goat fleas possibly on my head, I had to wash it." She continued to work her fingers through her soapy hair.

"No problem," He lied. "It was on the schedule for today. Didn't you see it?" He teased. Running his fingers through her beautiful mane was affecting him. They worked together until her hair was clean.

"Okay, time to rinse it." She gave instructions with no thought of the intimacy it created between them.

Pouring the last half of the third bottle, he opened the fourth one. "Close your eyes. I'm going to rinse the hairline."

She leaned back farther as he poured the water and worked his fingers through her hair. The shampoo came out, leaving her hair shining in the early morning sun that peeked through the leaves. Beau didn't want to stop. But the bottle was empty, and her hair was clean.

"We're done, Miss Bendale. Twenty-five dollars, please. Pay the receptionist before you leave." He put the lid on the empty water bottle.

Ringing the water out of her hair, she wrapped it in the blue gauze cloth she'd purchased. "We're not done."

"I don't do mani-pedis." He grinned.

"Always the comedian. Take that vest off and have a seat. You're next." She bossed him.

"No, I'm good. I'll get a shower in Bamako." He put up his hands in protest.

"But you smell, and it will cool you off. Sit and lean your head back." She opened the last bottle of water and wet his hair with about a third of it. She poured a few drops of water into the shampoo bottle and shook it before pouring it into his hair. "So, do you get your hair cut in France or America?"

Watching her would be too personal, so he closed his eyes. "Wherever I am when it needs cutting. Why?" He looked at her.

"When I met you, I knew you had the makings of a military man except for the length of your hair and that scruffy beard gracing your chin. Don't get me wrong, I like your hair, but it is a bit long for their standards." She wove her fingers over his scalp. "Now I learn you're military. What's up?"

"I was on another assignment that required a civilian look. The long hair and beard were my disguise needed for this assignment. It was an attempt to keep me from looking military." He looked at her. "Did it work?"

"Well, it worked until you jumped into action with your Kung Fu moves and SEAL tactics, saving the day." She started humming as she washed his hair.

He had a difficult time tracking the words of her song as she moved her magic fingers through his hair. Knowing this wasn't a good idea, he took a deep breath and blew it out slowly. He would never forget the moment. "You about done?" He didn't want her to stop but knew he was in dangerous territory under this scrawny tree.

"Time to rinse." She worked her fingers through his hair as she poured the water until the bottle was empty. "It's squeaky clean, Bond, James Bond. Doesn't that feel better?"

Shaking the water out of his hair like a dog after a bath helped rid him of the effect she had on him.

"Whoa there, Hooch. You're raining on me." Ellie took her hair down, pulled out a brush, and worked it through her long strands.

Watching her, he was mesmerized. He ran his fingers

through his wet hair. "It does feel better. Thanks." He checked his watch. "Want a soda before we mount up?"

"Only if I can make another pit stop."

"I'll be right back." He asked a shop owner if there were any cold drinks in the village and returned with two cold Cokes. "Coke okay?"

"Absolutely. It's my favorite." She took it. "It's cold. You're my hero." She gave him a quick hug, grabbed the Coke, and took a long drink. "That's wonderful."

"They—they have a refrigerator they run with kerosine." Beau needed to dodge her hugs from here on out.

"Kerosine. Well, it's a nice surprise." She finished every drop and endured the outhouse again before following Beau into the blazing sun. "And, we're off. To ride smelly camels to Bamako—to the angry soldiers anticipating our arrival— probably loading their guns at this very moment."

"I'll keep you safe." As they approached the camels, Beau slowed their pace. "Don't rush up to the animal. These camels don't seem as calm as the ones in Timbuktu."

Ready this time, she took a deep breath, blew it out, and held on. She was flung forward and then hung on as the camel threw her backward. Once upright, she threw her hands in the air. "I did it! Did you see that?"

"You are a pro. That was well executed." He applauded.

Beau hung on as his dromedary stood and left the others behind.

"I think they're ready to go. Here, catch." She rolled up the blue gauze cloth and threw it to him. "Make yourself an air-conditioner. You can pull off that tough-guy persona again once we're back in civilization."

"So, I don't need to impress you right now? Is that what you're saying?' He twisted the cloth into a headwrap and put it on. "How's that?"

With her camera ready, Ellie took his picture when he smiled in her direction and struck a pose.

"That cannot go into your article, Ms. Bendale." He gave her a stern look.

"But it might look good in the middle of a dartboard." She showed her mischief.

Grabbing his chest, he said, "I'm wounded at your sarcasm."

"You're tougher than that, Beauregard. Or, at least, you think you are." She laughed.

12

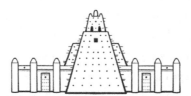

Once the village was in their rear-view mirror, the dunes began to look alike. Waves of sand were rippled from the last windstorm. With scorpions and lizards the only signs of life, it was sand, sand, and more sand. Time inched by as they made slow progress, seemingly going nowhere. Drinking water and eating their snacks only took a few minutes out of the hours dragging by.

"Hey, Beau."

"Yeah." He glanced at her.

"Do they ever get lost out here?"

"Not a chance. Didn't you read the road signs?" He grinned.

"Very funny. But seriously. We are going to get there, aren't we?"

He faced Ellie. "I promised to get you back to Bamako. And I will. We'll be there by one or two this afternoon. Don't worry."

She held eye contact, longing to soak up some of his bravery.

"What?"

"Will they be waiting for us?" Tears clouded her eyes. "Will he try to kill you this time?"

"I hope not."

"Me too." She decided to use the time to pray for the Lord to protect them.

Hours passed in total boredom. Making their escape while laying side by side in a dug-out canoe or thrown together in their cubicle of hay in a stinky lorry was much more invigorating. But this was safer for his heart. While keeping her in the friend category, he had to get her to Bamako, to her hotel, back to her life—so he could return to his routine of following orders, fighting bad guys, and making the world a safer place to live for everyone—but him.

A small village came into view when they topped a hill. It would feel good to walk around for a few minutes. And he was hungry.

"Ellie, when you start to get you off, wait for me. Okay?" Beau caught her gaze.

"You don't think I can dismount my ride?" She asked.

"Trust me just once," he begged.

"That's what got me here in the first place. But I'll humor you." She smiled and obeyed.

Beau dismounted and shook his legs a bit, then strode to her camel. "If you're not used to it, riding on an elephant or a camel for a long time can cause a numbing of the nerves in your hips, like when your foot goes to sleep when you sit on it. Throw your leg over and slide down."

With her bag over her shoulder, Ellie slid into Beau's arms. Her legs felt like jelly. She tightened her arms around his neck and hung on. "Beau! What's wrong with me? My legs aren't holding me up!"

Picking her up, he walked toward a bench in front of a

kiosk. Ellie put her head next to his. Her closeness was messing with him.

Her breath came in and out quickly. "Please tell me I'll be back to normal soon. This is scary." Scanning his face, she waited for an answer.

Putting distance between them, he sat beside her. "It will take a few minutes, and the feeling will return. You'll be good as new."

"Thanks. I would have been an ugly mess in the sand." She removed her headwrap and wiped her face with it.

"At your service, *mademoiselle*." He bowed. "I will scope out the area and find you some facilities and a snack. Don't stand up until I get back." He waited for a response.

Ellie saluted and grabbed the bench that threatened splinters if she held on too tightly.

Feeling her eyes on him as he walked away, he gave himself a pep talk. *I know her too well. She's a distraction. And that's not good when I'm trying to protect her against a serious enemy. Beau, get your head in the game and finish this mission.*

The village had maybe ten small buildings with rusty tin roofs and rickety boards as walls, one being a sorry excuse for a restaurant. Beau ordered bread and boiled eggs and returned for Ellie, casting short shadows with the sun directly overhead. She took his picture as he approached.

"Give me your hands." Beau held his hands toward her.

Placing her palms against his larger ones, she tightened her grip, then looked into his eyes.

"Okay, stand up slowly. You should be fine." He pulled her up in front of him. "Give it a minute."

"Yay, I can walk again." She reached up and patted his cheek. "Thanks, de La Croix." She stepped back and grabbed her bag. "Now, lead the way, Mr. Tour Guide."

It took him a minute to move. For a man who prided

himself on keeping his body fit, he shouldn't let the feel of soft skin and silky blonde hair be his undoing.

"You coming?" Ellie had walked a few steps and turned back.

"Since I'm your fearless leader, I should lead the way." He hitched his backpack on his shoulder and escorted her to their dining destination, two rickety chairs by a table that seemed slightly slanted, wiped with a dirty wet rag as they entered. He pulled out her chair like the gentleman that he was. "Your chair, Elliana."

The floor was dirtier than the desert, if that was possible. She kept her bag in her lap. "What's on the menu at this fine establishment? Filet mignon?" She smiled, awaiting his response.

"How about a baby chicken and a pile of crumbs?" He smiled.

"You're kidding, right?" She wrinkled her nose.

"Yeah. It's boiled eggs and a loaf of bread. But the bottled water is cool."

"Nothing but the best. You know how to show a girl a good time." She pulled out two tissues.

"And your sarcasm knows no bounds."

Ellie's laugh was a perfect mix of joy and nervousness.

Their food was served in a plop-down fashion. Ellie gave him a tissue to put on the table and peeled her eggs.

"I'm glad they let us peel them ourselves. It feels safer to eat." She put her hand on his arm and prayed over their food and for their safe arrival in Bamako.

After her eggs were peeled, she used the screen on her camera to capture their amazing restaurant while she ate without bringing attention to her actions.

"Ever the photojournalist." Beau watched her.

"There's always a story, if you look for it."

She put the camera to her eye and took his picture, then checked the shot on her screen and showed it to him.

"What's that story?" He asked.

She stared at his photo. "I see a ruggedly handsome man consumed with one assignment after another, protecting the weak, righting the wrongs, saving the masses—while trying to forget his losses and keep personal pain at bay." She pocketed her camera. "How did I do?"

"You're quite observant." He drank the last of his water and asked for another one.

"It's in my job assignment." She used his words against him.

He opened her bottle of water. "Drink up. We're leaving in a few minutes."

Her eyes widened. "Will my legs quit working again?"

"Probably, but I'll help you till the feeling returns."

They finished their meager meal and returned to the dromedaries chewing their cud, looking as if they planned to stay there for a long rest.

"Look at those eyelashes! I could make a fortune creating false eyelashes with those." She got a closeup of the camel's face.

"Are you going to do that as a side job?" He put a bottle of water into his backpack.

"Nope. Too busy for that."

Cupping his hands, he offered her a step up so she could mount easier. "You think you could ride side-saddle when we see the lights of Bamako?"

"I'll try. Will that help my legs have feeling in them?" She hung her bag over the horn of the saddle.

"Yeah." He paused. "But hang on. I wouldn't want you to fall off." He left her to get on his ride.

"But I liked you coming to my rescue, McGarrett." She winked and rubbed sunscreen on her arms. "Don't forget to drink your water and put your turban on. I wouldn't want you to have a heat stroke, and I'd have to give you mouth-to-mouth." She laughed at her words.

"I think you're having fun at my expense." He rubbed his hands through his hair.

"What's the matter, tough guy? Having a hard time keeping up?"

"You're the winner, hands down, E." He mounted his camel and hung on as it threw him forward then backward like the tug-of-war his heart was having toward a certain feisty blonde. He busied himself, creating the wrap for his head. He had it tucked in the back when the drivers made the caravan move toward the next dune, leaving the village in the distance.

Ellie took a few photos of the village as it diminished like a moment in time.

———————

As the sun burned bright overhead, causing heatwaves to radiate skyward, the city of Bamako appeared on the horizon. Ellie had mixed emotions. Relief that they'd made the journey without incident, mingled with the icy dread that Hussein would be waiting for Beau. Her stomach tightened as sadness flooded in.

Her time with the handsome Frenchman was coming to an end. She'd grown accustomed to his presence, his protection, and, if she was truthful, he'd claimed her heart. She sat side-saddle on her camel with her back to Beau and prayed for divine protection, for the right words to say, and for strength to walk away.

"Are there taxis near the camel lot to take us to our hotel? I'm ready for a hot shower and a warm meal." She finished her bottle of water, knowing a lady's room was in her near future.

"Yeah. They should be lined up for you as if royalty is arriving at the airport." He smirked.

"No, they won't." She spouted back.

"I'll get you to your hotel. Don't stop trusting me now." His gray eyes begged for her trust.

"Okay. You've done great so far, except for the stinky goat situation and smelly fish gut ride." She hung on as she turned the other way on her camel. "Should I mention those things in my review? I'd hate for you to lose other interpreter gigs because of my three-star rating."

"Three stars! I made sure you got the photos you wanted, added adventure to your excursion, and washed your hair. What more do you want?" He grinned.

"Maybe a chariot ride to my hotel. Can you arrange that?"

He tipped his imaginary hat again. "I'll do my best."

After thirty more grueling minutes of camel riding, Ellie watched Beau gradually slip into protector mode. His sniper focus scanned the horizon on high alert for terrorist soldiers or the glint of a rifle pointed in their direction. He surveyed the camel lot as they approached, loaded a clip into his gun, and returned it to the holster at the back of his waist. After guzzling the last of his water, he zipped his backpack and took a deep breath.

"A man on a mission."

"What?" He asked not taking his eyes off the city they were approaching.

"You're stepping into hero mode again." She spoke the truth as a shiver snaked down her spine.

"I can't fail. It costs lives. That hurts too much. I'll finish this assignment—complete this mission. Stay close to your camel when you dismount. Okay?" Concerned shadowed his eyes as his brows drew together.

"Yes, I will, Beau."

The camels picked up their step as they caught the corral in their sights. The drivers opened a gate and led the caravan inside. Men were waiting to unload the goods they'd transported and to bed the animals for the night.

They instructed Ellie's camel to sit first. She watched Beau's diligence in his protector's role. Her heart went out to him for the pain he'd experienced and the loss that drove him. Being a hero put him in constant danger, his life in jeopardy. It was no way to live.

Standing by her camel as Beau instructed, her hands were clammy, her stomach in knots. An eerie sense of dread settled over her. A bird cried out from a nearby tree like an alarm. Ellie searched the area for signs of danger. Not seeing anything amiss, she fanned herself with the flight itinerary she'd pulled from her bag as the heat of the day intensified the smell of dung in the corral.

When Beau's camel was down, he hurried to her side. "Let's get you into the lean-to while I pay the driver. Then, I'll escort you to the hotel." He put his arm around her as they left the camels and steered her to an old chair. "Sit here, E. I'll be right back."

"I won't move." She promised.

Beau hurried to the main driver and began negotiations to pay for their trip. It seemed he wanted more than Beau had agreed to pay.

Aware of his absence immediately, she kept her eyes trained on him. Thirty feet away, she could hear his voice. The owner of the corral was also bargaining with the driver, probably to get paid for the use of the corral.

Watching their transactions was amusing. Beau argued in French using exaggerated hand gestures. As she reached for her camera, the cold, hard barrel of a gun jabbed into her back —again.

"Don't say a word, or your boyfriend is dead. Stand and go right, behind the lean-to. Now!" Hussein hissed.

Ellie stood, praying Beau didn't notice the movement.

Certain he was outnumbered since Hussein wouldn't come alone, she did as the man instructed and came face to face with the guy whose nose she broke with her jiu-jitsu moves in Timbuktu.

"Oh great, not you again." She groused in a low voice. He probably didn't know English, but he got the message.

"Silence!" Hussein grabbed her hands and tied them together before leading her to an old Hummer. "Get in." He gave her a shove.

Once the doors were closed, they took off, with Ellie as their hostage.

Now she was scared ...

After settling on a good price, Beau tipped the driver and headed back to Ellie. But stopped abruptly. Dust rose at his feet.

"Ellie!" Her chair was empty. Her bag was on the ground. "E, where are you?" He ran, picked up her tote, and pivoted, searching for her. As he rounded the lean-to, a Hummer slung dust in the air as it sped away. Hussein had Ellie.

"No!" He kicked the ground scattering sand.

With his heart beating double time, Beau searched for a taxi, a truck, or a motorcycle, anything to give chase. One old taxi was idling across the road. He ran to it and jumped in giving instructions to the driver in French. The driver revved the engine and chased the dirt settling behind the kidnappers. Dust was all he had.

Knowing when they got to the main road, the tarmac would eliminate his clues, he prodded the driver. "Hurry! We can't lose that vehicle."

He punched the numbers on his cell. "Chief Auguste, call me ASAP. We just returned to Bamako, and while I was paying

SHIRLEY GOULD

the caravan driver, Hussein kidnapped Ellie, the photojournalist. I'm following the dust they're leaving in their wake. I need help! Do you have any idea where he would take her—I'm desperate! He will kill her!" He punched END.

The dust dissipated in the breeze. Beau had the driver stop the taxi when they reached the main intersection. He jumped up on the battered hood and searched the traffic for the Hummer. He saw it in the distance, jumped down, and gave the driver directions. He might not catch up, but he could limit the search area by continuing to follow.

His phone buzzed. "Hello."

"Beau, I just got your message."

"Dakir Hussein has Ellie, sir! We're still on the trail but losing them fast." Beau leaned forward, watching for the taillights of the vehicle.

"Where are you? I'm leaving the Embassy now." Auguste sounded out of breath.

Looking for street signs, he spoke, "We came into Bamako from the east side at the stables. We are driving west on Prem des Angevins. He's taking a right onto Bulavard du Peuple. Now he is turning into a busy area. I can't see a street sign—but I'm losing him!" Panic tightened Beau's throat as he white-knuckled the front seat with clenched fists.

"I'm heading your way now. Stop where you are and describe the area." Auguste demanded.

"Chief, it's mostly businesses with a few houses. I got some intel from McCabe in D.C. Hussein has a property in an industrial area. We may be close. But I don't see street signs on these roads. The dust is settled on this road, so it's the wrong one." Beau raked his hand through his hair.

"But you have given us the right area to search. Stay where you are. I'm mobilizing my men as I drive to you." Auguste said.

"No sirens, okay? That could put Ms. Bendale in more danger." Beau had his driver stop the cab. "Chief, I'm in an old blue taxi." Beau got out, paced the area, and Auguste's radio squawked.

"I'll find you. I'm about five minutes away." Auguste ended the call.

Beau leaned against the taxi and wiped his sweaty brow. Waiting was excruciating. *Lord, I haven't spoken to You in a long time, but I need You right now. Direct us, Lord. We need your help, Your guidance. Please don't let me lose her, Lord. Please!*

Trembling as they drove through the city, not slowing for potholes or pedestrians, Ellie yelled when they barely missed an old man walking along the road.

Hussein jerked around and faced her, pointing his gun at her face. "Let's get this straight. You make noise—you die. Be quiet—and if Dubois will exchange places with you—you might live another day. He has a tendency to fall for the women I kill." He smirked. "Not my fault. I have an agenda, and he keeps getting in my way. So, how this ends is up to you." The heavy frown and harsh mouth matched the evil in his eyes.

"Why kidnap me?" Ellie kept her voice soft.

"Bait! You're the incentive I'm using to draw in de La Croix. To catch the big fish, you use the perfect bait. He has thwarted our moves numerous times in the last several years. It's time to end him. And I will, thanks to you." He let out a haughty laugh and turned around.

Scanning the area, Ellie saw a few people and several businesses. Some looked deserted. All the properties had tall fences around the perimeter and large gates concealing what was inside. She would be well hidden—difficult to rescue. Tears filled her eyes as her gut tightened.

Before long, the Hummer skidded to a stop at a large gate covered with rusty tin. The gate creaked painfully as it opened, and a cloud of dust caught up with them. The driver proceeded and then stopped, jamming the Hummer into Park.

The gate screeched as it closed when they were inside the compound, then slammed shut. Ellie jumped. The enclosed area, about two acres, had a guardhouse by the gate, one building with stucco walls, and several shacks. A few scrawny trees gave bits of shade from the midday sun. Chickens scratched in the dirt. An old man sat on an overturned bucket peeling potatoes.

Three armed soldiers rushed toward the Hummer with AK-47s on their shoulders and bands of ammo across their chests. It resembled a scene she'd seen in a war movie, but this was real—very real.

A guard locked the gate. Leaving this compound undetected would be impossible. She sucked in dusty air.

"Get out. And keep quiet." Hussein opened her door and barked orders. Ellie did as she was told. He spoke in French, and everyone hurried to do as he demanded. One of the soldiers grabbed Ellie's arm and led her to the small stucco building.

"Can I use the facilities? I've been on a camel for hours."

Hussein ordered a soldier to allow her request. He led her around the building to a smelly outhouse in the back.

She held her hands out for him to untie her. He loosened the knots keeping his gun pointed in her direction. Ellie took care of business and used the opportunity to scope the area as the soldier escorted her back to the building. She was surprised they didn't tie her hands again. But surrounded by guns, she knew an escape attempt would be met with death.

"Water, please." Ellie knew she was irritating him but didn't care. He stomped out and returned with a bottle of water.

"Leave this room, and I shoot." He made his point.

He left the door open, which allowed a slight breeze. Ellie was thankful as she surveyed the room. Concrete walls and floor, barred windows, a table with two chairs, and an old army cot. Laying on the cot, she did the only thing she could. She prayed for rescue, for Beau's safety, and for wisdom about how to get out of this nightmare alive. She needed a miracle. And needed it soon!

13

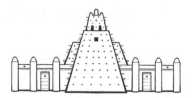

Beau grabbed his backpack and Ellie's bag, then slapped money into the hand of the taxi driver as he left the cab. "Thanks, man. You did great." He threw his French comments over his shoulder as he hurried to Police Chief Auguste's Toyota SUV. "Sir, they're in this area. Any idea where to start looking?" Beau put their bags in the SUV.

"Was the Hummer camouflaged or solid green?" The Chief asked.

"Camo."

Dax Auguste clicked a button on a microphone and spoke to his team. "The Hummer is camo. Eyes open, everybody. We have to find her quickly and make our move before nightfall. Explore your assigned grids, then check in. And hurry!" He punched a number on his cell and gave their location to someone.

"A helicopter is searching the area. Unless the Hummer is in a garage, we will find it." Auguste unfolded a map of Bamako and circled the area in question. They were parked in an industrial area of businesses with a few houses interspersed.

"So, what can we do? I can't just stand here and wait for

something to happen." Beau massaged the tight muscles on the back of his neck.

"By the photos you've been sending me, you've uncovered the last remnant of the terrorist cell in Timbuktu. That's something, Beau." He squeezed Beau's shoulder. "Great work. Mission accomplished." He gave Beau a slight smile.

"But it's not great if we lose Ellie. I turned my back for twenty seconds, and she disappeared." He should have never let his heart soften toward Ellie. "This can't happen again!" Beau kicked the dust, sending it flying. He paced the length of the truck back and forth, wracking his brain for a plan of action, the next step.

The chief's radio squawked with static. Beau hurried back to the SUV and listened to the helicopter pilot's voice.

"Chief Auguste, I've located a Hummer matching the description you've given. It is located inside a two-acre compound half a kilometer from your current location on the back road of the Missira block. The area is walled on all four sides. There is no sign of a blonde American female. I see three guards with AK-47s, one at the gate, one outside a building, and one walking the perimeter. I do not have a visual of Hussein. I await your instructions, sir."

"Thanks, Phillips. Continue to circle the area. I will get back to you." He replaced the radio and rubbed the scruff of a beard shading his chin, letting out a breath.

Beau waited, his anxiety at its peak. "What do we do, Chief?"

"Our next moves are critical for many reasons. We must be strategic. Take out Hussein and his men while protecting Ms. Bendale. I've got to think this through." Auguste spoke into the radio again. "Phillips, case the area. Is it highly populated? Are there children playing in the streets? Are there businesses nearby? And see if you can ascertain where they are holding the hostage. Get back to me with more info."

He punched a number in his phone. "Officers, let's converge at headquarters immediately." He fastened his seatbelt. "Get in, Beau. We have work to do."

Beau rushed to the passenger side, jumped in, and slammed the door as the Chief pulled into Bamako's traffic. He turned his lights and sirens on to assist their rush through the congested streets.

"We must move strategically. I expect to hear from Hussein any time now with his demands. If you're a praying man, now would be a good time to talk to the Man upstairs." Auguste down-shifted the SUV and passed a traffic jam using a field by the side of the road.

Taking several turns through the city, he wheeled into the police headquarters parking lot on the same property as the French Embassy. Other cars arrived, one after another.

"Dax, trade me for Ellie. I'm who he wants," Beau begged.

"But what's going to keep him from killing both of you? It's too risky." He got out of the truck. Beau followed suit. Auguste's phone rang. "Hello." He waited. "Put the call through on this phone." He motioned two of his captains to come close. "Hussein is coming on the line. Stay close, but don't speak." His phone rang again. "Hello, Chief Dax Auguste here."

"Afternoon, Chief Auguste, are you ready to talk business?" Hussein's voice was husky and gleeful, his breathing heavy. "I think I have something you want."

"Yes, you've kidnapped an American woman who is visiting Mali. I need you to release Ms. Bendale unhurt within the hour," Auguste demanded.

"I'm sure you do. But I had a purpose in taking the American woman. I want to make a deal, a trade. You can have the journalist in exchange for Beau Dubois de La Croix. I'm sure he's listening—waiting for his chance to take me out. But you will do this my way or de La Croix will lose another woman he loves." He paused.

"I saw the helicopter—so you know where I am. Listen—I have a plan, and this is how this will go down. Chief Auguste, you and de La Croix meet me on the road in front of my compound in two hours. If I see anyone else or hear the helicopter again, I will kill the American woman. She is of no consequence to me. Do you understand?"

The sound of Hussein's voice ground Beau's nerves. His gleeful taunting mixed with brazen arrogance betrayed his Jekyll and Hyde tendencies. At the slightest whim, he could kill Ellie just to laugh at the anguish her death would bring.

"Two hours. I understand." Auguste ended the call and picked up his radio, "Phillips, I need you to land the copter ASAP. I need you at headquarters."

"Fifteen minutes, sir." The pilot signed off.

The chief met with his main men for a few minutes. Beau paced and prayed. When the helicopter pilot and his co-pilot rolled into the parking lot, Beau rejoined the conversation.

Phillips had a sketch of the compound to show Dax. "Sir, this is an industrial area with no residential dwellings within a quarter-kilometer radius. It is a fortress, probably where they're storing guns and ammunition, so take precautions—it could be explosive. I did not see the American woman, but a soldier is watching the door of this stucco building with an AK-47." He pointed to the area on the diagram.

"Then that's where she is." Dax stared at the sketch. "What is behind the compound?"

"A garbage dump," Phillips said.

"What is across the street and on either side?" Auguste asked as he made notes on the diagram.

"A body shop is across the street, and the building on the left is a pipe factory. The business on the right is deserted, looks empty." Phillips showed him the one he was talking about.

"That's good." The chief motioned for his men to move

close. "I want all six of you to get into plain clothes and hurry back for your orders."

The officers hurried toward the locker room.

"How are we going to do this, Chief?" Beau awaited his orders.

"Play it carefully. This is our one chance, and we can't mess it up. How good a shot are you?" He eyed Beau.

"Top of my class." Beau didn't flinch.

"I'm counting on it." He clasped Beau's shoulder.

When the officers returned wearing plain clothes, Auguste barked orders. He sent two of them to warn those in area businesses to stay off the street and then enter the compound from the pipe factory. Two were sent to the garbage dump to breach the back fence and take out the guards, then search the premises for weapons.

The last one was told to go to the deserted property and approach the compound from that angle, as a sniper on the roof. All of this was synchronized with the time Beau and Auguste were to face Hussein and Ellie on the dusty road.

Once the men left, Dax turned to Beau. "You ready? You know we're going head-to-head with a powerful terrorist, correct?"

"I've faced him before. I'm aware of his agenda and the lengths he'll go to for success." He kills without remorse." Beau took a deep breath and wiped the perspiration off his forehead.

"Since he called me, let me negotiate this exchange and try to get Ms. Bendale out of harm's way. If that doesn't work, we have to take him out. Understand?" He waited for confirmation.

"I understand, sir. The stakes are very high." *Lord, I need your help here. I'm desperate. Protect Ellie. Help us see this through ... without loss of life.*

Ellie lay on the cot, praying for a miracle. *Lord, I need divine intervention for my safe release, for Beau's protection. Give Beau and the police wisdom to deal with this volatile situation. Without your help, this could end badly. I'm trusting You Lord—.*

Angry voices interrupted her prayer. The small window above the cot gave her a view of soldiers hurrying to bring food, water, and ammunition to Hussein. He sat under an awning having his meal while loading several guns. One plain-clothed man changed the bandage on Hussein's arm. Blood stained his thigh where Beau had shot him. Ellie sucked in a shaky breath. Hussein was preparing for battle. Against Beau.

Checking the other window and the door, she realized she was surrounded. Escape wasn't possible. She returned to the cot to stare at the ceiling.

The soldier guarding her stuck his head into the room and looked around. Not seeing anything, he mumbled something and left.

Strategizing, she planned if noise erupted, she'd escape through the roof and try to climb over a wall or hide until this was over. When she surveyed possible exits, she found tall walls covered in tin. Unclimbable. Pole vaulting wasn't in her skill set. She stretched out on the cot, praying again.

After an hour, Hussein appeared in the doorway. Ellie sat up.

He wiped his mouth on his sleeve. "de La Croix will be here in an hour to offer himself in exchange for your release. You must have made quite an impression on the Frenchman." A pompous smile slithered across his face like a reptile. He turned his back to her. "I want to see de La Croix's blood spilling in the street today. My plan will work."

"No!" Tears filled her eyes. "Don't do this," she begged.

Laughing at her plea, Hussein walked away. "de La Croix has thwarted my plans too many times. It's past time to eliminate him, my nemesis."

Chief Dax Auguste and Beau stood on the dusty road when they heard the gate unlock. Beau took a breath, blew it out, and took a military stance, planting his feet while clasping his hands behind him. A rooster crowed in the distance, appropriately announcing it was time. Vultures circled overhead. A donkey brayed in the distance. The screech of the metal gate opening pierced the air, sending a shiver up Beau's spine.

Hussein stepped into the entrance with his bandaged arm wrapped tightly around Ellie's neck. Her wide tear-filled eyes pleaded for help. She was terrified, desperate—and rightfully so. This was a life-or-death situation with her future on the line. The next move was critical, and the terrorists were in control.

The arrogant leader limped, favoring his wounded leg, until he and Ellie were on the road about twenty feet from Auguste and Beau. Blood seeped through the bandage on his thigh as evil radiated from his eyes. With anger in his movements, he jerked Ellie around in front of him, loosening his hold a bit. He braced his feet, readied for battle, and smiled with an angry gleam in his bloodshot eyes.

"So, de La Croix, we meet again." He hesitated. "I usually go into battle with my men by my side, but I want to be the one who ends you." He looked down at Ellie and then at Beau again. "You choose lovely women, Dubois. This one has served her purpose. Now I have your undivided attention. You are in my clutches." He released a condescending laugh.

Chief Dax Auguste stepped forward. "This is an act of war, Dakir Hussein. Not Sharia Law. There's no need for civilians to be involved. Let's handle this exchange like the soldiers we are. In an act of goodwill, I ask that you let her go immediately." He stood firm with one hand on his weapon.

SHIRLEY GOULD

"You're in no place to make demands, Chief. I control this negotiation. She matters not to me. I have Beau Dubois de La Croix in my sites. She was excellent bait." Hussein's brow furrowed as he glared at Beau. "When his blood is spilling in this sand, I will release the American woman."

Beau was in attack mode, using great restraint as flames raged through his veins. Poised for action, his jaw clenched, ready to strike. "Let her go. She's not part of this. I'm willing to take her place." He stepped forward, planted his feet, braced for battle. His insides tightened as if being squeezed by a python. The sun's heat added to the intensity of the stand-off as a warm breeze stirred the sand at their feet.

"Oh, you're wrong. She is serving an important role in how this will play out, Dubois." Hussein smirked. "You don't release the bait until you reel in your catch." He laughed.

Auguste eased forward. "Ms. Bendale's safety puts you in control, Hussein. What's your plan?" He waited, staring at the enemy.

Hussein pulled a pistol from a holster at his waistband and held it to Ellie's temple as he tightened his hold with the other hand. "de La Croix, let's do this without ending this woman's life. You come halfway, and then I'll release her and turn my gun on you."

"I agree to your terms, Hussein. We'll do this your way. Can I speak to her first?" Beau asked.

"Oh, a sweet farewell. How touching. Yes, but make it quick." Hussein grinned.

Beau focused on Ellie's eyes. "E, trust me."

She nodded slightly.

"*Chini. Sawa?*" Beau spoke to her in Swahili saying, down and okay.

She gave a small nod.

"*Moja, mbili, tatu.*"

On three—in Swahili—Ellie hit the dirt as Beau drew his

pistol firing at Hussein. The terrorist leader landed right behind Ellie, writhing, as blood stained his shoulder. He yelled for his men to attack as the hemorrhaging spread, but no one rushed to his rescue. He shouted again as he reached for his gun.

Beau spun into action kicking Hussein's gun out of reach, then grabbed Ellie. She fell into his arms and sobbed.

Chief Auguste rushed forward, turned Hussein over and cuffed him, called for an ambulance, then retrieved the gun laying in the dirt. Auguste's men shot one of the soldiers who ran to assist Hussein, then apprehended the other terrorists.

The police officers searched the compound, shouting as they discovered weapons and brought them to the gate. The plain-clothed officers escorted cuffed soldiers out the gate as sirens wailed in the distance.

"Let's get you into the shade." Beau put his arm around her shoulders.

She trembled as tears rolled down her face. He led her to a bench in front of the business across the street. "You did great." He strengthened his grip on her in an attempt to quell her shaking, her fear.

"I'm glad you're a crack shot, Doc Holliday." She wiped her face and rubbed her hands on her khaki pants.

Sirens pierced the air as an ambulance arrived on the scene. The technicians worked on Hussein's soldier.

"This could have ended differently." Her eyes were puffy and red, but still beautiful.

"The Lord was with us," Beau said.

She stared at him. "You prayed?"

"I was desperate. You could have been killed. He had you in his grip. I think your faith has rubbed off on me." He gave her a weak smile.

With her face buried in her hands, she sobbed. "Thank you, Lord."

She leaned back and looked at him through wet lashes as more tears dampened her face.

"He did come through for us, didn't He?" His rough fingers dried her cheeks like a caress.

She nodded and drew in a deep breath. "I could use some water. Can you get me a bottle?"

"You'll be okay here for a minute?" He stood.

"Yep. I'm staying right on this bench." Around her the police shoved the terrorists into their cars.

When he returned to the compound, Beau bent over and took a couple of deep breaths. That was close. One day his luck could run out. He grabbed two bottles of water and returned to Ellie.

"For you, Ms. Bendale." He opened her bottle for her and then downed his own.

"I know why both countries vie for your service, you're a regular GI Joe, willing to go up against the number one enemy in the world."

"Wow! I should hire you as my agent." He laughed. "But it wasn't a one-man show. Dax Auguste put the plan in place, he had the compound surrounded and took out the terrorists. Planes are leaving within the hour to take out their stronghold in Timbuktu. Troops left earlier today to confiscate the weapons hidden at the mosque. So, I can't take all the credit for the success of this mission."

"Blah, blah, blah. Keep telling yourself that, but I've witnessed your tactics and know your strengths." She took a deep breath and realized she'd stopped trembling. "You did it again. Got me through my fear." She offered a small smile.

"How about I see when we can get you to your hotel? I'll have to give a deposition, but I will be there later." He took her empty bottle.

"That's the best thing I've heard all day."

14

Emergency workers rolled the gurney to the ambulance.

"How bad is Hussein's injury?" Beau asked.

"He'll live to stand trial after a lot of pain and suffering." One side of the chief's mouth lifted in a slight smile. "Great shot, Beau. Get one of my men to take you and Ms. Bendale to her hotel, then I'll meet you at headquarters for your deposition." Auguste turned to instruct more of his men.

"Thanks. I'll see you there." Beau arranged transport for Ellie and ambled back to where she watched the scene play out in the street.

"Are you ready for that hot shower?" He asked as he crossed the road.

"Yes. But first, you need to go get your knife back. It's in Hussein's pants pocket."

"Good idea." Beau winked at her then hurried to the gurney, stopped the techs from putting Hussein in the ambulance, and searched his pockets. The prisoner yelled in protest, but handcuffs kept him from retaliating.

"Hussein, you lose." Beau made a slight bow with a smirk on his lips.

Turning, Beau held up the knife so Ellie could see it. After retrieving his backpack and her bag from Auguste's truck, Beau motioned for her to proceed to her chariot, a dusty police car that smelled of cigarette smoke.

Emergency technicians loaded Hussein into an ambulance. Ellie jerked when the doors slammed. Beau knew it would take time for the effects of this experience to pass. He'd been there. Many times. War wounds people in different ways, but the Lord smiled on them today. He looked up to the clouds and sent a word of thanks after she was safe in the car. This day could have ended badly ... but God.

Elated to be back in her hotel suite enjoying the air-conditioning, the sense of safety, and a warm shower helped to melt Ellie's anxiety. She relaxed on her bed and drank an ice-cold Coke.

And forced herself to dwell on the good experiences in Timbuktu, her adventures with Beau, and waking up on his shoulder, wishing it could last forever. Along the way, she'd given her heart to the hunky hero—the one with no interest in a relationship. Par for the course. The memories would help her survive after she walked away. And walk away she would.

A few minutes after the restaurant started serving the evening meal, she entered. It felt wonderful to be clean and dressed up, with jewelry and makeup on. And blessedly peaceful to be safe in a classy restaurant with strains of Kenny G's saxophone adding to the ambiance of candlelight and flowers.

After ordering a soft drink, she visited the salad bar. Opting to wait until arriving in the States for a salad, she selected fruit.

Once back at her table, she picked up her stemware glass of water covered with condensation, holding it with a new appreciation for the small things, for being alive, and for the freedoms she enjoyed. Her experiences in this West African country challenged her as they adjusted her worldview.

The manager of the restaurant approached her table with a beautiful bouquet of roses and held them toward Ellie. "Ms. Bendale, there is a gentleman who would like to join you for dinner. He has sent these blooms to ask your permission. May he dine with you this evening?".

With a smile, Ellie accepted the bouquet and inhaled the fragrance. "Yes. Tell him he can join me for dinner—since he sent me flowers."

The manager bowed and hurried away.

Elllie's breath caught as Beau approached.

Bowing slightly, he took Ellie's hand and kissed her fingers. "You look lovely tonight. Thank you for the invitation to join you."

"You're welcome. A girl doesn't know when she'll need a hero. So, I'd better keep you close until I board that plane to Nairobi."

"At your service, *mademoiselle*." He winked. "If you'll order me a bottle of water and a Coke, I'll visit the salad bar and be right back." His masculine scent lingered after he stepped away.

The waiter was pouring his soda over purified ice when he returned. The ends of his hair were still wet from his shower.

"You look refreshed and smell good, finally, de La Croix. Did you enjoy your shower?" She sprinkled salt into her soup.

"The water was clean and warm and much needed." He drank some water.

"Is your assignment completed?" Ellie played with her soup spoon.

"Yes. I have two meetings tomorrow morning at police

headquarters, then I'll surrender my weapons at the Embassy and fly out after you do the next morning." He met her gaze.

"Let me pray, then we can eat." Ellie wanted to move things along.

He put his hand on hers. "No—let *me* pray." He bowed his head. "Lord, thank you." He paused and tightened his hold on Ellie's hand. "Thank you for helping us today, thank you for safety on our escape from Timbuktu, for this food and our time together. Amen." He released her hand and picked up his fork.

"You okay, Ellie?" He cut into a piece of juicy watermelon and took a bite.

"Yeah. The job assignment brought me here. I came wanting adventure, and you've given me that and then some. I'll need to get over being kidnapped by terrorists, but I have memories of a handsome hero saving the day. So, I'll be fine." She winked.

He drank half his Coke. "It takes time to debrief after an experience like you had today. How is your schedule in the coming weeks?"

Ellie wiped her mouth after taking a sip of her soup. "Oh, that's good. Here, try this." She gave him a taste using her spoon. "I'll fly to Nairobi the day after tomorrow and meet my friends, Olivia and Jocelyn. Olivia has resigned from her flight attendant position because she's marrying a widower she met in Zanzibar. He has an adorable little boy and has adopted a baby girl to give Olivia a child of her own. It's a sweet story," She took a drink.

"We'll have a day to relax in Nairobi before we work the late flight to America. Then I have a week off before I fly again. What about you?"

"I'll fly to Paris after you leave Mali. I have meetings, and mounds of paperwork waiting for my return. Where they will send me next—I have no idea." He finished his Coke and motioned to the waiter for another.

Their entrees were delivered.

"Hot food, cold drinks. Don't you love it?" Beau asked.

"Yes, I do." She cut into her meat. It tasted like a beef roast with gravy and vegetables. "What is this?"

"Ostrich. Isn't it great?" Beau took another bite. "Try it with some of the gravy on it." He poured some on her meat.

She took a bite. "It's wonderful."

"How's the article coming?" He reached for a roll from the breadbasket.

"Ask me that tomorrow. I'll be sunbathing and working on it at the pool." She cut another bite of ostrich.

"It's going to be amazing. Let me know when you get the offer from the magazine. I'll give you my email address." His expression turned pensive as he thanked the waiter, who delivered another Coke.

Did he regret offering her his email? "Sure, I can do that." She buttered a roll and turned quiet.

"What?"

"How much can I say about our dealings with the terrorists?"

"You are a writer with a nose for the news, but it would be safer if you could refrain from sharing those particular details. I don't want you ending up as a target in the future. Can you do that?"

"No problem. After what I've been through, I promise not to talk about it unless you're there to rescue me. And since we live on different continents, that's not likely to happen."

"You can speak about our adventures but under no circumstances mention the foreign soldiers. Okay?" His gaze held hers.

"Okay." She turned to check out the dessert bar. "Ready for something sweet to eat?"

"Sure." He stood and helped with her chair. "I think you deserve a reward for your bravery."

"It's not hard following your lead, Rambo. I'm not so brave."
She stood and led the way.

"But following orders takes effort for you. So, you get two
desserts tonight." He smiled.

He ordered his traditional half-chocolate, half-coffee drink
and some hot tea for her. Over dessert, their conversation went
from one subject to another like two old friends comfortable in
each other's company without a threat looming.

"I need to send you a few of the photos. You'll get a kick out
of them. I entitled the pics 'Beau at his Best.' You'll laugh."

"Send them to my email. I'll need something to smile about
after I finish the paperwork on this assignment." He stirred his
café.

Ellie yawned. "Sorry. I think I need to call it a night. I'm
pretty tired. You must be exhausted. I've slept a lot more than
you have." On his shoulder soaking in his strength and
masculine scent, wishing she could stay there forever, but she
didn't mention that info.

"It's catching up with me. I am tired" He put a tip on the
table and stood. "Enjoy your day tomorrow. How about dinner
again tomorrow night?" He helped Ellie with her chair.

"Sure." She breathed in the smell of her rose bouquet.
"Thank you for the flowers. And for saving my life." She
slipped her hand into the crook of his elbow.

"At your service, *mademoiselle*."

She smiled.

The smell of chlorine and the fragrance from a frangipani tree
filled the air as Ellie worked on her article. After putting some
of her edgy experiences in the prose, it took on a maturity she
hadn't written with before—a broader insight. She saw things
differently than she did eight days ago and felt changed in a

way she couldn't put her finger on. But it affected her work in a good way. She'd accept that for now.

Scanning her photos once more, she allowed the scenes to take her back to the desert. She clicked on a site and ordered canvases of the best shots. After selecting two prints for her parents and some for her siblings, she scanned the ones of Beau and ordered herself a five by seven of him on his haunches in the sand, looking in the distance with a caravan of camels trekking toward Timbuktu.

After pressing *SAVE* on her laptop, she closed her computer and placed it in her bag to protect it from moisture. She relaxed under an umbrella, ordered a cold drink, and applied sunscreen for the second time in an hour. Being near the equator caused the sun's rays to be ten times hotter. No sense in taking chances now after guarding her skin for days. Blistered shoulders would be miserable under her flight attendant uniform.

"*Mademoiselle*, would you like to have lunch at the pool today? I have a menu."

A waiter, probably melting in his uniform, smiled as he offered the placard.

"Yes, that would be nice." Ellie ordered, then relaxed, enjoying songs by Mariah Carey from the speakers. American music followed her on her trips across Africa. It was a good alternative to squeaky, off-key Kenyan tunes they played at the hotel she frequented with Joycelyn and Olivia in Nairobi.

Ibis flew overhead, squawking as their shadows crossed the ground. Her meal was served on a fancy tray with a sprig of bougainvillea. The waiter had a linen cloth across his arm while he removed a silver dome with flair as if she were royalty.

Ellie's mind went back to the bread, bananas, and bottles of water she shared with Beau as they escaped. It couldn't compare. Both experiences were extraordinary in her memories of Mali but were crowded by thoughts of

Beauregard. Deciding to focus on today, she enjoyed the lunch set before her and tried to let tomorrow take care of itself.

Her cell phone rang, and she dug for it in her bag. "Hello."

"Hey girl, this is Jocelyn. How was Timbuktu?" Their connection wasn't without static but didn't disconnect.

"Hot, adventurous, and very photogenic." Ellie tried to sound upbeat.

"Great! I can't wait to hear everything and read your article. Are you flying out in the morning as scheduled?" Jocelyn asked.

"Yes, I leave Mali and make one stop in Dubai, then I'll arrive in Nairobi mid-afternoon. Is everything still on schedule?" Ellie took a sip of her soda.

"Yes. The airlines put us up at Ole Serena this time. They're renovating the Nairobi Hilton. It's a gorgeous hotel built beside the National Game Park. Olivia and I love it. We'll have about thirty hours in Nairobi before we work the flight home," Jocelyn said.

"That sounds good. Is Liv okay?"

"Yes, but missing Eli and the kids terribly. These occasional flights have confirmed her desire to stay grounded and enjoy her new family."

Ellie understood missing someone you love. "I don't doubt that. I'll see you tomorrow."

"A room key will be waiting for you at the front desk. See you soon."

"Thanks, Jocelyn." Ellie ended the call. If this photojournalist opportunity offered something permanent, she would follow Olivia's example and put flying the African skies in her rear-view mirror, although it had been great working with her best friends.

Finishing her lunch, she relaxed under the thatched umbrella by her chair. The mixture of emotions of the last few days kept her from dozing off.

"*Mademoiselle*, a lemonade for you." The waiter served a tall stemware glass.

"But I didn't order this." Ellie sat forward and took a sip.

The waiter smiled. "It is from the gentleman on the diving board."

Ellie turned as a perfect specimen of masculinity stepped onto the board. *Beau.* Ellie lifted the glass and toasted it in his direction.

He stopped and bowed. "Enjoy." After a bounce on the end of the diving board, Beau executed an Olympic-worthy dive into the sparkling pool and swam toward her. He lifted his head from the water, slung his hair back like a model, and propped his elbows on the edge of the pool.

The drops of water on his eyelashes added an extra sparkle to his gray eyes. His physique resembled a body-builder's, except for a few scars, cuts, and bruises. But those gave him a rugged persona.

"Amazing lemonade. Thank you." She took another sip.

"You're welcome. You finish the article?" Beau rubbed water out of his eyes.

"I did."

"And—"

"And it's really good. Probably the best work I've ever done. With your help, I might add." Confidence coated her words.

"Hey, I was just the tour guide. You're the creative genius." He pointed at her emphasizing his point.

"Did you finish your work at the Embassy?"

"Yeah. For now. I'll face more depositions once I'm back in Paris, and my Washington D.C. boss has questions for me as well. It will take some time to put this thing to bed, as they say in the U.S." He pushed away a couple of feet from the side of the pool and treaded water.

"So, you're done for today?"

"Yes. I thought a swim would cool me off after sitting in hot offices all day." He shook his head, showering her with water.

"Beau!" Ellie grabbed her beach towel and dried her legs.

He splashed her again, then swam to the deep end of the pool, climbed the ladder, and dove off the board again. He swam the length of the pool, then got out and grabbed a towel. He dried off, turned, and waved. "I'll see you at dinner."

Watching his exit as she had many times this last week, she was apprehensive. He would exit one last time once they reached the airport. She sighed.

15

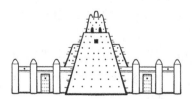

After a warm shower, Beau repacked his suitcase and confirmed his airline ticket. He requested the exit row, hoping to have legroom for his long flight to Paris. When dressing for dinner, he missed his weapons that were on their way to headquarters in Paris. He arrived at the table before Ellie.

"Will *mademoiselle* be joining you?" the manager asked as he lit the candle in the center of the table.

"Yes, but I'm early. Could I get a cold Sprite?"

He bowed slightly. "I will bring it right away."

Checking his messages on his personal phone while he waited was the first time Beau had relaxed since this assignment started. He was weary of being on guard but thankful they'd come through unscathed, except for the piece of his heart Elliana Bendale had hijacked. Goodbye would be a difficult moment. But he would say a final goodbye. It's what he did. Who he was.

"You're here. You could have called my room. I've been ready—just doing some packing. Some of my clothes smell like a fishy camel." She smiled.

"You may have to wash your clothes twice to get that odor out. After I packed, I had some texts to answer, but I didn't have any curios to squeeze into my luggage. Did the antique tent stakes fit?" He took another drink of his soda.

"No, but I'll hand carry those. As a flight attendant, I can bend the rules. It's a perk of the trade." She ordered a soda. "Are you ready to visit the fruit bar?"

"Yes. Just waiting for you." He stood and followed her to the display of colorful fruits and pastries.

Choosing watermelon, she smiled. "What I wouldn't have given for this a few days ago. I appreciate it more now than before our little journey."

"It gives a whole new meaning to being thirsty." Beau took two pieces for himself before following her to their table. Reaching for her hand, he prayed. "Lord, thank you for your protection, thank you for this food, and be with us as we go our separate ways tomorrow. Amen." He released her hand and reached for his napkin-wrapped silverware, then noticed her eyes were moist. It was time to lighten the mood.

"The officers sang your praises today. Your bravery under pressure impressed them. Most women would have been a weepy mess. But you stood strong." He raised his glass as if toasting her.

"You didn't tell them I ugly cry on occasion?"

"No. I kept your secret and painted you as a beautiful combination of grit and grace." Beau squeezed her hand still resting on the table.

"This melon is juicy today." She changed the subject.

"Or maybe our taste buds are dehydrated." Beau took another bite.

"You've got a point."

He peeled a small banana as they ordered their entrées.

Ellie sat back while Beau finished his fruit plate.

"What?" He put his fork down.

"Where is he?"

"Who?"

"Hussein. Will he be kept in Mali?"

Leaning back, he wiped his mouth. "I won't know for sure until I get to France, but he will probably be taken to a secure location in the States for interrogation before he faces war crimes."

"Can he escape?"

"No." He grabbed her hand and felt it tremble. "You're safe." He kissed her knuckles and released her, returning to his meal.

"Are you ready to go home?" She took a drink of her Coke.

"My bags are packed, and I'm anxious to put this chapter to rest. This will revive tourism for Timbuktu, and you were a part of that. Are you working a flight to America tomorrow night?" He didn't answer her question.

"No, I'll have thirty hours to relax with my best friends before I work a flight home." She took her last bite of melon.

"I'm glad. Extra time will help you recover from your scary experiences in Mali."

He paused. "I take extra days to decompress after difficult missions. Don't force the process. It takes time." He held her gaze for a long moment. "If you need to talk about it, to help process what you went through, feel free to email me, but don't use the word terrorist."

"All right. But I think I'll be fine once I get back to familiar territory. Thanks for protecting me." She sounded so sincere.

"It's what I do—beat the bad guys and save the damsel in distress." He laughed as their food was delivered. "Most subjects I've rescued are old pudgy men or stubborn grandmas who refused to believe there was any reason to hurry." He smiled. "Not a beautiful blonde with spunky sarcasm and quick wit.

"You've been a breath of fresh air for this soldier." He saluted her and picked up his steak knife. "This smells amazing." He took a bite, then cut her a piece. "You have to try this. It's great." He fed her the bite on his fork.

"You're right. I love it. You want to try my tilapia?" She cut a piece.

"Nah, I'm not much on tilapia. But thanks."

Beau kept their conversation light, sensing Ellie was getting weepy. Some of it was probably the stress of being kidnapped, but some of the tears were from their pending goodbyes. They'd shared life-and-death experiences, been thrown together physically during their escape, and gotten too close personally. This was going to hurt.

While enjoying dessert and hot tea, Beau broached the elephant in the room. "We need to be in the lobby at nine to leave for the airport. Do you want to get an early breakfast?"

"Sure, that works for me. I still have some of the funds I was given for expenses on this trip. Can I give it to you?" She reached for her bag.

"I don't know. That's confusing. I was given per diem as well. Let me text my boss, who put this arrangement together, and ask him. I'll tell you in the morning."

"Okay. Sounds great." She finished her tea. "I'm calling it a night."

"Me too." He tossed his napkin onto the table and helped her with her chair. They strolled together through the lobby. Beau stopped at the front desk. "You can go on up if you want. I need to talk to them about preparing our bills. Last time I almost missed my plane waiting for my receipt." He stopped at the receptionist's desk.

"I'll go on to my room. See you in the morning."

"I hope you rest well." He kept their interaction light.

"You, too, McGarrett." She left him at the desk.

"Hello, Grace, can you prepare the bill for the de La Croix room and the Bendale room tonight? We have early flights in the morning and will need our receipts before we depart."

The manager overheard his request. "We will not delay your departure, sir. It will be ready this time."

Beau smiled. "You remember?"

"Yes, with regrets. We appreciate your business. Have a good evening." The manager turned to Grace and discussed the two bills.

"Thanks." He headed to his room. It would feel good to be flat on his back, though sleep wouldn't come easy. It was best for Ellie to go to her room alone. Saying good night would have been tough.

Tears stained Ellie's cheeks as she slid to the floor and sobbed just inside her door. Watching Beau walk away would be excruciating. Somewhere along the way, she'd fallen in love with him. He'd captured her heart and had no idea how she felt —and it had to stay that way.

Lord, I need help. I can't do this on my own. I'm a mess. My heart hurts. I need emotional strength to walk away tomorrow. There's no room for me in Beau's life. He made that clear. Help me, give me strength, I pray. Amen

After donning pajamas, Ellie scanned her photos of this trip and allowed the tears to flow every time she saw Beau striking a pose. He'd helped her, even though she was an excuse to catch some evil men. He needed a ruse, a cover story to do his job. She was okay with that.

Burying her feelings, she would keep them from Beau and her friends. Saying goodbye to the one she wanted to spend her life with would take determination. But it had to be this way. She wiped her eyes, blew her nose, and took a deep breath. It was time to go home.

It was one of those nights when she felt she'd just fallen asleep when the alarm went off. Ellie punched the snooze button once, giving her ten more minutes before she faced the day. Ibis squawking as they flew over the hotel kept her from going back to sleep. When the alarm blared again, she let her feet hit the floor, got dressed, and closed her suitcases the final time. After stacking them near the door, she went to the restaurant for breakfast.

"Could you send a bellman to my room to bring my luggage down?" Ellie spoke to the lady she hadn't met before at the front desk as she handed her room key over.

"Yes, Ms. Bendale. I have your receipt ready. I hope you enjoyed your stay at Azalai Hotel." She spoke with kindness.

"It was wonderful. Thank you." She took the receipt and proceeded to the restaurant. After she ordered her eggs, she visited the breakfast bar.

The waiter delivered her tea. "Your friend ate much earlier."

"That's fine. We hadn't scheduled a time to meet." Ellie poured the hot water over her tea bag and bounced it in the water as it steeped. She spied the bowl they serve café' in along with a dirty place setting. *Beau's dishes.* He was already distancing himself. She knew it—felt his absence. Felt alone.

Once her eggs arrived, she prayed, then ate what she could. When the time of departure grew near, she left a tip on the table, shouldered her bag, and pulled her carry-on to the lobby. Beau was coming down the stairs with his luggage in tow.

"You ready?" He dropped his largest bag beside her suitcase.

"Yes. When will our ride be here?" She didn't look at him.

Beau spoke to the bellman in French. "He said the driver is entering the property now. I'll get our luggage ready to load." He moved their large pieces to the curb.

When the SUV pulled up, Ellie's eyes widened. "Wow. We're traveling in style this morning?"

"The Ambassador appreciates what was accomplished last

week. He sent his personal vehicle to transport us in the mode you're accustomed to." Beau bowed.

"Please thank him for me. This is nice." Ellie slid into the back seat and fastened her seatbelt. Her antique tent stakes were wrapped in a laundry bag the hotel supplied. She put them on the seat beside her.

Once everything was loaded, Beau got into the luxury SUV on the other side. He put his hand on the driver's shoulder. "We're ready, *monsieur*. To Kenya Air terminal and then Air France terminal, please."

The driver eased them out of the hotel parking lot and into the traffic flow. Silence hung heavy between them as they traveled through the city.

"Did you ask the Ambassador about the funds?" Ellie glanced at his profile.

"Yes, and he said to tell you to keep it as compensation for all you've been through. Consider it a reward." One side of his lip lifted in an attempt to smile.

"But it's over three hundred dollars." She reached into her bag to get the money.

"And it's yours. Spend it in the market in Nairobi." He winked.

"Okay. If you insist." She tried to smile.

His calloused hands tightened into fists. "Ellie, I've changed my mind about something." Beau's eyes met hers.

"Changed your mind? About what?" Ellie sucked in a breath. Her hopes soared.

His pause intensified the moment. "With everything you've told me about your two friends, I can tell you trust them completely. And you need to be able to debrief your experiences. So, if they promise to keep what you share with them in strictest confidence, you can tell them about the terrorist soldiers." He held her gaze.

Ellie blew out the breath she'd been holding and sighed.

"Thanks. I appreciate that. It will help me process what happened." She turned from his watchful eyes, peering out the window so he wouldn't see disappointment written on her face. *So much for wishful thinking, Elliana.*

The silence was palatable between them. Ellie was relieved when she spotted several signs giving directions to the airport.

"I appreciate all you've done for me." She bravely broke the silence.

Beau reached for the itinerary she held. "I'll put my email on here. Let me know what the magazine says about your article and photographs. I'm sure you'll be offered a position. Hands down." He smiled, then wrote his info on her paper and placed it in her hand.

She slipped it in her bag. "I'll email you after I hear from them." She looked out her window as the SUV slowed. "This is my stop." Perching her bag on her shoulder, she unfastened her seatbelt and grabbed the tent stakes. The driver opened her door. She got out, took a deep breath, and stepped onto the sidewalk.

After rolling her large suitcase to her side, Beau retrieved her carry-on roller bag. "Can you handle all this luggage?"

She raised the handles on both suitcases, rolled them in a circle until they were back-to- back, then propped her tent stakes on top. She looked up and smiled. "I'm a flight attendant with luggage skills."

"You do have skills, Ms. Bendale." His lip hitched in a smile.

The driver closed the back of the luxury vehicle and returned to the driver's seat as Beau stepped in front of her.

She scanned his grey eyes. "Beau, I'm not good at goodbyes, so, hug me and leave. Okay?" Ellie moved toward him.

Opening his arms, he embraced her. "Ellie, you're amazing."

"You're not so bad yourself, Rambo." She put her hand on one cheek and kissed the other, then stepped back. "Goodbye,

Beauregard Dubois de La Croix." She saluted, pivoted, and took a few steps, then paused. Waited.

She turned, ran toward him, threw her arms around his neck, and kissed him soundly. He responded, deepening the kiss. When he pulled back, her eyes filled with tears. She touched his lips one last time, turned, and walked away.

Right before going through the large glass doors, she looked back. Beau was still standing where she'd left him. She blew him a kiss as tears dampened her cheeks. Struggling to breathe, she kept moving toward the cue for her luggage to be scanned. She risked another glance to the sidewalk. He was gone.

But not forgotten.

Leaving was next on the agenda, though it was hard to get moving. After a hesitation, Beau slid into the front seat of the SUV and watched airport activity as they drove to his terminal. Taking deep breaths, he tried to pull himself together. His lungs stifled as if he'd been kicked in the gut.

Ellie was sunshine in his dark days. But it had to be this way. She could have been killed. He couldn't put someone he loved in harm's way again. He couldn't run far enough or do enough good to make up for what happened to Jazelle.

When the driver stopped, Beau realized they'd arrived. After grabbing his duffle, he shouldered his backpack and thanked the driver.

"The chief sent this for you, sir." The driver handed Beau a container.

"Tell him I said thanks." Beau opened the container and smiled. Baklava.

"Have a good flight."

Hitching his backpack onto his shoulder, he entered the terminal. Going home was all he could do now. Time would help their escape from Timbuktu to fade from his memory. But it may take a lifetime for Elliana Bendale to fade from his heart.

He hurried through the doors, sent his duffel through the security scan, and took his place in the checkin line. He checked the clock on the wall. Ellie would soon be boarding her flight. Leaving Mali.

Leaving him.

The view out her window gave Ellie a perfect line of sight as they lifted off toward the east. She took a deep breath when the Air France planes came into view. With the inertia gluing her to her seat, she attempted to breathe normally. As Bamako shrank in size when the pilot increased altitude, she thanked the Lord for helping with their goodbyes. There wasn't anything attractive about her ugly cry.

The flight attendant was overly attentive to her after seeing her tears. She kept soft drinks and snacks coming. Ellie accepted a magazine the attendant offered and thanked her for being kind. It was *Above & Beyond*, the magazine she'd written the article for, the one that sent her to Timbuktu. It was a great reprieve from her heartache—temporarily.

16

Walking the beautiful airport in Dubai felt like being in America. The stores, restaurants, and beautiful architecture soothed Ellie's tattered emotions. One curio shop had the best-carved camels she'd seen in African markets. They also sold replicas of Aladdin's lamp, like the ones in cartoons, where characters rubbed the magic lamp and a genie appeared. She bought one so she could rub it and make a wish from time to time. Maybe it would come true.

The flight to Nairobi was relatively short. Happy to be back in familiar territory, she boarded a taxi and hung on for a rough ride through downtown to Ole Serena. Jocelyn waited in the lobby.

"Yay! I'm glad to see you." She hugged her friend. "Where's Olivia?"

"In the shower. Let's get your things to the room, and we can talk until time for dinner." Jocelyn took the large bag, and Ellie followed with the rest.

Taking some deep breaths, she pulled herself together before she faced their questions, sure to turn into an interrogation, when they heard about her escape from Timbuktu.

Liv clapped her hands when Ellie walked through the door. "I'm so glad your back. Did you finish your article and get the photos you wanted?" Olivia had a towel wrapped around her hair.

"Yes." Ellie dropped her bag onto the bed. "The article is the best work I've ever done, and the pictures are amazing."

"I can't wait to read it." Olivia brushed the tangles out of her long brown hair.

"How about after dinner?" Ellie kicked her shoes off and got comfortable. "I want to hear an update on your wedding plans. How many days until you walk down the aisle?"

"Twenty-two. But who's counting?" Olivia turned the hairdryer on, drowning out her laughter.

"I think she's counting down the minutes, if you ask me," Jocelyn said. "You look tired, Ellie."

"Yeah. I am pretty worn out. I think the intense heat sapped my strength. It feels good to be in a cooler climate, even if the mosquitos are swarming." She reached for her laptop, brought up the main photo for the article, and turned the screen. "Look at this."

"That is amazing." Jocelyn pulled the laptop into her lap. "Can I look at the other photos?"

"Sure. The first ten are the ones I'm sending to the magazine." Ellie dug out her brush and fought with the tangles underneath her hair.

"This is your best work. Olivia, you have to see this. We have a professional in our midst." Jocelyn turned the laptop so Olivia could see her favorite.

Stepping closer, Olivia smiled. "These are fantastic. I love the sepia tones, but the full-color ones are breathtaking too." She scrolled through the photos and stopped on the one with

Beau squatted on the sand with the caravan in the distance. "Wow! And who is this?"

"Oh, that's Beau, my interpreter-slash-bodyguard." Ellie dropped her brush into her bag and stepped closer to the screen.

Jocelyn leaned in to see what the fuss was about. "You've been holding out on us, Ellie. He's a hunk!"

Both ladies stared at Ellie.

"What?"

They continued to stare.

"We're good friends. That's it." Ellie tried to keep things light.

"Oh, I think there's more to this story." Olivia put her hand on her hip.

"But for right now, it is time for dinner, and I'm starving." Ellie grabbed her shoulder bag. "Let's go, ladies." She slipped into her shoes, sashayed to the door, and held it open for them to proceed ahead of her.

Olivia twisted her still-damp hair into a messy bun as she trailed Jocelyn out the door.

"We *will* hear the story behind those sad eyes," Jocelyn announced, without facing Ellie.

Over dinner, they talked non-stop about Olivia's upcoming nuptials, Jocelyn's aspirations to help orphans in Swaziland, and Ellie's first camel ride.

"It was an adventure of a lifetime. Timbuktu is a diminishing oasis in the desert, but its future can blossom through revived tourism because of Beau's bravery." Ellie stared at her empty plate. "There are some disturbing details I'll share with you two in the privacy of our room. Let's just say, this experience changed me. I think I'll be processing it for a while."

"It sounds like part of it was difficult, and some of it stole your heart." Liv watched Ellie's facial expressions. "I'm right, aren't I?"

With tear-filled eyes, Ellie nodded as Olivia motioned for the waiter and signed their bill. "Let's move this conversation to our suite." She put her hand through Ellie's elbow. Jocelyn got on Ellie's other side as they stepped into the elevator.

"I don't think I've noticed the grandeur of this hotel before. The airline gives us the best accommodations—a safe place to rest and relax."

Olivia and Jocelyn looked at each other, and the latter shrugged her shoulders.

"What is it?" Ellie asked.

"Did you leave your sarcasm in Mali, my friend?" Jocelyn put her hand on the elevator door, holding it open.

"No, it's in my suitcase." She tried to smile. "I'm just tired."

"And heavy-hearted. I have your favorite candy bar in my luggage. It will cheer you up in no time." Jocelyn pulled out her key and opened their room. "Get your pajamas on, and I'll find some sweets."

"Perfect." Then Ellie's eyes filled as she planned to delete that word from her vocabulary.

As Beau stepped inside his front door, he dropped his bags and gathered the mail from the heap by the slot. He set it aside to thumb through later and stepped over to the window, then pulled the drapes to the side and stared at the Eiffel Tower. A couple under a red umbrella posed for a photograph with the tower in the distance. *Elliana.* He closed the drapes.

Opening the fridge, he sighed. What was in there was either wilted, dried up, or had mold growing on it. He gave up and headed out to the corner market for a few things.

As he walked, he called Alex. "How's my brother?"

"Beau, are you back in France?" Alex asked.

"I can hear you stirring something."

"Yeah, I'm running a restaurant. Or have you forgotten?"

"No, I haven't been gone that long. Just got back, I'm hungry, exhausted, and I smell like a camel."

"You want to stop by for some free food?"

"Not tonight. I have some serious jet lag since I haven't slept in days." Beau stopped on the sidewalk in front of a pizzeria. "I just wanted you to know that I'm home safe. Are you and Vivienne okay?"

"Order up!" Alex shouted. "We are doing great. Our neighbor's wife just had a baby. I'm afraid it's putting thoughts in her head about starting our family. When can we get together, Beau?"

Joining the cue, Beau placed his order. "How about next week? Debriefing takes days, and I need to do my laundry or buy some new clothes. These are rank." He laughed.

"I'll feed you. Call me, and let's set up a time."

"What are you stirring now? I can hear you hard at work." Beau enjoyed getting into his brother's world, even if it was just for a moment.

"This one is a *velouté,* which is a roux and white stock used over a stuffed chicken recipe. Sound good?"

"Sounds great and will probably taste amazing. Tell Vivienne hi for me. I'll call you next week. Later, Bro." Beau ended the call.

The fragrance of pepperoni made his mouth water. He took a seat outside to wait for his order. Strains of Moulin Rouge filled the street at a romantic sidewalk café, where couples sat holding hands and whispering to each other. One couple had a red umbrella leaning against their table. Beau ran his fingers through his hair, stood, and stepped back inside to put a rush on his to-go order.

With pepperoni pizza in hand, he hurried home, put his groceries away, and ate the pizza while it was still warm. His thoughts didn't drift again until he opened his cold Coke.

"Lord, I'm going to need help here." He spoke into his empty apartment. He popped the final pepperoni in his mouth, threw away the box, unpacked, started his laundry, then took a shower. He planned to get a haircut and be clean-shaven before he reported for duty. It was time to get back to work.

Stretching out on the bed, Ellie started the story at the scene where she was getting her toes broken in the Bamako airport by Steve McGarrett's clone. "Then he stole my taxicab and sped away."

"You were standing there with two broken toes, and he cut you off and took your cab?" Jocelyn sat up from her reclining position. "Did he know who you were?"

"No. We hadn't been introduced yet." Ellie shared her adventures from dinner with Beau when he assumed the photojournalist he was meeting was a man, L. E. Bendale, to finishing her assignment in Timbuktu. "He helped me get the photos I wanted, even if I needed to get up on his back to get a shot from a higher elevation."

"Physical contact. Did you two become more than friends?" Joycelyn asked.

"Beau isn't open to a relationship. Several years ago, he asked the love of his life to wait for him in a restaurant in Paris. When the bombings took place—she was killed. He vowed to never let that happen again. Love hurts too much." Ellie paused as a knot lodged in her throat. She would not cry again.

"But you lost your heart to him and had to say goodbye." Liv moved to Ellie's bed to hug her. "I'm sorry."

"At this point of the story, I still had my feelings in check. But when things turned deadly, and we had to make our escape with terrorist soldiers on our tail, I fell for my hero."

"Did you say terrorists?" Jocelyn moved to sit closer to Ellie.

"Beau said I could share the whole story with you two, but you can't repeat what I'm saying to anyone. Promise me. It could be dangerous enough to paint a target on my back."

"You know we'll keep it between us," Jocelyn said.

"Absolutely." Olivia moved back to the other bed in their room and got comfortable. "Were you in danger, Ellie?"

"Yes, but Beau kept me safe. He's like a SEAL, a double-agent for the U.S. and France. I think he's called a commando in France. He took this assignment as an interpreter for me, to keep me safe while he scoped out terrorist activity in Timbuktu. I wasn't aware of his assignment until we were attacked by the soldiers."

Ellie loved telling the part about how she put her self-defense skills to good use by breaking the soldier's nose. She painted Beau as the hero, then added the details of the smelly canoe ride and the crocodiles, the trucking experience, and the goats, then the camels, hitting the highlights.

"And during hours of close contact and heart-to-heart conversations, you fell in love with him," Olivia spoke with a voice of experience.

"It happened gradually. I understand." Liv reached over and squeezed Ellie's hand.

"Yeah, I was guarding my heart, but he stole it while I wasn't looking." Ellie sighed.

"But how does the story end?" Jocelyn asked.

"When we reached Bamako, while Beau was paying for our camel ride, I was kidnapped by Hussein—by the terrorists. I was taken to their compound in an industrial part of the city." With the undivided attention of her best friends, she replayed the events of that afternoon.

"It was like one of those moments in a movie where you didn't know how it was going to play out. But Beau spoke to me in Swahili, telling me to drop to the ground when he counted to three. I did, and he shot the leader. So, Beau is alive, I'm safe, and the terrorists have been run out of Timbuktu."

She took a drink of bottled water. "The rest is pretty straightforward. We parted as friends. He hugged me. I kissed his cheek, turned, and walked away. But I went back and really kissed him. Then I left."

"Did you look back?" Jocelyn reached for the tissue box on the bathroom vanity.

"Yes, and he was still standing where I left him, watching me leave. I blew him a kiss and caught my plane."

"And cried all the way to Nairobi." Jocelyn finished her sentence before she put the tissue box on her bed. "Are you okay? Olivia experienced a kidnapping in Zanzibar and is just now getting past it."

"With Hussein using me as bait to get Beau in his sites, it wasn't me he wanted to kill, it was Beau. Big difference." Ellie tried to downplay the danger.

"But we're talking about terrorists. You had to be terrified." Jocelyn stood and paced their suite.

"Yes. I was petrified and very aware of the danger. But I knew Beau would find me and exchange his life for mine. That's who he is. A valiant warrior, an expert marksman, Rambo in the flesh." She attempted a smile. "And he didn't let me down." She wiped her eyes. "Hey, can we talk about this tomorrow? I'm sure you'll have more questions. But I need to get some sleep."

"Good idea." Olivia grabbed her pajamas from her suitcase.

Jocelyn seemed lost in thought. "Did Beau find you pretty? Did he enjoy your wit? And did he appreciate your talents?"

"Yeah. He mentioned traveling with a beautiful blonde and complimented my blue eyes. He loved my photography and seemed to admire the way I broke that guy's nose. I made him laugh a lot. I called him McGarrett, Rambo, 007, Tarzan,

Indiana Jones, MacGyver, and Hooch when he shook his hair like a dog after I washed it for him." She smiled.

Jocelyn met Olivia's gaze across the room.

"What?" Ellie asked.

"This story isn't over yet, Elliana. You can trust me on that." Olivia smiled. "Jocelyn Cate, one day, you and I will meet the infamous Beauregard Debois de La Croix."

They laughed and soon turned out the lights, but for Ellie, sleep wouldn't come. She was haunted by the look on Beau's face as she walked away.

After a haircut and a shave, Beau donned his uniform and left for headquarters. It felt good to be back in some kind of normalcy, driving his truck, sleeping in his bed. Returning salutes after clearing security, he proceeded to the elevator, passing fellow soldiers along the way. Once he reached the fifth floor, he proceeded to the colonel's office. A line of those waiting acknowledged his arrival. Some saluted. A female in the group smiled.

"Hey, de La Croix. You made it back in one piece, I see." Francois saluted.

Returning the salute, Beau stepped forward and shook hands with his friend. "Francois, how are things in your high-tech world? Still creating drones for warfare?"

Francois shook his head. "Yeah. We have a new model making heads roll during the demonstrations. You'll like it."

"That's good to hear. Having eyes in the sky saves lives when our men are pinned down in combat." Beau advanced into the waiting area beside Francois.

"Are you here to debrief?" He took a seat and motioned for Beau to join him.

"Yeah. I'm ready to close the chapter on Timbuktu." Beau

rubbed his shaved chin. "It got pretty sticky. People could have been killed."

"I'm glad you were successful, but I didn't doubt you for a moment."

Beau's name was called, taking him from the back of the queue to the front. A soldier diverted him into a conference room instead of the colonel's office.

"Come in, Beau. I had them bring you in here. After your exhausting assignment, I didn't want you to wait for our appointment."

"Thank you." He stepped forward. "Good afternoon, Colonel. It's good to see you again."

Colonel Philippe Leroux stood and returned Beau's salute. "I'm glad to see you, DuBois. You did a fine job and ended a critical threat to that region of the world. I'm sorry the young lady was in danger for our mission." He straightened some paper on the conference table.

"Just following orders, sir, and Ms. Bendale is quite safe. She flew out of Mali right before I boarded my plane." The memory stung, but Beau didn't flinch.

Leroux motioned Beau toward a seat, then got comfortable in another chair. "You did a meticulous job. And as you suspected, the Imam was hiding guns and ammo for Hussein. He was being blackmailed and did as they demanded to keep the soldiers from killing everyone in Timbuktu." His brow furrowed with that bit of info.

"So, it's over?" Beau ran his hand over his new haircut.

"Yes, the threat to Timbuktu is over. Their tourism can now be revived, and Timbuktu can become the metropolis it once was." Leroux gave a hint of a smile. "But you will need some downtime to decompress. And so will Miss Bendale. Have you checked on her since she returned to the States?"

"No, sir. But I did encourage her to take a break and to talk to someone in case she has issues getting past it. She understands the importance of not mentioning that terrorists kidnapped her. I also offered my email address in case she needed to talk about what happened with someone who was there." Beau took a deep breath and sighed.

"Has she contacted you yet?"

"Not yet. But she is quite capable. I don't expect to hear from her." He paused. "I'm glad tourism in Timbuktu can now be rebuilt." Beau leaned forward with his elbows on his knees. "What's your next assignment for me, sir?"

"Your first order of business is to pick up your weapons, get some rest, fill out this stack of reports on the mission, and then we will talk." He hesitated. "Your five-year tour of duty is almost over. Are you signing on for another term?"

"I've not given it much thought, sir. I've been a bit preoccupied." Beau leaned back in his chair.

"Well, you're great at what you do." He paused. "I'd hate to lose you, and so would Axel McCabe in the States, but it is your decision."

"I'll think about it." He picked up the stack of forms. "I'll get these back to you within a week, sir." He stood.

"Thank you for your service, Beau. Mission accomplished." Leroux saluted Beau.

After returning his salute, Beau left the office. Down the hall, he ran into a friend.

"Hey, Beau, I didn't know you were back in Paris." Louis shook Beau's hand.

"I got in late yesterday. I haven't had time to connect with anyone yet, except my brother with a quick phone call. Still shaking Mali's dust off my boots. I was here to debrief, and now I'm facing mounds of paperwork." He held up the stack of documents he'd been given.

"The guys are meeting later for dinner. You want to join us?" Louis put his hand on Beau's shoulder.

"I'd love that, but I'm on a strict deadline." Beau hesitated. "How about one evening next week?"

"We can do that. I'll tell them you're back safe. Get some rest. You look wiped out." Louis smiled and headed in the other direction.

"From you, I'll take that as a compliment." Beau moved toward the main door. It was time to start the paperwork, as painful as it would be. This was one part of the job he dreaded. He would have to relive the experiences, the close contact he and Ellie shared for hours during their escape. Getting it done was the only way he could begin to forget her ... if that was possible.

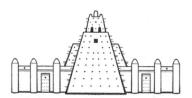

17

"Can you two put a rush on it? I'm starving." Ellie was dressed in her white gauzy sundress and sandals. Her toes had finally quit hurting, though they were still blue and green. She waited by the door for Olivia and Jocelyn.

"Go get us a table. We'll be right behind you." Jocelyn yelled from the bathroom. "I'm almost ready."

"I'll walk down with you." Liv reached for her cross-body purse and joined Ellie. "Let's go." Her capri pants matched her flip-flops, both adorned with small flowers.

The five-star hotel, Ole Serena, boasted a circular staircase in the lobby with soaring ceilings, pieces of sculpture, and extravagant lighting. The gift shop displayed a variety of high-end curios from the area. Plush carpet cushioned their steps as strands of Kenny G's saxophone filled the air.

"I wonder if Kenny G knows he is heard all over this continent," Olivia said.

A host led them to a table on the veranda where they ordered their eggs before visiting the fruit bar.

"It will be hard to go back to a bowl of cereal when I get

home. I get spoiled in these hotels." Ellie checked out the choices of jellies on their outdoor table. The orange marmalade gave her pause as she chose berry jam when the waiter placed a basket of toast on the table.

Their eggs were delivered as Jocelyn joined them.

"I'm going to order mine. Be right back." Jocelyn ordered coffee for them when she passed a waiter.

Bowing her head, Olivia prayed, "Lord, thank you for keeping Ellie safe during her trip, and thanks for this food. Amen." Olivia squeezed Ellie's hand. "I'm glad you're okay." She removed the napkin from her silverware and put it on her lap. "I think we've kept our guardian angels busy."

"Are wedding plans helping you forget what happened in Zanzibar?" Ellie took a bite of mango.

"They are, and Eli has been amazing, but the counselor has helped. You should see her. Her name is Jessica. I'll send you her contact info. She's given me methods to help process my emotions and move past the trauma." Olivia buttered her toast.

"Give me her number when we get home. Beau said I needed to debrief so I wouldn't carry this experience into the future."

"That's great advice."

Jocelyn took a seat at the table.

"Wow, you look good. Is that a new outfit?" Ellie asked.

"Olivia has been cleaning out her closet. This fits me, and I love it. Her designer clothes are amazing." Jocelyn smiled at Olivia. "Thanks, Liv."

"You're welcome." Olivia sipped her juice and turned to Ellie. "I saved a few outfits for you to consider."

"Don't go dressing her up, Liv. I have to work hard to keep up with you two beauties." Jocelyn smiled.

"You put me in the shade, J. Don't kid yourself." Ellie hugged Jocelyn.

They enjoyed breakfast and lingered, catching up on each

other's lives while they watched the animals in the game park. Ellie focused her Sony lens on a herd of cape buffalo grazing as they eased by. White birds were perched on their backs, eating insects. As they meandered along, some antelope followed, foraging for the shorter grass they left behind.

"Look at the dazzle of zebra coming in this direction." Ellie focused in their direction.

"A dazzle?" Liv asked.

"That's what groups of zebra are called. Did you know when a zebra is born, the mother keeps the newborn in the bushes away from others for a week until the colt learns her ways, her smell, the sound of her voice, and the pattern of her stripes? It prepares the foal to make it on its own in the wilds of Africa." She took another picture. "The time together just the two of them bonds them for life."

"Hmm, Liv. Is she still talking about zebra?" Jocelyn smiled. "I think a week together bonded Ellie and Rambo. That's what I think."

"Let's not change the subject." Ellie gave them a stern look.

"Are you finished taking photos? We need to make a plan. Do you ladies want to visit the market or take a tour today? We have five hours until we put our uniforms on again." Jocelyn looked from Olivia to Ellie for an answer.

"The pool looks divine. We could also lie by the water and relax. What would you like to do, Ellie?" Jocelyn moved her plate aside and put her crossed arms on the table.

Not wanting time to dwell on Beau today, Ellie wanted to keep moving. "I think I'd like to take a cab to the mall and buy some of those *Kizuri* beads indigenous to Kenya. And let's get more seasonings for our kitchen. Some are getting low." Ellie put some shillings on the table for the waiter.

"That's a good idea. I should buy a supply of those myself, since I'm moving away from the condo." Olivia glanced at Jocelyn. "Are you okay with this plan?"

"Sure, sounds great to me." Jocelyn stood and pushed in her chair.

They left the restaurant while Liv told them the latest antics of her fiancé's son. Their laughter was good medicine for Ellie. They were her safe place but didn't compare to the security she'd felt with Beau—her hero. But that was in the past, where it had to stay.

Within three days Beau completed the final report and was relieved the questions stopped at the apprehension of Hussein and his men. Reliving the departure scene at the airport would have been gut-wrenching. He happily placed the stack of reports into a large envelope for safekeeping. The process had been grueling, but he could see the Lord's protection at every turn.

After a few nights of trying to sleep, tossing, and turning while dreaming of Ellie, Beau was ready to meet the guys at their favorite eatery. Being in various military positions, they understood the classified nature of the assignments they executed, which made their comradery comfortable and safe, and the details of their assignments were never in question.

Louis waved him to their corner table in the back. "Hey, Beau, Come on back."

Making his way through the restaurant, Beau met Arthur, Adam, and Ethan, who motioned to the waiter they were ready to order.

Slaps on the back, strong handshakes, and insults thrown in jest surrounded him. He settled in for a good time. They ordered without seeing the menus.

"Beau, glad you're back." Adam greeted him. "I was up for that assignment but couldn't get back in time, and I hadn't seen the wife for two weeks. How was your jaunt with the photojournalist?"

"It went well. She was good at her job and pleasant to work with." He chose his words carefully.

The guys stared at him as if waiting for details.

"And?" Louis asked.

"What?"

"She was either an old hag or drop-dead gorgeous. Which was it, de La Croix?" Adam pressed.

The men waited, unflinching.

"You know I can't talk about our missions." Beau tried to get the focus off himself.

"I knew it! She was gorgeous. I should have volunteered for that op." Arthur slammed his palm on the table.

"Did she get under your skin?" Louis waggled his eyebrows.

"After Jazelle, I closed my heart to relationships. But if I was interested in pursuing someone, she'd be a great candidate. I'm just not there yet." Beau kept his tone firm.

The waiter delivered their round of ginger ale. The conversation went from one topic to another. Beau was glad to be out of the spotlight. Catching up on the comings and goings of his comrades led to some exciting stories from different ports of call. With so much indecision in his life, this interaction soothed his soul.

Once Adam, Ethan, and Arthur left, Louis stayed with Beau. "You okay, man? I know you're still pretty tired, but I sense you're struggling with something else." Louis reached for his soda and finished it, giving Beau a chance to consider his answer.

He took a deep breath and blew it out. "Yeah. I've got a couple of heavy issues on my mind right now. It's time to decide whether I want to re-up for five more years. I have three months until my tour is over, but Colonel Leroux wants an answer soon."

"That's big. Which way are you leaning?" Louis pushed his plate toward the busboy clearing their table.

"Right now, I'm in the middle weighing the pros and cons. I've always felt like I was a career man. But today, I'm not so sure." Beau held his hand up, letting the waiter know he didn't want a refill.

"But there are so many posts that don't have you walking into a war zone on every assignment. You're great at what you do, but with your experience, you could name the job assignment you want. Other positions could be as equally fulfilling. You don't have to be a commando forever."

"Haven't given that much thought."

"You said a couple of issues, which means more than one—so, what's up?" Louis leaned back and settled in.

Being in his unit, Louis knew where Beau had been sent and that his mission had been accomplished. But he didn't know the personal aspects of the assignment.

"Her name is Elliana. On my assignment, she was kidnapped by terrorist soldiers and used as bait to draw me out into the open. Her kidnapper was the same soldier who killed Jazelle." His throat tightened. She could have been killed. I won't have someone I care about hurt again because of a relationship with me." He blew out a breath.

"That won't happen twice, Beau—"

"It almost happened. He held a gun to her head." Beau threw his napkin onto the table.

"I saw the report in Colonel Leroux's office. You wounded him. And she didn't die. It sounds like you have another chance at love. That doesn't come along very often. Don't throw it away." Louis leaned his elbows on the table.

"It's a lot to consider. I need to pray about it." Beau stood.

"And get more rest. You have some big decisions to make and an adventurous road ahead. You just have to decide which direction it goes and if you're traveling alone." Louis stood and walked out with Beau.

"Sounds easy enough." Beau stopped on the sidewalk. "Say a prayer for me, Louis."

"I will." They went in opposite directions toward their cars. "Beau."

"Yeah." Beau turned around.

"Call if you want. I'm here." He waved and got into his vehicle.

Beau waved back.

It felt good to be on an airplane, in uniform, seating passengers, and answering requests. Being busy and in charge helped Ellie put the Mali mayhem out of her mind. Olivia kept telling her to focus on the magazine article. Ellie tried. But her mind strayed occasionally. Her heart kept leading her thoughts down memory lane.

"You okay, Ellie?" Jocelyn asked.

"Yeah, why?" She retrieved some trash from a passenger.

"It's past time to serve dinner, and you haven't started yet." Jocelyn looked concerned.

"I'd better get moving." She rushed to the galley.

"Give me your bread baskets, and I'll serve for you."

"Thanks." She gave her the bread and began serving the dinner trays at breakneck speed, followed by drink service to her passengers. After picking up the trays and collecting trash in her area, Ellie was ready for a break. Thankfully, most of the travelers were either watching movies or settling in for a long nap. She went to the galley to rest and have a snack.

"You saved me. I didn't realize I was behind schedule."

"You're welcome. You've been through a lot, and I'm glad to

help. You need some downtime." Jocelyn handed her a snack tray and a Coke.

Ellie's eyes blurred with tears. "I hope you're right." She ate the food, not tasting it, but she knew it would be hours before she got another break.

Screaming babies, an airsick woman, and some rowdy teens kept Ellie busy for the final hours of the flight. She was thankful when the last passenger made his exit.

"Come this direction." Olivia beckoned her toward first class.

When Ellie got there, Jocelyn and Olivia were waiting.

"Sit in a comfortable chair." Jocelyn guided her into a seat. "Breathe for a few minutes before we face the next leg of our journey."

Kicking her shoes off, Ellie settled in. "These seats are so comfortable. I could sleep right here for a week."

Olivia served her a soda in stemware, like she was royalty.

"Thanks, Liv."

"The next flight isn't supposed to be as packed as this one was," Jocelyn said.

"You two are good to me. I'll be okay. I just need to sleep it off, cry a lot, and put my feelings on the shelf." She took a drink of her soda.

"Lean back and relax. You've got about fifteen minutes before we need to leave first class. Olivia and I will get your bags." Jocelyn moved to the back of the plane.

The quiet relaxation did wonders for Ellie. She stretched her worn body.

"You'll be okay after you have some popcorn, your fluffy slippers, and some chick flicks." Olivia took her empty glass into the galley and handed Ellie her shoes. "After you work the next flight, we can get you home. You ready?"

"As I'll ever be—just no tear-jerkers—only comedies, okay?" She slipped her feet into the pumps and stood. With her carry-on and bag of tent stakes, she reentered the terminal following her friends—reminding herself to keep moving. It would get easier in time.

She hoped.

Beau saluted as he entered Colonel Leroux's office.

"de La Croix, I'm glad you're on time. I have McCabe on a video call, and he'd like a word with you." Colonel Phillipe Leroux spoke with the authority his full uniform demanded. He returned the salute, then pivoted for Beau to follow.

Beau removed his hat and sat in front of Leroux's desk as the colonel turned the laptop in Beau's direction. He saluted the man on the screen, and Axel McCabe returned the gesture.

"Hello, sir." Beau moved his chair closer to the desk.

"It is good to see you've survived another mission. Very successfully, I might add. Great work." He smiled.

"Thank you, sir." Beau put the thick envelope on the desk. "I have the completed documents for you. I'm ready to put this assignment behind me. If that's agreeable to you."

"I'm sure you've finished this task with excellence as per your norm," McCabe responded.

Beau slid the completed documents toward Colonel Leroux.

"I'll review these and send you a copy before day's end, McCabe," Leroux spoke to McCabe, then eyed Beau. "We were discussing your future." Leroux paused. "I'd like to keep you in France and assign you another mission, but he wants you to consider an assignment in the States."

The States? Moving forward in his chair, Beau looked at McCabe on the screen. "I understand serving both of your agendas when you send me to take out a common enemy, but where would someone with my skillset fit in your unit?"

Axel McCabe looked Beau in the eye. "I always need men of integrity and strength of character such as yourself. It would be a change of assignment, a promotion in rank, utilizing your leadership skills. You would be teaching and advising the heads of our military branches concerning terrorist activity and best practice strategies for successful missions. It would require you to accept a post here in Washington D.C., but there would be some travel involved."

Pausing, Beau considered his offer.

McCabe cleared his throat. "I've taken the liberty of sending Colonel Leroux a brief on this assignment. Will you at least consider this offer?" Axel McCabe waited.

After making eye contact with Colonel Leroux, Beau focused on the laptop screen. "I'm honored you would consider offering me a position of this magnitude. I am at a pivotal point in my military career that requires me to make a decision soon. When do you need an answer, sir?" Beau took a deep breath and blew it out in a nervous huff.

"Can I hear from you within the next two weeks? I know this is a big decision, but the position needs to be posted by the end of the month."

"Yes, sir. I'll make sure you have my answer before two weeks are up." Beau sat back.

The Colonel leaned in to see Axel face to face. "Do you have any questions for Beau about this last assignment?"

"I'll wait to read his reports. If I have anything to discuss, I'll set up another call. Again, de La Croix, great work out there. Mission accomplished." He ended the call.

Leroux closed his laptop. "I also have assignments and positions that might be of interest to you, if you want to stay in Paris since you have family here. I've prepared these job descriptions and opportunities to be thrown into the mix." He gave Beau several folders.

"Take your time. You've got some weapons to clean, duties

to execute for your commanding officer, but think this through and get back to me." He handed over the files and picked up the envelope Beau had completed.

Putting the files under his arm, Beau stood and saluted Leroux. "I will consider these offers, sir."

"Good day, de La Croix." He returned the salute.

Beau pivoted and left the room. His mind spun with questions—more questions than he had when he'd walked into the building. How do you make such a life-altering decision in a short amount of time? *Lord, I need some help here. What do You want for my future—which direction should I go? Your Word says You have plans for me. Can You let me know what those plans are? And soon?*

18

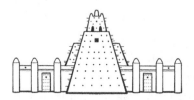

J et lag had Ellie awake until the wee hours of the morning and sleeping until noon, especially with raindrops hitting her window. Days off were her favorite. With her laundry done, she wanted to prepare the tent stakes to hang.

The stakes showed great woodgrain but were rough to the touch. Replaying her market experience with Beau, she spent an afternoon sanding them. It was therapeutic to work. And sanding the stakes kept her mind busy.

"Ellie, a package came for you." Olivia pushed the box from the foyer into the kitchen.

"Already? That was fast. I'm excited!" Ellie grabbed some scissors and opened the box. "Look at this, Liv." Ellie pulled out the canvas of the child drinking milk from a gourd.

"That's amazing. I love it" Olivia held up the canvas to the pendant light hanging over the kitchen table. "This could win a prize."

"Check out this one. I sent it to the magazine with my article." Ellie held up her favorite photo of the camel caravan.

"I'm calling this one 'The Ships in the Desert.' Do you think they'll like it?"

Olivia clapped her hands. "It's magnificent! Yes, they're going to love it." Olivia held it up to a wall. "You're right. This is the best work you've ever done. That tour guide must have been inspiring."

"His heart for the history and his love for the people came through as we toured the city. Beau believed in me and pushed me to dig deep inside of myself to reach my potential." She paused. "I miss him, Liv."

"I know you do."

Cleaning up the packaging material, Ellie glanced at the clock. "Don't you have somewhere to be?'

"Yep, and if I don't hurry, I'm going to be late and frustrate my wedding planner." She grabbed her keys as she slung her purse strap over her shoulder.

"Bye. Drive carefully."

"I'll be meeting Eli for dinner. See you later." Olivia rushed out the door, letting it shut behind her.

After removing more of the wrapping, Ellie eyed special photos transporting her thoughts to West Africa, back to the scenes and sounds, back to the heat, and back to Beau. She took a deep breath and let herself remember.

With a hammer in one hand and several small nails in the other, Ellie hung her canvases on the wall of her bedroom beside her antique tent stakes. After working to level them, she stepped back and surveyed her handiwork.

"Wow, I love it. Do these make you miss Timbuktu and G.I. Joe?" Jocelyn sidled up to the wall to touch the tent stakes.

"They do. The trip stretched me in many ways. But I'm better, stronger for the experience." She sighed. "Allowing my heart to get tangled with the handsome Frenchman was my doing. I should have kept my emotions in check." She closed her box of nails and picked up the hammer.

"It would be difficult for any of us to be close to a man like Beau and not get infatuated." Jocelyn straightened one of the canvases. "Ellie, I've watched your photography improve over the years, and these are the best."

"Thanks."

"I'm going to the garage, are you through with the hammer? I'll put it back in the toolbox." She held her hand out.

"That would be great." Ellie gave her the hammer and nails and went to her laptop to send some photos to the other side of the world. She selected her best ones and added some humorous shots to an email for Beau choosing her words carefully ...

> *Beau. Thanks again for our wonderful adventure. I'll never forget our time together. Here are the pictures I promised to send. I hope you like them. I haven't heard from the magazine yet ... Ellie*

> *P.S. I sent your photo to the magazine. I knew you wouldn't mind since your face wasn't showing. You don't mind, do you?*

Keeping it short and sweet was difficult. She would rather beg him for his undying love and affection, ask him to throw his strong arms around her and kiss her senseless for the rest of his life—but who was she kidding? He was probably gearing up for his next mission, where he would singlehandedly save the world. He didn't have time for an Elliana in his life or room in his wounded heart.

She pressed SEND and sighed.

Smelling popcorn, she joined Jocelyn in the living room for a movie. It was just the two of them today since Olivia was with her fiancé.

"Are you okay? I see tears."

"Yeah, I sent photos to Beau. I'd promised him I'd send

some. I sent a short note leaving out the part about my broken heart and how much I miss him." She wiped her face.

"Now you can move on. Time will be your friend." Jocelyn cued up the video.

"You got your heart broken almost a year ago. How long did it take you to get over Jimmy?" Ellie grabbed a throw and covered her legs.

"I'll let you know."

"That's encouraging. You're still missing him." Ellie threw a pillow at her.

Jocelyn laughed.

"Hey, ladies, come quick!" Ellie was standing in the foyer with the front door still open.

"What is it? I heard the doorbell. Is something wrong?" Olivia hurried in from the kitchen, wiping her hands on a kitchen towel.

"I'm coming!" Jocelyn wrapped her wet hair in a towel as she reached them. "What's up?"

"Look at this. It's a check—a big one! And a job offer! They loved my work!" Ellie was stunned. Frozen in shock. "And they're using the picture of Beau on the cover of their next issue!"

Applause and squeals erupted among hugs and high-fives, as they celebrated.

"Congratulations, Ellie. This is the break you've been waiting for!" Olivia reached for the letter. "Can I read it?"

"Sure, Liv."

Olivia read it out loud as Jocelyn shut the front door and listened. Taking a seat on the arm of their leather sofa, Ellie smiled as Liv finished, folded the letter, and handed it to her.

"It's really happening, isn't it?" She looked at her friends.

"Yes, it is. What's the timeline? When do you start?" Jocelyn asked.

Ellie scanned the letter and check again, then found a sticky note attached to the back of the check. "This says, 'Call me for details, and we can make a plan sometime after the third Monday of the month. I'm on a cruise until that date.' So, I guess I'll know a timeline then." She refolded the letter and put it back in the envelope.

"This is so exciting—E. L. Bendale, Photojournalist with *Above & Beyond* magazine." Olivia smiled at Ellie, then noticed Jocelyn's expression. "What's wrong?"

"I'm losing both of you within a few months. I don't do change well. You're getting married. And I'm over-the-moon happy for you. Then, Ellie gets her dream job. She'll end her career with the airlines soon. Your lives are shifting in great ways, but I'm being left behind." Jocelyn's eyes filled with tears.

"Our lives will change. We'll go in different directions, but we're joined at the heart. Best friends forever. You're still going to Swaziland, aren't you?" Olivia asked.

"Yes, in four weeks." Jocelyn wiped her cheeks. "I know you're right, Liv, but I've loved this chapter of our lives."

"Our futures will be fun too. Just different." Ellie tried to sound encouraging, though it took effort. "And I'll still be living here with you." There was no promise of romance in her future.

"I'm glad. Let's focus on looking gorgeous at the wedding of the year when Olivia walks down the aisle to her happily ever after." Jocelyn high-fived Olivia.

"And we'll both be trying to catch her bouquet with the promise of being next in line."

Ellie held in a sigh as she headed to her room.

"Lasagna. Can you stir some up for me?" Beau put the menu down and gave his brother a grin.

"You don't stir lasagna, Beau. But I knew you would order that, so I've layered meat sauce, a mixture of cheeses, and some great pasta, just for you." Alex pivoted and returned to the kitchen.

"And can I have a salad, please?" Beau checked his email on his phone while he waited. "With that homemade dressing you gave me last time."

His breath caught. An email from Ellie. She'd sent a short note and some photos. He shouldn't expect a long missive— they'd said goodbye. He took a deep breath bracing himself for the pictures. Scanning through them, he laughed at the funny ones, stared at the amazing pictures of Timbuktu she used for her article, and stopped at the selfie she took of them in the goat-filled truck. The laughter in her eyes held him.

"So that's what's got you tangled in a twist." Alex looked at Beau's phone. "Wow. She's a looker." He approached the table with a tray, placed two plates of sauce-covered lasagna with bread and butter and two salads on the table, then took a seat across from Beau. "What's her name?"

"This is Elliana Bendale." Beau locked eyes with his brother, his best friend. "She goes by Ellie, but I call her E. She's amazing."

"And that's a problem?" Alex passed the breadbasket to Beau.

"That's one of them. I have to decide if I'm signing up for five more years. And I've been offered an opportunity that would require me to relocate to Washington D.C." He took the bread. "Those are my problems. I hope you're serving answers at this restaurant." He bowed his head and prayed over their food, then met Alex's eyes. "What?"

"You prayed." Alex looked stunned.

"I was desperate. Ellie was going to die because of me." He took a bite of his garlic bread.

"So, you opened communication with the Man upstairs. I have to say that makes me happy. You've been diving into danger on your own for a while. Now you have the Lord on your side." He tasted his lasagna. "That's good. Even if I cooked it myself."

Beau took a bite of his entree. "It is great, Alex. Thanks."

"You're welcome. Now spill it."

"My lasagna? Not on your life." He smiled.

"No. Tell me your story, Beau. Start from the beginning. I'm not needed in the kitchen until the dinner shift." Alex took a drink of water and ate another bite of his lasagna.

Stabbing his salad, Beau told Alex his story between bites. "My assignment was to act as Ellie's interpreter as she toured Timbuktu. It served as a cover to get me into Timbuktu." He gave Alex a play-by-play of their time together." He took another bite of pasta.

Alex dropped his fork. It clanged against the table. "You're talking about the number one enemy in the world, and you were doing this alone?" He spoke in a forced whisper.

"Just getting information—until I met the leader face to face in an alley." He filled him in on their escape from Timbuktu.

A waiter refilled their glasses and removed the empty dishes. "Beau, do you want *crème brûlée* or chocolate banana crepes?"

"Crepes." Beau smiled.

Alex asked for two orders of crepes and two cups of café. "Okay, when did things get out of hand?"

"While I paid for our camel rides, Dakir Hussein, the leader, kidnapped Ellie. Then it got really scary. I won't lie to you. I was desperate." He locked eyes with his brother.

"And by this time, you'd fallen for the blonde." He leaned

back for their dessert and café' to be served. "Since you're sitting in front of me, I know you didn't die. And you're still mooning over the blonde, so she is alive. Did you kill the terrorist leader?"

"I shot him and rescued Ellie, put her on a plane, and returned to Paris." Beau sampled the crepes.

"Reading between the lines here, but let me recap. You did your 007 act and rescued the blonde from enemy number one, then let her go because you're afraid to risk your heart. And this tug-of-war inside you is making your other decisions harder to make." He sipped his brew. "Am I close?"

"Yeah. I hope you have some words of wisdom for me." Beau took a sip of his café. "I can't see my way forward."

Alex sighed. "After we lost our parents, we took some hard hits at those first two foster homes. When Hazel took us in, we were in bad shape. But she loved us as if we were her biological sons and helped us recover. We survived because we had each other, but her love gave us a picture of what it means to have a real family. We were blessed."

"Yes, we were." Beau sat back and eyed his brother.

"After losing Jazelle, you reverted into that broken person again. You fear loving someone, and I understand, but what you want is a family. You can't have one without the other." Alex spoke with a voice of reason.

"The Lord knows your history. I think He orchestrated this turn of events to get your attention. You take risks and face the most dangerous enemies, taking out the bad guys—you stop wars. And I'm proud of you. But the Lord wants this war inside you to end. I think it's time to take a risk. Embrace a future with promise. But it's up to you, Bro."

"When did you get so smart?" Beau sipped his café.

"What do you mean? I've always been smarter than you." Alex laughed.

"Yeah, right,"

"If you hang around two more hours, Vivienne will be here, and I can cook you some dinner."

"That's a great offer, but I have work to do. I've been asked to analyze some confidential documents for the colonel by tomorrow." He stood and put his hand on his brother's shoulder. "I appreciate the lunch, Alexandre. You're a great chef."

"You're welcome. Hey, if you want to talk, call me. And let me know what conclusions you reach on these decisions."

"Later, Bro." Beau left the restaurant, feeling the need to pray, and he was a bit out of practice.

The job is mine, Beau. Thank you again
for your help ... Ellie

Pressing *SEND*, Ellie spun her words into cyberspace. Her last contact with the hunky hero was done—the decision was made. She'd closed the chapter.

With her uniform on and her bag packed, she glanced at Beau's photo one more time and shut the door. It was time to fly the African Skies.

"You two ready?" Ellie raised her voice to be heard through their condo. She waited for them in the foyer, eyeing a scripture Olivia had framed and hung as their motto. *Trust the Lord with all your heart and lean not on your own understanding ...* It caused her to pause, to question her actions. She'd been figuring things out for herself. Was the Lord reminding her to trust Him?

After slipping her jacket on, Olivia pulled her bag to the front door. "It's hard to let the Lord orchestrate your future. But He knows what's best."

Ellie pasted a smile on her face. "So, are you ready for your last trip as a flight attendant?"

"I'm sad but peaceful. A handsome man will be waiting for me at the end of the aisle in two and a half weeks. I'm ready to marry my Prince Charming." Olivia smiled and reached for her luggage.

"We're both thrilled for you, but you'll be missed." Jocelyn joined them.

"Let's keep our tears at bay and get to the airport before I miss my final trip as a flight attendant." Olivia led the way.

They loaded their luggage and made the drive to Houston's Intercontinental Airport. Going through their routine, they parked, went through security, and strolled to the gate. Jocelyn was quiet, contemplative. Olivia was on the phone with her fiancé one more time before they got on the plane. Ellie savored the togetherness of the three of them this final time.

Once the plane was boarded, the trio was overly busy. Ellie dealt with airsick passengers because of excessive turbulence. She had to hold on as she delivered and retrieved dinners, pacified nervous travelers, and tried to convince a drunk that he'd consumed enough. The flight smoothed out an hour before they landed, and the aisles were crowded with passengers needing the facilities. When the 'fasten seatbelt' sign came on, she and her friends had to coax passengers back into their seats.

"That was a rough flight. How was it up here is the champagne section?" Ellie chided Olivia as she plopped down in one of the first-class recliners. "I'll be glad when we get to Nairobi. I'm beat already."

"Sorry." Olivia was finishing her checklist. "It was pretty calm up here. But if you say yes to the magazine, you'll be leaving the airlines, unless you're seated in first class on your way to an assignment."

"I'll try to remember that if the next flight is as bad as this one." Ellie smoothed her hair and applied fresh lipstick—a routine all flight attendants followed to give a good impression as they paraded through the airports.

"You ladies ready to roll?" Jocelyn stood at the open door.

Ellie retrieved her luggage. Liv pulled hers from the overhead bin and followed them to the restaurant they frequented on their way through Europe. After ordering, Ellie kicked her shoes off and relaxed. Her toes still ached when she wore heels.

"We have three and a half hours until we board the flight to Nairobi. You want to go to the lounge or shop, or just walk for a while?" Jocelyn looked at her watch.

"I think I'll go to the lounge and stretch out for an hour." Ellie leaned back for their drinks to be delivered.

"Well, since I won't be in Holland again anytime soon, I think I'm going to buy some tulips to take home for my yard and then a toy for each of my babies. Eli loves their chocolate. But after I do that, I'll come to the lounge and rest too." Olivia smiled. "Here comes my food. Nobody cooks herring, or *broodje haring*, anywhere else like they do in Amsterdam."

Jocelyn salted her entrée. "I think I'll walk with you, Olivia, if you don't mind, and get my steps in for today."

"Sure, I'd love that." She bowed her head and prayed over their food. She looked up and smiled at her friends.

"What do you want to do in Nairobi on our layover, Olivia?" Ellie reached for the breadbasket. "Jocelyn and I talked, and we're going to let you choose this time."

"Well ..." Olivia finished chewing. "I think Massai market and lunch at Java House, since I want two of their mugs and some of their coffee to take home. Then let's visit the elephants we adopted."

"That sounds good to me," Jocelyn said as she lifted her water goblet to toast with her friends. They touched their glasses together one last time.

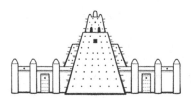

19

"**D**id you bring another suitcase to pack with all this stuff you've bought, Olivia?" Ellie smiled around the packages stacked beside her in the van.

Pushing another sack under her van seat, Olivia laughed. "I did get a little carried away, didn't I?" She sat down and exhaled. "But I won't be back. And did you see the toys I got for Judah? They're African animals with wheels on them. He'll be thrilled."

"I think he likes anything with wheels on it." Jocelyn shut the door of the van. "Driver, take us to Java House for lunch."

"To answer your question, I brought an extra piece of luggage. I put one piece inside of another so I'd have room for my curios. And I knew I could squeeze things into your suitcases too."

"Sure. I'm glad to leave my shoes behind just to get your treasures to America." Ellie patted Liv on the shoulder.

"Anything to keep a smile on the bride's face. That's my motto." Jocelyn put three fingers to her brow like a Girl Scout.

Over amazing guacamole and steamy fajitas, they competed for floor time to be heard. Ellie's sarcasm had returned, and

Liv's wedding jitters were coming on strong, while Jocelyn verbally planned her trip to Swaziland. The waiter had to wave to get their attention. Their banter displayed their differences as it bonded their hearts.

"So, Liv. What's the plan? Are you moving to your house in the Woodlands soon or waiting until after the honeymoon?" Jocelyn asked.

"No. I'm letting Eli and the children move in there since he'll start working on Monday. His parents are staying there while we're on our honeymoon, and my Aunt Jana will be keeping the kids some while we're gone to give Eli's mom a break. I'll make my move when we get home."

Ellie winked at Jocelyn. "We'll have your things waiting on the sidewalk."

"But you forfeit everything in the fridge," Jocelyn announced.

"You're heartless. You can't wait to get rid of me! This is a fine way to treat someone who took you off the streets!" Olivia laughed. "It's a good thing I love you two."

Beau opened the drapes in his flat and stood in his T-shirt and jogging pants, enjoying the thick rug under his feet. Feeling more rested, he missed Ellie all the more. As the sun descended on the horizon, the lights on the Eiffel Tower shone in the evening mist. Beau wanted her to see this, to experience Paris. But it would mean he had to open himself to a permanent relationship with her. *Am I ready for that?*

He grabbed a cold Coke and got comfortable on his couch, feet propped on the coffee table. After taking a long drink, he opened the offer from Axel McCabe. It was a prestigious position with perks and a salary worth considering. He read every line and thought long and hard about the implications and sacrifices it would require. Leaving Paris hadn't been on his radar ... until now.

While finishing his soda, he read the offers and opportunities Leroux had thrown into the mix. Three of them he set aside immediately without giving them a second thought. The other two possibilities had merit. He paced his living room and thought through the offers. Not reaching a decision, he changed his tactics and added prayer to his pacing. Soon his angst was replaced by a quiet confidence. He didn't have an answer, but he'd narrowed his choices down to two offers.

His phone rang, and he checked the screen. Alex. "Hello," he answered as he made café.

"Just checking on you. You haven't mooched any food in a couple of days. You okay?"

Beau pushed the button on his coffee maker. "I'm good. I've been reading through the information on the offers I'm considering. I have eleven days to give them my decision on the U.S. offer. Are you still at the restaurant?"

"No. I let the staff close up tonight. Business was slow, and I like to get home early a few days each week. So, have you made any life-alternating decisions since we talked?"

"I've narrowed it down. One is here in Paris. The other one would require a move to America." Beau prepared the hot chocolate to add to his coffee. "Both are great offers with higher pay and fringe benefits."

Alex cleared his throat. "Would these offers take you out of harm's way? No more risking your life to save the world?"

"Yes. I'd still carry a gun but wouldn't have opportunities to use it." He took a bowl from the cabinet while the coffee maker finished. "I may miss that part, but I would like to live without a target on my back."

"I'm glad to hear it. Is Ellie playing into your decision?" Alex spoke to Vivienne, then returned to the call. "Sorry about that. Viv is cooking for me, and it will be ready in ten minutes."

"I'm trying to make the right choice, so I've tried to keep her out of the mix until I decide on my career move. But she is never far from my thoughts. If there is a future between us, she could work from anywhere in the world with her magazine job. I've been asking the Lord for clarity. What do you think, Alex?" Beau mixed his coffee and chocolate and poured the café into a bowl.

"It sounds like you're thinking it through in a good way. I don't know what I could add to the process. I just wanted you to know I'm here if you want to talk."

Beau got comfortable on his couch again. "That means a lot. How about you make me a pizza for lunch tomorrow, and I'll let you go over my options."

"Great. I'll see you then. I'll have it ready to go in the brick oven when I see you come through the door."

"Thanks." Beau savored his café and let his mind go to a beautiful blonde with dazzling blue eyes. He reached for his phone and brought up her picture, staring at her smile.

Lord, do I have this all wrong. Should she be the main deciding factor and the job be secondary? I need wisdom. Lead me, Lord.

A fine mist had just begun to wreak havoc with Ellie's hair. "Hurry girls. If my hair gets damp it won't stay in my required airline up-do. I wish they would let me wear my signature messy bun." Ellie stepped under the awning and rushed through the doors to the security belt.

"Your hair looks fine." Jocelyn put her luggage on the belt to be scanned. "If they let you wear your messy buns, you would ask for your expensive holey jeans to be a part of your uniform."

"And what would be wrong with that?" Ellie laughed and followed Liv and Jocelyn to the check-in counter.

Once they had paraded through the crowd of passengers to their boarding gate, they joined the other flight attendants at the head of the line to go through security again before boarding KLM Flight 566.

"Are you ready for this—your last flight?" Jocelyn asked as she and Ellie followed Olivia down the long jetway.

"Except for missing you two, I'm ready to start my next chapter." Olivia sighed. "But it'll be sad to disembark the last time once we reach Houston."

"Well, I hope you have an easy flight." Ellie turned toward the coach section and stored her carry-on and jacket.

Jocelyn followed suit as they began to prepare the cabin. Ellie organized the magazines while Jocelyn started coffee in the galley. Once the passengers started piling in, the flight attendants didn't have a chance to visit until they landed in Europe and every passenger had left the aircraft.

Just as they finished their prep duties, passengers entered the aircraft.

Thankfully, the flight went off without a hitch. Mere hours later, they landed, and the weary travelers disembarked.

A tall man caught Ellie's eye. Her breath caught. It couldn't be. Not Beau. But his hair and build were right. She rushed after him.

"Come on, Joe." Another man called to him.

Ellie's steps faltered. Not Beau.

"Are you ready to get some food?" Olivia touched her arm.

Wiping her eyes, Ellie put her jacket on.

"What is it, Ellie?" Olivia stepped closer.

"That last guy who left the plane reminded me of Beau." She pulled out her luggage and lifted the handle." I miss him, Liv. I knew he didn't want a relationship. But I let my guard down."

Olivia put an arm around her. "I'm sorry. Heartbreaks hurt. Let's feed you. Food always helps. It puts heartache on the back burner."

Joining Jocelyn at the door, they walked the jetway into the terminal.

Ellie tried to enjoy their time together but her heart wasn't in it.

After a quick dinner, with no time to waste, they proceeded to the gate for their next leg of the journey. The flight to New York was full. Ellie's cheap seats were occupied by a group of loud, large men who'd obviously already visited the bar at the airport and had a few too many. They were too flirty for Ellie's taste. One man needed some cold water spilled on his lap. Though she was tempted, she refrained. But it took effort.

Babies cried, kids knocked over their drinks, and the men continued to be obnoxious. When the last one left the plane, Ellie grabbed her makeup bag out of her carry-on. She refixed her hair and freshened her makeup in the tiny restroom.

"Sorry to keep you guys waiting. That was an exhausting flight. I'm glad we have three hours before our last flight of the day." She took a deep breath and blew it out.

"Most of my passengers slept during that flight," Olivia said. "Maybe you needed to be busy, and the Lord sent them to keep your mind occupied."

"I don't think the Lord sent nine flirty drunk men to keep me busy!" She smirked.

Olivia laughed as she put her arm around Ellie's shoulder.

"Let's get you a Coke, Ellie." Jocelyn led the way.

"I may ask for something a lot stronger!"

Laughing as she caught up with Jocelyn at customs, Olivia stopped behind other flight attendants waiting in line and turned to Ellie. "You have to trust the Lord with the desires of your heart. He was with you and Beau on your escape from Timbuktu. He orchestrates amazing things. I know this from personal experience. Tell Him your life is in His hands and rest in that." She hugged Ellie.

"Thanks, Liv. I'll try."

"Hey ladies, you're holding up the line." Jocelyn motioned for them to close the gap in the customs line.

Ellie followed the pack of flight attendants through customs and into the terminal. The other attendants gathered to bid Olivia farewell and good wishes on her wedding before they went in different directions for the domestic flights.

Looking up, Jocelyn checked the signboard and pivoted to Ellie and Liv. "Ladies, it's either Five Guys Burgers and Fries, Wendy's, or McDonald's. Which is it?"

"Five Guys and Fries," Olivia answered quickly. "Eli loves that place." She led the way. When she reached the counter, she turned, "Place your orders—my treat. Let's end this chapter in style with lots of ketchup on top."

"Aren't you glad we're not working the domestic flight today? I'm bushed." Ellie stretched and yawned. "Jet lag is tough on my beauty sleep."

"A good-looking Frenchman is the culprit stealing your sleep." Olivia smiled at Ellie.

"Well, I won't deny that. He is a dreamboat." She reached for her phone. "You want to see his picture again?"

Jocelyn held her hand up. "No. I think I have it memorized."

"Okay, show me again. He is handsome." Olivia leaned close to Ellie's cell phone. "Yep. He looks just like he did the last time you showed me his picture."

"You two are impossible." Ellie put her phone away. "You're supposed to *ooh* and *ah*."

"Okay. He is ruggedly handsome. A real catch. I don't blame you for losing your heart." Jocelyn put her hand on Ellie's. "But I'm concerned about you. You're hurting."

"I'll be okay. In time." Ellie reached for the ketchup.

Enjoying their meal was a great way to end this chapter of

their lives. Ellie felt tears threatening. "So, for the next few weeks, let's focus on Olivia's showers, bachelorette party, and wedding."

"And honeymoon!" Olivia added as she stuck her last French fry in her mouth.

"So, we get to go on your honeymoon too?" Ellie chimed in.

"I don't think so!" Olivia blushed a bit. "I think it's time to get to our gate." She stood and threw their trash away.

"Do you have a fever, Olivia? Your face is red." Jocelyn teased her.

Ellie laughed and high-fived Jocelyn. "This gives a whole new meaning to *blushing bride*."

She dozed during the uneventful flight. The three friends occupied empty seats all over the plane for their free ride home. It took a few minutes for Olivia to make her way into Houston's Intercontinental airport. Ellie and Jocelyn waited for her.

"I'm ready for my bed." Jocelyn yawned. "How about you, Ellie?"

"Popcorn and a movie for me. I took a nap on that flight. You can sit with me and fall asleep on the couch. Liv will probably be with Eli." Ellie said a little too loudly.

"I think he'll be at baggage claim." Olivia smiled.

"I have no doubt." Ellie led the ladies into the first restroom they found. They touched up their makeup and hair—their flight attendant's protocol. "I think I'll wait for Judah to grow up and marry him. He's adorable."

"But that would be robbing the cradle. And he may want someone who still has their teeth." Jocelyn laughed.

"But I have very strong teeth, two crowns, and several caps. They'll hold up."

"Forget it." Olivia dried her hands and led the way to baggage claim with a spring in her step.

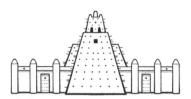

20

"Do you want me to go with you, Ellie? I have time, and your mother doesn't scare me." Jocelyn was in her sweatpants, reclining on the sofa in their condo and enjoying a cup of hot tea with the latest Melissa Tagg novel.

"Thanks for the offer, but I need to settle this with my mom once and for all. It could get tense, so I'll spare you the drama. But my brother might be home, and he roots for me when I need a cheerleader." Ellie grabbed her keys and slipped her purse over her shoulder.

"Okay. Be safe. Call me on your way home." Jocelyn returned to her book.

Ellie touched the fob, unlocked her Mustang, and shut the front door of the condo. Her letter from the magazine and a copy of her check were in her purse. She knew it was time to end the debate about her future and hoped her gifts would ease the blow and diffuse the debate. She prayed for a dose of confidence when she faced her mother.

Entering River Oaks, one of the most prestigious areas of Houston where the *crème de la crème* of real estate was located, her stomach tightened. It was the only place her mother wanted to reside. It made her all the more intimidating, like a queen on her throne.

Ellie parked her baby blue Mustang in the circle drive and turned the car off. She stared at the enormous mansion. The shadow of the structure covered the perfectly manicured front lawn and her car.

Determined to bring things into the light with her parents, Ellie let herself into the foyer with her key. "Mom, Dad. Anybody here?"

She left her scarf-stashed purse and a stack of canvases with a bag of knives on a chair in the living room and headed toward the outdoor living area. As she drew close, she could hear voices. She opened the French doors leading to the veranda.

"Elliana!" Anne Bendale, dressed in a striking spring ensemble complete with matching jewelry, sandals, and nail color, hurried toward Ellie and gathered her in an embrace. "You're early. I'm so glad to see you, honey. It's been too long." She air-kissed both cheeks, preserving her lipstick.

"My favorite, Ellie." Bruce Bendale hugged his daughter as soon as her mother stepped back. He kissed her head as he'd done since she was tiny.

"Dad, you call each one of us your favorite," she chided him.

"Because you *are* my favorites." He grinned and put his arm around her shoulders. "Come see your brother."

"He's here?" She spotted him and took off running. "Austin!" She threw her arms around his neck.

He grabbed Ellie and swung her in a circle. "My world-traveling sister. Glad you could spare us a few moments of your time." He let her feet touch the pavement.

"Says the one who disappears on a regular basis. How long are you home?" Ellie sat beside him in their mother's swing, and he set them to rocking.

"I'm not sure yet. But we'll talk about that later. How was Timbuktu?" Austin always supported Ellie's adventures, despite their mother's constant disapproval.

"It was hot, challenging, adventurous. And I loved it!" Ellie grinned.

"I'm sure you have pictures. I want to see every frame." He grabbed her hand.

"Thanks, Austin." She paused. "I've missed you."

"We need to talk more often."

"I'd like that." She leaned her head on his shoulder.

The youngest of the siblings, Marissa, arrived promptly at the dinner hour. Wearing a stack of clanging bracelets, a broom-stick skirt, and a peasant blouse, she resembled a gypsy. As per her normal, she floated into their presence, air-kissing her parents. Her fake eyelashes and perfect makeup added to her sophisticated look. After happy greetings and hugs, the family gathered for a meal on the veranda.

Bruce Bendale prayed over their meal before they were served barbeque brisket, potatoes au gratin, corn on the cob, and sugar snap peas.

"This is a great meal, Mom." Ellie smiled at her mother. "Did the new maid cook it?"

"No. She's off for two weeks. I prepared this meal, my dear." Anne tapped her lips with her napkin, careful to leave a hint of her lipstick in place. "Thank you for the compliment. It's good to have all three of you here at one time. I was glad to pull out some family recipes for this occasion."

Patting her hand, Bruce complimented his wife. "Great job on the meal, my love. You haven't lost your touch." He loaded his fork with potatoes. "This spread looks like a page from a magazine."

Ellie choked on her water. Austin patted her on the back.

"It went down the wrong way." Ellie covered her nervousness. "Marissa, are you still working at the trendy dress shop in Katy?" She hoped putting the spotlight on her sister would keep things from turning to her own employment debate.

Tossing her long tresses over her shoulder, Marissa smiled. "As a matter of fact, I'm now part-owner of Lynn's Lace & Leggings. I'm an entrepreneur! Can you believe that?" Marissa clapped her hands.

"Congrats, Mar. Way to go!" Ellie hugged her as their father and brother applauded.

"That's wonderful, my dear. But where did you get the money?" Anne Bendale looked down her nose at her youngest daughter. "You've never stayed at one job long enough to accrue any capital." She tapped her lips again. "If I'd known you wanted to get into investments, I could have helped and assured you a sizable return." She looked to her husband for support. "Tell her, Bruce."

"We've been talking about showing our support to the kids in whatever they chose to do. I'm proud of Marissa and this new endeavor." He paused. "Aren't you proud of her, Anne?"

"Yes, I am. I hope she has success in her little dress shop." Anne conceded.

"Just because I don't sit behind a desk every day doesn't mean I don't have business sense." Marissa reached for the bread. "I made some wise investments along the way, and they've paid off splendidly. I used my earnings to buy into this high-end dress shop. I think two of your friends, Louise and Evelyn, were in the store last week. They said to say hello to you." Marissa popped a piece of bread in her mouth, signaling the end of that conversation.

"I'm happy for you, Marissa." Bruce put his hand on her shoulder.

"Thanks, Dad. That means a lot." Marissa turned to Austin. "What about you, hotshot military man. Are you upping for another tour?"

"That's one reason I came home for a couple of months." He looked around the table. "I may leave the Navy, start my own business, and use my master's degree."

Huffing, Anne shot a questioning look in his direction. "But I've told all my friends that you were going to be an admiral one day. You're not going to make me look bad, are you?"

Dropping her fork, Ellie earned her mother's frown when it clanged. "But Mom, he can't make life decisions based on the fact that you've bragged about him to your society friends. Let him follow his dreams and do what he wants to do."

"I know that. I just want what's best for you three. And a proud mother boasts about the accomplishments of her children. I can't help that your father and I run in prestigious circles." She sighed and took a drink of water.

"Thanks, Ellie." Austin paused and looked at his father, then his mom, "It is a big change. In two months, I have to give my final decision."

"Then you would be in the States. That's wonderful news." Ellie high-fived her sister.

"But what would you do?" Anne looked shocked.

"I've been praying about it and giving some serious thought about my future. I'm doing a lot of research and have also invested wisely, giving me the funds to make this kind of change." He took a deep breath and blew it out. "I'm excited about being stateside."

Leaning forward, Anne asked, "Is there a young woman involved in your decisions, Austin?"

"No, Mother. But I want there to be. I want a family of my own someday." Austin finished his last bite and pushed his plate away.

"Son, I'm proud of the man you've become." Bruce put his hand on Austin's arm. "I'll be praying with you about this decision. It is a big step, but I have no doubt you'll succeed in whatever career you pursue."

"Thanks, Dad."

Being at the end of the agenda, Ellie's turn was next. She took a deep breath and blew it out with trepidation.

"Tell us about Timbuktu. And I'm sure you have a few pictures to show us, don't you?" Austin asked.

"You just want out of the line of fire, I'm on to your moves, Bro." She whispered.

"Why don't we move into the den, so Edward can clear these dishes and serve our dessert." Anne stood and led the way, and as per custom, they followed.

Retrieving the photos she had brought as gifts, Ellie presented the canvases to her family, allowing them to choose from a selection.

"These are amazing. The best you've ever done." Austin raved about each picture.

"I want the cactus blooming in the desert, Ellie." Marissa chose first. "I have the perfect place for it by my Christmas cactus." She hugged Ellie, thanking her.

Her father looked from one photo to another. "These are phenomenal. Did the magazine buy them?"

"Yes. And they offered me a job. I'm now a photojournalist with *Above & Beyond Magazine*." She took the letter along with the copy of her check from her purse and showed her dad. Austin stood and read over his shoulder.

"But, what about your stewardess job, Elliana?" Anne gave her a disapproving look.

"They're called flight attendants, Mom. And I'll be resigning from my job with the airlines to take this assignment."

"Wow! Is this your first paycheck?" Austin asked as he waved it in the air.

"Yes. They bought the article and my photos, and one of my pictures will be used on the cover." Ellie held her breath.

"So, you've already accepted their offer without talking to me? What about the position we've been holding for you at the company? Did you give that any consideration?" Her mother shot her a pointed look.

Her father spoke up. "Anne, if you'll look around this room, you'll notice our children are talented adults with minds of their own. It's time for you to let go of your plans for their futures and let them pursue their dreams. I've wanted to sell the company for years. Let's do it and enjoy our retirement." Bruce spoke tenderly but didn't leave room for discussion.

"But, Bruce—" Anne touched her nose with a tissue.

"Dear." Bruce covered Anne's hand with his own. "We've raised three amazing young people. They're spreading their wings. Let's cheer them on. Shall we?"

"I suppose you're right, dear. I'll try." She blotted her eyes, though Ellie couldn't see any tears forming.

Austin held Ellie's letter and the copy of her first check in front of his mother, saving the day. "Look at this."

She read the letter and glanced at the check. Then did a double-take. "That's a lot of money." She offered a slight smile. "I had no idea they paid so well."

"Your work must be good to get this position. Which pic did they choose for the cover?" Marissa asked.

Ellie brought out her photo of Beau squatting on his haunches, watching the camel caravan in the distance.

"That's amazing, Sis." Her brother took it from her. "Who is the guy in the photo?"

"My interpreter on the trip. He's a Frenchman named Beau de La Croix." Ellie watched a knowing look come over Austin's face but kept the conversation moving. The magazine hired him to carry my bags and help me when my French was lacking."

"You speak French?" Marissa asked.

"Yep—as much as you do. I can say *croissant, merci, mademoiselle, oui, bonjour*, and French fries." Ellie grinned.

They laughed, and Ellie put Beau's photo away. "Oh, I also

have something for each of you." She gave the knives to her father and brother, a scarf to her mother, and a bracelet for her sister that added to the noise her accessories already made.

"This is amazing. I'll keep it on my desk. Thank you." Bruce hugged his daughter.

Holding his two knives up against a wall, Austin smiled. "These are great, Sis. I love them."

She winked at her partner in crime. "I'm glad. I knew you would."

Anne thanked Ellie for the scarf and then fanned herself as she took her seat, ignoring the gifting of the knives. "Too many changes for me to process. Let's have dessert and coffee, shall we?" She motioned for Edward to serve.

"In France, they serve café, which is half black coffee and half hot chocolate. And they drink it from a bowl." Ellie told Marissa.

"Let's try it sometime." Marissa accepted a cup of coffee from Edward.

Over dessert, Ellie relaxed, hoping the worst was over. It helped that both her siblings had life-changing news to add to hers. God's timing. *Thanks, Lord.*

When the dessert dishes were cleared from the room, Marissa stood to leave. Ellie joined her, with Austin following close behind.

Bruce hugged each of them in turn. Anne saw them to the door.

"Loved the dinner, Mother. And the pie was superb." Ellie hugged her and turned to retrieve her purse and the photo of Beau.

"Please come more often, Ellie," her mom said.

"I will, Mom. Love you, Dad." She stepped through the front door and pressed the fob on her Mustang. She took a deep breath and let it out slowly. She was released from her mother's domineering thumb. It felt good. Freeing. Beau was right.

"Hold up, Sis." Austin hurried to her car.

"I'm glad I got to see you again, Bro." She hugged him.

"We need to talk. You free for lunch on Saturday?" He opened her car door.

"I'm free." After sliding into the driver's seat, she looked up at her handsome brother. His muscular build, blond hair, and stunning blue eyes made him a very eligible bachelor. "But what do we have to talk about?" Ellie put her key in the ignition.

"It's time for a heart to heart. You're different. I didn't hear one sarcastic remark all evening. And you didn't let Mom have her way. I know Dad stepped up to the plate for all of us, but especially for you. And I'm glad. I want to talk about the Frenchman. There's more to that story."

No doubt, he saw the tears gathering on her lashes.

"I'm right, aren't I?"

"Text me the time and place, and I'll see you on Saturday." She shut her door and pulled out of the circle drive in front of her parents' mansion before she let the tears flow. Austin knew her too well.

The fragrant aromas in Beau's brother's restaurant kept him returning. The checkered tablecloths with drippy candles in the center displayed the true style of a Paris-Italian dining facility. The smell of oregano and garlic increased the desire for Italian cuisine, while the soft music added romance to the setting. His brother had proven his worth.

Beau smiled and waved at the waitress as he barged his way into the kitchen. "All right, everybody, get to work! Clean this place up! It's a pigsty. Throw this chef out! He is worthless!"

Alex opened the oven and put Beau's pizza in. "Beauregard!" He put his hands on his hips. "I'll have you know, we have a perfect report from the health department, and we're being featured in another magazine next month. So, back off!" Alex grinned at the sight of his older brother.

"Take over, guys." Beau grabbed Alex in a headlock and forced him out of the kitchen. "He's out of here."

The staff applauded and laughed as they worked on the pending orders.

"Sometimes I hate that you're stronger than me." Alex straightened his clothes and stuck his head back into the kitchen. "Hey, Julia, bring the pizza to our table when it's done. And bring two Cokes. Thanks, guys."

Seated at the back booth they usually occupied, Beau shoved a chair out for Alex with his foot as he reached the table.

"You're a bully. You know that, right?" Alex wiped Beau's footprint off his chair and took a seat.

"But you love me. And they think it's funny." Beau smiled with a look of mischief on his face.

"It is good to see you more relaxed. You bring those papers?"

Beau put a folder on the table and pushed it toward him.

Looking at the Paris offer first, Alex read it and then set it aside. Their drinks were served as he started reading the American offer. When he closed the file, he took a drink of Coke. "The American offer has more potential for advancement. Besides, the salary and benefits are amazing. The Paris job doesn't hold a candle to it."

Their pepperoni pizza was delivered, along with parmesan cheese and peppers to top it off.

Bowing his head, Alex prayed. "Lord, thank you for this food." He paused. "And thank you for Beau. Help him follow Your plan for his life. Amen."

"This smells amazing." Beau slid a piece of the pizza masterpiece Alex had created onto his plate and doused it with parmesan cheese. He reached for Alex's plate and served him.

"The best offer is in the U.S. Ellie is in the U.S. It's a no-brainer. You're a traveler and can visit us often. Distance doesn't destroy families."

"Your pizza is getting cold."

Alex took a bite and sat back, waiting for Beau to speak, then gave up and finished his lunch. "I make great pizza."

"Yes, you do." Beau took another slice for himself and grabbed the cheese.

"So, tell me. What's keeping you from saying yes to the offer in America? I want to know."

Beau sat back and met his gaze. "You."

21

The digital clock in her Mustang let Ellie know she was early. She parked at Joe's Crab Shack in Humble, Texas, and got a table for two away from the noonday crowd. She sipped her sweet tea until Austin arrived.

"You're looking quite summery today with your ponytail and shades, Miss Bendale." Her brother took a seat by her and picked up the menu. "You want to share the bucket of shrimp like we did last time?"

"Sounds perfect to me. Order for us."

Motioning to the waiter, he gave their choices and turned his gaze to his sister. "Where do you want to start? What have you done—gone and fallen in love with a Frenchman?"

Tears filled her eyes. Her bottom lip trembled. "Yes."

Austin sat back. "I was kidding. But you're serious." He offered her his napkin. "Don't cry. Here, blow your nose and start from the beginning." He waited.

After taking a deep breath, Ellie told him the story from Beau breaking her toes to her time in Timbuktu.

"But this sounds like a routine assignment. What changed?" He took a drink of his Coke.

Nervous about how much to say about the kidnapping, she paused. Hesitated.

"What are you not telling me?" He tossed a hush puppy into his mouth.

"We ran into a little trouble and had to escape from Timbuktu—running for our lives."

"Wait! Is this guy de La Croix? Beau Dubois de La Croix!" He almost choked, coughed a couple of times, and took a drink.

"Yes. Beauregard Dubois de La Croix." She knew her secret was out. Austin was Navy and would have heard about the mission's success.

Austin leaned close to her and kept his voice to a forceful whisper. "Elliana—you were kidnapped by a terrorist leader, enemy number one against the world. I don't believe this!" He rubbed the back of his neck and breathed in a deep breath. "You could have died! I heard about this op before I came home. Sure, we were happy about the success of the mission, but I never considered the American put in harm's way was you! My sister. What was he thinking?"

"Calm down, Austin. You're getting loud."

"I'm angry."

"Don't be. He was following orders. You, of all people, should understand that. He needed a ruse, a cover to get him into Timbuktu to spy on the stronghold. Working with me gave him that. I was unaware of his dual objective until we were attacked the first time. The arrangement was made with our government and the French. Beau never intended to put me in harm's way. He protected me, rescued me—put his life on the line to save mine."

Austin sat back in his chair. "And you fell in love with him on the journey."

"Yes. But he isn't interested in a relationship. He lost his fiancée in the bombings in France several years ago. Beau says it hurts too much to lose someone you love. He won't risk his heart again. So, I kissed him on the cheek, wished him well, got on my plane, and cried."

"It's a good thing he's five thousand miles away. I'm pretty miffed." He paused. "I understand war. But I don't want you to be caught in the middle of it." He took a drink of his sweet tea. "So, what now?" He leaned back for their food to be delivered, huffing out a breath. "Will you see him again?" He served her plate from the shrimp bucket.

"I doubt it. He lives in France. I won't be running into him on the streets of Houston anytime soon. Right now, I'm focused on Olivia's wedding, then quitting one job and accepting my new assignment." She peeled her shrimp.

"I'm proud of your success. You've found your niche and will enjoy the challenge. But I'm sorry for your heartache. de La Croix is a decorated soldier—the best of the best. You chose well, Sis."

"But he didn't choose me. We were thrown together, literally, by difficult circumstances and—"

"He was a hero when you needed one." Austin squeezed her hand. "The Lord will help you through this."

"Thanks, but before we leave that subject, I want to tell you about the first attack." Ellie smiled. "Hussein was coming for Beau while another soldier was closing in from behind. Beau went into attack mode, and I braced my feet, twirled around, and hit the soldier with my elbow. I broke his nose! You should have seen it! It was awesome." She laughed. "Blood went everywhere."

"So, your self-defense course paid off?" Austin laughed.

"Yep." She smiled briefly.

"I wish I could have been there for you." He sighed. "I joined the Navy to protect people, to make a difference. While I served on the other side of the world, you were kidnapped by a terrorist leader." He lowered his voice on that last part.

"You can't always come to my rescue." She laid her hand on his arm. "You've patched up my scraped knees so many times."

"But I wasn't there when a gun was held to your head." He furrowed his brow.

"Let's change the subject. I want to talk about you. What are you going to do? Are you leaving the military and becoming a civilian like us peons?" Ellie asked.

"That's the question of the hour. They want me to be a career military man, and you know how Mom feels. But I want the white picket fence, the wife and kids, and a dog. The Great American Dream. I want to build a successful business."

"I don't blame you. I'm shocked Mom didn't pressure you to take the head position at their business. It's been her dream. I think she wants to continue being in charge." Ellie sipped her tea.

"Oh, she did that before you arrived, but Dad shut her down."

"It's one of the reasons I don't visit them much." Ellie dipped her shrimp in cocktail sauce. "Now, quit hogging the shrimp!"

Dress fittings, bridal showers, and bridesmaid teas kept Ellie busy. She and Jocelyn hosted and entertained until they were exhausted. As the big day approached, the bachelorette party was in full swing. They chose to have it the weekend before the wedding, with petit fours and chocolate fountains displayed among a vast array of culinary creations. Olivia was all smiles as she prepared to walk the aisle toward the love of her life, Eli.

All the wedding talk sent Ellie's mind spinning into overdrive with missing Beau. She kept envisioning how her wedding would be ... someday.

"Hey, are you ready to watch Olivia open her gifts?" Jocelyn came through the kitchen with her arms loaded. One gift slipped off the top. "Help!"

"Got it!" Ellie caught the gift before it hit the floor. She took a couple more off the pile and followed Jocelyn into the party room. "Let's get this show on the road."

Olivia, a very happy bride, was delighted with the negligees, lingerie, and personalized gifts she received.

"Here are a few more plates." Jocelyn carried them to the counter.

"I'll get them into the dishwasher. Are there any more punch cups in there? I'm missing three cups." Ellie scraped cake crumbs off the plates.

"I'll look around." Jocelyn hesitated. "You okay?"

"Sure, why wouldn't I be?" Ellie dried her hands on a towel. "It was a great shower, and Olivia was over-the-moon happy."

"Yeah, we did good, and on Saturday, she gets her happily ever after. But you're hiding your heartbreak behind a smile right now. I can see it."

Tears filled Ellie's eyes. "I'm trying. I love Olivia and couldn't be happier for her."

"But—"

"Missing Beau hurts sometimes. Heartache amid all this bridal bliss is a tug-of-war."

Jocelyn stepped forward and hugged Ellie, letting her cry. "I'm so sorry. You're doing a great job of putting up a brave front at a hard time."

"Thanks. Help me finish this. Okay?" She wiped her cheeks with the dishtowel.

"Absolutely. We'll get those two married, then we can sort out your love life. Deal?"

"Deal." Ellie sniffed again and got back to work. It's what one did when unhappy in the middle of wedding celebrations.

The week passed in a blur of lunches, brunches, final fittings, and nail appointments, along with the wedding rehearsal and dinner. The sun shined bright in a cerulean blue sky on Olivia's wedding day. After one last breakfast together, Olivia, Ellie, and Jocelyn made final preparations.

The day was filled with hair and makeup appointments, then an hour of photos. Before they knew it, the wedding music had started, and it was time to line up for their walk down the aisle. The church sanctuary was gorgeous with candles, white gladiolas, white roses, and toile. It was like walking into a fairy tale. A quintet of strings serenaded the crowd of family and friends gathered for the wedding.

"It's magical, like a fairytale where dreams come true." Ellie peeked through the back doors of the sanctuary. "And you're stunning, Olivia."

"Thanks. You and Jocelyn are glowing. Those iridescent blue gowns with the off-shoulder look are gorgeous." Olivia smiled.

Stepping forward to escort his daughter, John Stone kissed her cheek and offered his arm. The music changed, and the wedding coordinator sent the flower girl and ring bearer down the aisle. In a graceful stroll, Jocelyn and Ellie walked the long aisle in front of Olivia.

Eli's eyes glistened when he saw Olivia. Their vows to each other were heartfelt, and the ceremony was touching as two lives became one.

As they were pronounced husband and wife, Ellie wiped a tear from her eye. The processional set things in motion. There were photos and photos and more photos. Then, the reception with a five-course dinner, ice sculptures, chocolate fountains, and an ornate cake with a water fountain in the middle of it. The chandeliers sparkled as love songs filled the air. The bride glowed with joy competing with the happiness on Eli's face.

As things began to wind down Ellie knew it was time for

her speech. She took a deep breath, then picked up a crystal goblet and tapped on the side of the glass getting everyone's attention.

"Ladies and Gentlemen, as Maid of Honor, or should I say one of the Maids of Honor, I want to wish Olivia and Eli the very best life together. They radiate love for each other and those two babies, Judah and Becca. The Lord orchestrated their love affair and is making this four-some into a beautiful family.

"Let's raise our glasses and toast to a happily ever after for Eli and Olivia. May they have enough challenges to keep them turning to the Lord, enough joy to give them laugh lines, enough energy to keep up with two babies—" Everyone laughed. "And a thriving relationship to keep them clinging to each other." Ellie raised her glass higher. "To Olivia and Eli." She took a drink and smiled.

The best man stepped forward and made his speech. As Ellie left to take her seat, Jocelyn waited her turn. This reception was exactly how Olivia wanted it.

Slipping off her stilettos, Ellie wiggled her two aching toes. It had been a long week—no it had been a long month. But Olivia was one happy bride, and everything went off without a hitch. Checking her watch, Ellie knew the limo would be arriving soon. This evening was coming to an end. She sighed and put her heels back on. It was time to paste a smile on her face and see the happy couple off on her honeymoon.

When Jocelyn finished her speech, everyone applauded. Ellie caught Olivia's eye and motioned to her watch. Olivia nodded her head, and Ellie stood. "Okay, all you single ladies, let's gather at the staircase just outside this reception hall. It's time for Olivia to toss her bouquet."

Getting a thumbs-up from Olivia, Ellie joined Jocelyn and the other single ladies.

"Okay, Ellie, let's catch it!"

"This isn't a team sport." She smiled and edged Jocelyn to the side.

"Now, who's acting competitive?" Jocelyn laughed.

"Wait." Eli leaned around his bride and pulled a perfect rose out of the bouquet for Olivia to enjoy later. "Now throw it." He smiled at the waiting ladies.

"Ready, set, go!" Olivia tossed her bouquet toward the waiting throng of hopefuls raising their arms, wiggling manicured nails, as they reached for the gorgeous display of roses, pearls, and ribbon.

As the bouquet descended, Ellie did her famous jump shot and snagged it.

"Yay!" Ellie waved the bouquet in the air celebrating her victory.

Jocelyn smiled at Ellie and made an announcement. "Okay, men. Let's have all the eligible gentlemen gather to catch the garter. It's your turn."

As per custom, Ellie stepped aside for the men crowding in to catch the garter Eli was preparing to toss.

"Stay here, Ellie. The photographer will want a picture of you with the guy who catches the garter," Jocelyn said as she moved to the side.

"Stay close, Jocelyn. I don't want to be surrounded by all this testosterone alone. Ellie grabbed Jocelyn's arm.

"Is one of these eligible bachelors catching your eye?"

Her smile faded. "I'm not interested. You should have caught the bouquet."

The men were getting restless and loud—excited to catch the garter.

"Okay gentlemen, are you ready? Here it comes," Eli shouted before the garter went airborne as he launched it like a slingshot.

Sailing through the air, a guy in the back caught it. The

crowd of available men cheered and then parted so the lucky man could step forward.

Ellie waited. The bride and groom looked on as an uninvited guest stepped forward with a tentative look on his face and the garter in his hand.

Beau.

22

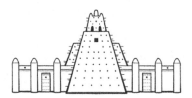

"**D**e La Croix?"

Those gathered quieted, the newlyweds waited —time stood still—as Ellie took a few slow steps toward the man before her. He was clean-shaven with a military haircut in his gray French military uniform with a chest covered in medals, his hat under his arm, and a garter in his hand. *Perfect.*

"Elliana." Beau gave a slight bow while holding her gaze.

As the men moved into the reception hall, Jocelyn stepped forward. "Ellie, could you and your friend pose for the photographer, so we can get our newlyweds off on their honeymoon?" She pushed Ellie toward Beau. "Get closer together, turn in this direction, and smile for the camera."

Beau stepped closer to Ellie and placed his hand on her back as she turned to face the photographer. They posed —smiling.

Ignoring the people milling around them, Ellie pivoted. "What are you doing here? Did you take a wrong turn in Paris? Shouldn't you be out saving the world? I thought you'd have brought world peace by now—"

He pressed his finger to her lips, stopping her diatribe. "Normally, I would be on another assignment, but—" He removed his finger.

"But—" She tilted her head.

"You ruined it for me." He relaxed his military stance.

"How did I do that?" Ellie warned her heart not to get ahead of her again.

He gently gripped her bare shoulder. "Ellie, I can't get you off my mind. You've invaded my thoughts, my world, and changed everything. I can't sleep, can't eat, can't function—and you're responsible." He was serious. "I'm miserable. I am so in love with you. I can't—"

She kissed him, stopping his speech. He lifted her off her feet, spinning her around as he deepened the kiss.

Easing her arms around his neck, Ellie leaned back. "Hello, McGarrett." She grinned. Hearing applause, she leaned back to see they had some interested bystanders. But she didn't care. Beau was back, and her happily ever after loomed.

"Hey, guys. This is Beau."

Letting her feet touch the floor, he kept his arm around Ellie and focused on her friends.

"The newlyweds are Eli and Olivia. And this is my friend, Jocelyn."

Eli shook Beau's hand. "I've heard a lot about you. Glad you could make it."

"I got here as quickly as I could." Beau turned his focus on the bride as he took her extended hand.

"It's about time you showed up, G.I. Joe." Olivia, stunning in her wedding gown, smiled at Beau. "I hope your intentions are honorable. We get pretty touchy when it comes to Elliana."

"Completely honorable, I assure you."

Jocelyn eyed Beau from head to toe. "Ellie said you're McGarrett, Rambo, 007, and Hooch all rolled into one. Is that true?"

"Am I the only one she abuses with sarcasm?" Beau grinned.

"Nope." Jocelyn laughed and shook his hand. "So, you better get used to it, Hot Shot, if you plan to stick around." Jocelyn checked her watch. "But for right now, Eli and Olivia, your limo is waiting. You need to get your things and kiss your babies goodbye. We'll meet you on the sidewalk in fifteen minutes for your grand send-off."

Jocelyn straightened Olivia's train as she ascended the stairs, arm-in-arm with her groom, before she hurried to check on the limo.

"I like your friends. They're protective of you, and I'm glad you have them in your life." Beau gazed at her as if admiring the view. "You look gorgeous, Elliana."

"Thank you. You look pretty amazing, yourself," She ran her hand over his medals.

"G.I. Joe?" He shook his head.

"I've been telling them I had my own personal hero." She cupped his face in her hands. "I can't believe you're standing here."

"Believe it. I couldn't stay away." He kissed her hand. "I feel like we're on display. Would you have dinner with me?"

"Yes. As soon as this shindig is over, I'm all yours. The reception is winding down." She slipped her hand through the crook of his elbow. "Let me introduce you to my family."

Sauntering into the wedding dinner-slash-reception with Beau, Ellie led him to her family's table. Her parents stood.

"Who is this, Elliana?" Anne Bendale, the picture of wealth in her designer gown, flashed her array of diamonds as she extended her hand.

Taking her hand, Beau bowed slightly.

"Mom, Dad, this is Beauregard de La Croix. My friend from France. He kept me safe in Timbuktu." Ellie smiled at her parents.

"It's a pleasure to meet you." Her dad led the conversation. "And thank you for taking care of my girl." He clasped Beau's hand.

"I'm honored to meet you, sir."

"It is always good to meet one of Elliana's friends. Are you here on assignment?" Anne pried into his business.

"A military man cannot reveal the purpose of his mission." Ellie's brother stood to greet Beau. "I'm Austin Bendale, Ellie's brother. That uniform is well decorated." Austin saluted Beau, and he returned the gesture even though Austin wasn't in uniform. "Ellie, get Beau some cake and punch. There's room for you both at my table." Austin pointed to the next table.

"It was my pleasure to meet you both, Mr. and Mrs. Bendale." Beau gave another bow in her mother's direction before leaving their presence.

Ellie leaned in and whispered. "You just impressed my mother. Was that your plan?"

"I need her as my ally," Beau smirked.

"You're fired from the war, Rambo. Didn't you get my memo?" Ellie tucked her hand through his elbow.

"I've missed you, E." He drew her close and kissed her temple.

"You want some cake?" She looked into his grey eyes. "How about some punch?"

"Can we get it to go?" Beau grinned.

Ellie laughed. "That can be arranged. Stay right here. Don't move."

He winked.

"Isn't he gorgeous?" Ellie grabbed Jocelyn's arm. "He wants to take me to dinner. What else needs to be done before I can leave?" She looked back at Beau.

"Yes, he's handsome. Sounds like you're in a hurry." Jocelyn grinned. "As soon as we send the bride and groom on their honeymoon, you can go. I'll pack up their gifts, retrieve the top layer of their cake and get it into the freezer for their first anniversary. Give me the keys to your Mustang, and I'll get your things out of the dressing room." She held out her hand palm up.

"You're the best. Thanks." Ellie hugged her. "First, let's go see the bride one more time." They linked arms and proceeded to the bridal dressing room.

As Ellie walked away, Beau remembered her in khaki clothing with her hair in a favorite messy bun.

"I can tell you're smitten with my sister, de La Croix." Austin broke Beau's concentration.

"That's an understatement. I'm in love with her." Beau eyed Ellie's brother. "You okay with that?"

"Let me level with you. When I put two and two together, I was livid. I was read in on the Timbuktu op, but didn't see the whole picture until I had lunch with Ellie."

Beau sat up straighter in his chair. "She told you what happened?" Beau asked as he read Austin's facial expressions.

"No. The truth dawned on me when I remembered the timing of Ellie's trip to Mali, and I added that info to the debriefing I received at headquarters." Austin drank the last of his punch.

"It was not the plan for Ellie to be in any danger. I was following orders from our governments to save lives in Timbuktu when it turned dangerous. I did my best to keep her safe and send her home in one piece." Beau paused. "I promise you, this will not happen again. I've recently taken a position with your government—in Washington D.C." Beau rubbed his hand through his hair.

"Relax, Beau. Your gallantry is being proclaimed among the ranks. Your integrity isn't in question. I'm just concerned that you'll break her heart."

"Her heart is safe with me. I'll never purposely bring a tear to her eyes."

"I'll hold you to that." Austin stood and handed his business card to Beau. "Call me when you get settled. If I'm in D.C., you can buy me a cup of coffee." Austin motioned for Ellie to take his seat at the table. "Now, I think I'll get another cup of punch."

"Will you help Jocelyn load my car, Austin? She's got a lot of things to take to our condo. I'm leaving with Beau."

"Sure. I can do that." He wiggled his eyebrows. "She's gorgeous," Austin hurried away.

Ellie tugged his hands, and Beau stood willingly at her insistence, then slipped his arms around her waist and Austin's card into his pocket.

"Jocelyn is finishing my Maid of Honor duties, so I'm free to leave after the bride and groom depart. Everyone is gathering out front to see them off. Are you ready?"

"More than ready. Lead the way." He smiled. "Let's bid your parents a good night."

With the newlywed's limo fading into the sunset, Beau motioned for his driver to approach. "Your chariot, Elliana."

He opened the door for her before sliding in next to her, making her feel like a princess.

"To the restaurant, Allen."

"Yes, sir." The driver closed the window between them and pulled the limousine into Houston's traffic.

"How many bags of potato chips did you buy me?" Ellie laughed. "There's a pile in here."

"Remember, I'm all that and a bag of chips."

"And I'll think of you as I enjoy every package." She picked up several packages and tossed them in the air.

"As long as they make you smile."

"You did that by showing up." Ellie turned toward Beau so she could meet his gray eyes. "I've missed you so much it hurt."

"Well, you've made my life pretty miserable." He ran his fingers down her cheek. "I think we need to remedy this situation."

"What do you have in mind?" She touched his lips with her fingertip. "I like the thought of finding a remedy." She kissed him softly and stayed close, feeling his breath on her face. "So, what are you doing here?"

"I came for you." His brow furrowed. "Life is hard without you."

"It hasn't been easy on this side of the ocean either." Ellie leaned in for another kiss.

Beau wrapped his arms around her and held her close. Did I tell you how gorgeous you look this evening? When the crowd parted, and I saw you, I couldn't breathe. You're exquisite."

Smiling, she ran her fingers down his cheek. "I love you."

"Remember, I'm the one who said it first." He touched his finger to her lips. "I traveled halfway around the world to see you. And it is worth it."

"And I'm so glad you did."

The limo slowed, stopping in front of Brennan's of Houston. "Are you hungry?"

"Yes. I was too busy to eat at the wedding." She grabbed her evening bag.

The driver opened their door, and Beau escorted her into the restaurant. "de La Croix, table for two, please. We have a reservation."

The lady smiled and picked up two menus. "We have your table ready. Please follow me." She led them into a luxurious dining facility with plush carpeting, high-backed chairs, chandeliers, and soft music. Their table was in a quiet corner, with a dozen roses and candlelight.

"Very romantic." Ellie smiled.

He helped her with her chair. "Remember that slanted table and rickety chairs in Mopti?"

"Sure, I do."

"I was trying to find an improvement over that setting."

"You succeeded." She pulled her linen napkin out of its fancy fold. "This is lovely."

"Let's order, then we can talk." Beau looked for their waiter.

After delivering their sweet tea in stemware and fresh bread on a board, the server took their orders.

Curious, she gazed at him until he looked up.

"What?"

"How did you find me?"

"It was a challenge, but I have amazing detective skills, and you're all over social media." He tapped his phone and showed her his view of her Facebook photo. "I was a man on a mission." He served her some bread. "I wasn't sure crashing a wedding was the best time to return, but this was the first weekend I could get free."

Reaching for the butter, she spread it on her bread. "What a perfect grand entrance. Catching the garter was a great touch."

"I lucked out on that one."

The waiter chose that moment to serve their appetizers. "Sorry to interrupt." He placed a shrimp cocktail in front of Ellie and a plate of cheese sticks and steaming marinara before Beau.

Beau leaned back. "It smells good."

When the waiter left, Beau reached for Ellie's hand and

prayed for their food and their time together. He squeezed her hand before releasing it to eat one of his appetizers.

"It's good to hear you pray." Ellie reached for a shrimp. "So, as I see it, we have a geography problem."

"Yes, we do. But I may have the solution."

"Meeting halfway is out of the question. It's all ocean, and I get seasick."

"That's not what I had in mind. I've been offered an amazing opportunity." Beau took a drink of tea. "That sauce is hot." He paused. "I've been offered a position with the offices of the *Defence and Armament Attachés*. I'd be advising the Pentagon on French defense policies and keeping the Ambassador abreast of current defense issues. It would require that I live in Washington D.C."

"D.C.? Wow." She clapped her hands. "I'd be thrilled for you to move to the States." She hesitated, and her smile faded. "But your brother lives in Paris."

"That's true."

She held a shrimp by the tail. "I have one question. Would you, being the macho man you are, be happy leaving your world of chasing bad guys, rescuing damsels in distress, and being a hunky hero to sitting behind a desk and dealing with stuffy bureaucrats?" She dipped the delicacy and took a bite.

"Well, the real question is, would you still love me if I became one of those stuffy bureaucrats?" A smile tugged at his lips.

"One thing do I know—you'll never be stuffy, de La Croix." She winked at him. "So, you're serious about moving to the States?"

"I'm serious about our relationship."

She sat back and eyed Beau. "You're willing to leave life as you've known it—willing to leave Paris and your brother —for me?"

"Yes." He reached for her hand.

Ellie's eyes filled.

Beau reached up and caught a tear as it moistened her cheek. "Don't cry."

"But I love you so much and want you to be happy."

"You make me happy, E."

"But—"

"Don't overthink it. Let's enjoy our dinner. You've got one more shrimp." He nibbled on a cheesy appetizer. "So, what are your thoughts on me making this change in geography?"

Pushing her empty cocktail dish to the side, she met his gaze. "I'm humbled and overwhelmed by the sacrifice you'd be making." Tears clouded her eyes again. "It makes me feel your love." A tear escaped, but she ignored it. "It's a dream come true."

"Would you be willing to live in Washington D.C.?"

"Yes. With my new job, I can work from anywhere. If you'd asked me to move to Paris, I'd have been on the next plane, so moving to D.C. is a definite *yes*." She smiled.

"Now you tell me," He teased.

The restaurant manager delivered their entrees. "For the lady." He served Ellie. "And for the gentleman." He set a platter in front of Beau. "Can I get you two anything else, sir?"

"No, we're good. Thank you."

Picking up his fork, he took a bite. "This is much better than that goat you tried to eat."

"You mean the goat I spit out. I was so embarrassed." Her face grew warm at the memory.

"You know what I thought at that moment?"

"That I was disgusting?"

"No. I thought you'd probably be a classy puker too." He laughed.

After enjoying reconnecting over amazing food by candlelight, Ellie grew quiet when their flan was served.

"When do you leave, Beau?"

"I have to be in D.C. for a meeting on Monday morning. I fly out tomorrow evening. I took the last flight out so I could spend as much time with you as possible." He took her hand in his and stroked the back of it with his thumb. "When do you fly again?"

"The flight leaves mid-day on Wednesday for our regular jaunt over the African skies." A beat passed. "What's on your agenda for tomorrow? I'm going to church in the morning, then to my parents for lunch with the family. Are you up for that?" She took a bite of her flan.

"I want to spend the day with you, so sure." He pulled out his cell phone and texted their driver, then turned the phone in her direction and took her picture. "You are one beautiful woman. And I want to love you forever and a day." He leaned over and kissed her lips.

"That can be arranged."

23

W hen Beau got into his hotel room, he checked the time. In Paris, Alex would be getting up to start his day. He dialed the number, connecting on the second ring.

"Morning, Bro. I have a question for you."

"Well, hello to you too." Alex yawned. "What has you up so late tonight? That beautiful blonde?"

"As a matter of fact, yes. I've made some decisions. I'm taking the job here in D.C., and Ellie is very happy about it. But I have a question?" Beau stepped out of his boots.

"Okay. I'm awake. What's your question?"

"Do you want my flat?" Beau waited.

"What? You're kidding, right? Don't you want to keep it?"

"No, it's paid for, and if I could use one of the bedrooms when we come to visit, I'd love for you to have it."

"Man, that's too big a gift. Vivienne would be thrilled. It's a block from her job and so much bigger than our place. But— but I can't afford it yet. There's no way we could manage it right now." He hesitated. "I can keep an eye on the place for you. It's your flat, and you love it."

"Listen, Alex. I mean it. I want to give you my place. You'll need a larger place when your family begins to grow. I'll sign the deed over to you."

"It's too large of a gift." Alex's voice cracked.

"You're my family." Beau took a deep breath. "I want to do this for you."

"How can I ever thank you?"

"Just keep being my brother. Don't let a little geography come between us, and keep feeding me when I'm in Paris. Okay?"

"Anytime. I'll miss you, but I'm at peace about you accepting the position."

"I'm glad. That means a lot." Beau ran his hands through his hair. "I need to get some rest. I'm still in jet lag. But I'll call you in a couple of days. Okay, Bro?"

"Okay. Call when you can. Beau?"

"Yeah?"

"Thanks."

"You're welcome."

Under partially cloudy skies on Sunday morning, Ellie pulled her Mustang in front of the Hyatt Regency Hotel near the Intercontinental Airport. She got out and opened the back for Beau to load his luggage. He looked amazing in black dress slacks, a button-down dress shirt, and a sports jacket.

"Good morning, Elliana. You look great this morning." He loaded his luggage.

"Thank you. I had to ditch the evening gown. These duds will have to do." She wore dress pants, strappy sandals, and a boyfriend jacket with a ruffled tank underneath. She got into the car and faced him. "Is that your GQ look there, McGarrett?"

"Yeah. I'm trying to impress you. Did it work?" He fastened his seatbelt.

Absolutely!" She leaned over, pulled him toward her, and kissed him. "Good morning to you too."

She put the vehicle in gear and got them to church without incident, even though Beau grabbed the dash a couple of times. "Driving in America will take some getting used to."

"Our church will be different for you. It's lively and loud but filled with wonderful people, and our pastor preaches powerful messages."

"Lead the way." He opened Ellie's door. "Churches in France tend to be stoic, so this will be interesting." He shut her door.

"Is the assignment in Washington D.C. confirmed?"

"Yes. It is decided. I'm making the move." He stepped ahead of her. "Let me get the door for you."

"Thank you."

"At your service, *mademoiselle*." He gave a slight bow.

She stopped in the church foyer—truth dawning. "I've seen that in *The Princess Bride*."

"What?" He tried to look innocent.

"When did 'at your service, *mademoiselle*,' become 'I love you'?"

"During our escape from Timbuktu." He winked at her.

The joined her family in their usual pew. Her parents greeted Beau, and Austin saluted. Beau returned the gesture and took a seat by Ellie then leaned close. "I can't tell if your brother likes me or wants to take me out."

She whispered. "He's very protective of me. Maybe it's his military training."

"Or your mother hired him."

Slipping in just as the worship music started, Marissa eyed Beau. "Oh, hello. You must be Ellie's handsome heartthrob. I'm Marissa. The black sheep of the family. Nice to meet you." She shook his hand and joined in the singing.

It must have been a culture shock experience for Beau, but he seemed to enjoy the hour and a half of music and inspirational speaking.

"What did you think?" Ellie pressed her key fob.

"I've never experienced anything like it, but I loved it."

"Well, brace yourself. If you thought Hussein was a challenge, you haven't seen anything yet. You're about to face my mother on her turf." Ellie laughed and put her 'stang in gear.

Though the mansion was pretentious, and the veranda was decked out in high-class finery, Beau held his own among the Bendale family. He aced her mother's interrogation with finesse. His manners were pristine—unshakable when in the line of fire. Ellie smiled as she watched the interaction.

As the dessert dishes were being cleared, Anne turned to Ellie. "You've been quiet, Elliana. I know you've accepted the new job with the magazine, but how does this handsome soldier fit into your plans?"

Ellie put her and Beau's dessert plates on the tray Edward carried. She stood and motioned for Beau to join her as she slipped her hand through his elbow. "Beau, would you wait for me by the front door?"

He nodded. "Thank you for a wonderful lunch." Beau bid her family goodbye and left the veranda.

Facing her family, Ellie put her hand on her hip. "Look, it's too soon to answer questions about my relationship with Beau. I don't know how this is going to play out—but Austin, I think I've found the X on my faded map." She winked at her brother. "And I'm hanging on to the treasure."

She grabbed her purse. "Beau has a plane to catch. Thanks for lunch, Mom. We can talk later. Gotta go." She smiled as she escaped the interrogation sure to commence, then stopped inside the door to slip her shoes on while listening to her family's conversation.

"When we were kids," Austin spoke up. "We would hide things in the backyard and draw maps so we could find our treasure again later. Ellie always said one day she would find the X on her faded map when she found the man of her dreams. I think you let her play Barbies way too much, Mom."

Marissa clapped her hands. "Ellie's in love."

With a smile plastered on her face, Ellie joined Beau at the door as he finished a call on his cell.

When the door was shut, Ellie stopped on the porch, turned, and kissed Beau. "Congratulations. You survived."

Throwing his head back, he laughed. "You are a piece of work. You enjoyed shocking your mom, leaving her with a plethora of unanswered questions."

"I sure did. Now, let's make our escape." She tossed Beau her keys. "Want to drive my car?"

"Absolutely." He caught the keys and opened the passenger door for her, then slid behind the wheel. After adjusting the seat, he cranked the sports car and revved the engine. "Sweet." He smiled and pushed the button to slide the top down and lowered the windows.

"So, you like my ride?" Ellie grabbed a scrunchie from the cupholder, caught her long hair into a ponytail, and put it in a messy bun.

"Yes, I do." He pulled out of the driveway and drove to the entrance of the prestigious subdivision. "I got a call from the manager of the hotel. He said I left something. Can we stop there on the way to your condo?"

"Sure. Follow the signs to Beltway 8. I'll tell you where to turn."

Beau maneuvered the shiny Mustang into traffic flow with ease. When he propped his wrist on top of the steering wheel, it took Ellie back to driving with him in Timbuktu, except the steering wheel was on the opposite side of the vehicle. She smirked.

"What?" Beau glanced at her.

"Looking good behind the wheel of my car, McGarrett." She squeezed his other hand, resting on the gear shift. "I think rain is coming this way, but we can outrun it. Your hotel is on the left, about five miles down this road."

"Getting accustomed to driving on this side of the road may take some time. But I'll be careful with your ride."

"Do I look worried?"

"No. You look amazing. I'd gotten used to dusty sundresses and khaki pants. You clean up great and make my mind wander." He pulled the car under a portico and left it running. "Be right back. I'll run in and check with the manager."

Ellie pushed the button to slide the top up and grabbed the lever on the right to secure it. Knowing the lever on the driver's side was more difficult, she looked around the car for something to use as a hammer. Her stilettos were on the floorboard. Jocelyn must have missed them when she emptied the car. She grabbed a shoe, got out of the car, went around to the driver's seat, and used the heel to force the lever into place.

As she hit it one last time for good measure, the passenger side door opened. "That was fast—"

Holding the shoe mid-air, she realized the man getting in her car wasn't Beau. He'd moved fast—catching her off guard. His was a face she never wanted to see again.

The car door slammed, and he locked it. "Hello again." With a revolver pointed in her direction, he demanded, "Don't make a sound!"

She froze—stifling a scream. Unable to take him down with her stellar moves while sitting in a sports car, her mind raced through her options.

"Drop the shoe. And put your seatbelt on."

She obeyed, dropping the shoe out the window before she reached for her seatbelt. Her phone was in the side pocket where she put it while securing the top. Reaching down, she pressed Beau's number, the last one entered into her phone. With the seatbelt in her hand. It took three attempts to fasten it with her hands shaking.

"Get it done and drive!" He jabbed the gun against her shoulder.

Putting the Mustang in gear, she hit the gas, hoping Beau would hear the squealing of the tires. "Hussein. How did you get out of prison?"

"Not hard with loyal followers planted in the system." He smiled in a sinister sort of way. "It will take them a while to realize I've been replaced. By then, Dubois will be dead."

Sucking in a breath was a mistake. Hussein smelled sweaty and wore a prison guard uniform. The feel of his gun against her skin was very familiar. "You want to draw Beau out again, Hussein, but it won't work this time. He doesn't know Houston and has no resources to help him find me."

"Stop talking and keep driving." He huffed out a foul breath. "I need to think."

"Where are you taking me? Kidnapping is a felony. You know that, right?" She prayed Beau was hearing their conversation. Panic knotted her stomach. He didn't know where to find her and was unarmed with no transportation. She was on her own with a very dangerous man. Pressing the accelerator, she exceeded the speed limit, hoping to attract a police officer.

Reaching the Interstate, she glanced at Hussein. "Which way, north or south?"

"North—away from the city."

She put her blinker on and turned left. Taking the entrance ramp, she joined the traffic flow pushing the speed limits and changing lanes often. *Where's a cop when you need one?*

"Sorry for my delay, we had a fire in the dumpster in the back. Kate says you received a call to come here. I'm the manager, but I didn't call you. There must be some mistake." The squealing of tires out front had the manager looking in that direction.

"The call came from an 866 area code." Beau's cell buzzed with another incoming call.

The receptionist overheard their conversation. "That call came from an anonymous number."

"This is strange, but thank you for trying to help. Sorry to have troubled you." He turned from the reception desk and answered the call. "Hello." He waited. "Hi. Is anyone there?" He heard a distant conversation—Ellie's voice.

He kept the phone to his ear and took off running, arriving curbside in time to see the Mustang's taillights as it disappeared into traffic. *No!* Ellie was gone! He reached down and picked up her stiletto. He turned back toward the hotel.

"Hussein. Now we can add carjacking to your list of crimes."

That name stopped him in his tracks.

"Kidnapping is a felony. You know that, right?"

Beau rushed back inside the hotel. "My girlfriend has been kidnapped. I need to use a phone. Now!"

The manager led Beau into the office center and pointed to a desk phone.

"Thanks." He pulled Austin's card out of his pocket and dialed his number.

"Austin, this is Beau. Where are you?"

"I just left my mother's house. What's wrong?"

"I'm at my hotel, the Hyatt Regency on Beltway 8. Get here quick. Ellie has been kidnapped! By Hussein."

"No! He's supposed to be in custody. I'm on my way—be there in ten."

Beau heard the roar of the engine of his Jeep.

"Do you have any idea where they've gone? Of course, you don't. You're not from here."

"But Ellie left her phone on, and I can hear their conversation."

"Ellie's smart. She's feeding you vital info. Keep listening. I'm almost there."

"I'm out front."

"Where are we going?"

"Just keep going north."

"What are you going to do with me?" Her voice cracked.

"Just use you again. Don't be making any wedding plans." He let out a haughty laugh. *"I will succeed this time."*

Hussein's harsh voice sent fire through Beau's veins. Austin pulled in front of the hotel, and Beau bolted inside the vehicle.

"Has Ellie given you any idea where they're going?"

"Not yet. Just north."

"Then she's driving toward Kingwood, where she lives." Austin looked up a number on his phone and activated the call.

"Jocelyn. This is Austin. Ellie's been kidnapped, and she's driving north on I-69. If they come there, call me and leave by the back door—and pray." He listened. "Yes. I'll call you back." He ended the call.

"Can I use your phone to call my boss?"

"Trade with me. I'll listen for clues."

They swapped phones, and Beau reported the incident to McCabe, letting him know Hussein had escaped. He gave him an update and their current location. "I will keep you updated, sir." He ended the call and then took his phone back—but Ellie was quiet.

"Austin, are you carrying?" Beau needed a weapon.

"Always. And my backup is in the console. Put a magazine in it."

Beau grabbed the weapon and loaded it.

Austin made another call. "Joe, are you on duty right now?" He paused. "Great. I need help. My sister has been kidnapped, and the guy is taking her north on sixty-nine. They should be entering your jurisdiction within ten minutes. She's driving a light blue Mustang. The man holding a gun on her is a terrorist, who escaped custody. Can you get eyes on her?" He listened. "No—don't step in—just follow at a distance and call me back. Thanks."

"Won't a police car bring attention and put her in more danger?" Beau scanned the area.

"Joe's a savvy detective in an unmarked car. What did McCabe say?" Austin picked up speed.

"No one knew he escaped. McCabe is contacting the powers that be to find out how this happened and calling in forces to apprehend him again."

"Is Ellie saying anything?" Austin changed lanes again to up his speed.

"No, all I hear are traffic noises." And all he had left was a blue stiletto ... Cinderella's glass slipper.

"I'll need gas if we're traveling very far." She stayed in the left lane since it's frowned upon in Texas, hoping to get pulled over. But no luck.

"No need for petrol. We will stop soon." He stared at an app on his phone.

"So, you have a plan?"

"I always have a plan." He watched the side mirror, probably for anyone following them.

Seeing red taillights in front of her, Ellie slowed her speed. "Something has happened up ahead. What do you want me to do?"

Speaking Arabic, Hussein was apparently frustrated at this delay, and Ellie was glad she didn't understand his language. She leaned to the left. "It looks like there's been a wreck."

"Act normal, and don't think of trying anything. I won't

hesitate to shoot you and let Dubois pick up the pieces." He moved his gun out of sight but kept it aimed in her direction.

"There's been a wreck on the interstate ahead of them, and it's slowing them down." Beau fed information to Austin.

Grabbing his phone, Austin made a call. "Joe, they're in the slow traffic that's waiting for a wreck to be moved off the Interstate. Do you know that location?"

"Yeah, it's about six miles ahead of me. I can approach with my lights on since there has been an incident. I'll get eyes on her and call you back."

"Thanks." Austin hung up. "Joe is going to access the situation for us in a few minutes and call me."

"Great." Beau took a deep breath and let it out slowly.

"Hussein threatened Ellie's life if she tried anything."

"She's strong and can hold her own."

"But she hasn't had time to get over the last time she was kidnapped by this monster. Austin, get me close, and I'll take her place. It's me he wants."

"It's too late. Ellie loves you. She'd step in front of a bullet to save your life. We have to let this play out and use our heads as we make a plan for her rescue." Austin reached for his phone. "Joe, sitrep, please." He put the phone on speaker. "How does she look?"

"She's okay. Tense with a tight grip on the wheel, yet focused."

"Can you stay in the area and keep an eye on her?" Austin asked.

"I'll find out who's on the scene leading the investigation and ask to keep the traffic stopped so they can't pass. I'll get back to you."

"Thanks, man. I owe you." He ended the call.

"The Lord sent him to help us today." Beau massaged the back of his neck.

"I think you're right." Austin handed Beau his phone. "Update McCabe."

"Good plan, Bendale." Beau made the call and started a chain of action that would send help immediately. Hussein was surrounded—he just didn't know it yet.

24

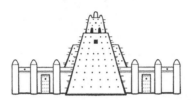

Praying for Ellie's safety and for wisdom, Beau hung on as Austin maneuvered the traffic. "We are getting close. I see taillights up ahead."

Austin's phone rang. "Joe?"

"Man, who's in that Jeep with you? He has clout."

"It's Beau de La Croix, why?"

"A special unit has been deployed, arriving in an ambulance. I'm going to start going from car to car, showing my badge, and updating the drivers. Tactical help will arrive before I reach your sister's car. Local police are working to reroute the traffic to get vehicles out of harm's way. I'll update them about you two approaching the scene. When you get close, park off the road and approach the wreck in stealth mode."

"Thanks, Joe." Austin ended the call. "Clout, huh?" He shook his head, pulled to the right lane, and drove on the shoulder of the road, getting them closer. When he found a secure spot, he stopped the Jeep. "You ready to do this?"

"Let's move." Beau put the borrowed revolver in the waist of his pants and followed Austin down the Texas Interstate. Smelling exhaust, feeling the heat radiating from the tarmac, they moved closer to the scene, with the stealth of lions. Beau scanned the area, acquainting himself with the terrain. "What's this area called?"

"We're just past Kingwood, where Ellie lives. Not far ahead is an area called Roman Forest. There are a few acres of forest between the two."

Sirens wailed in the distance. Finally.

"A man wearing a badge is going from car to car, probably telling them about the delay."

Hussein leaned over to watch the officer. "What is in this area?"

She looked around. "We just passed Kingwood. I know that area, but I haven't been this far north."

Sirens blared as an ambulance passed, followed by two wreckers. "There must be injuries. I can see another ambulance coming behind us." She watched in her rearview mirror. "It could take a while before the traffic gets moving." A helicopter circled overhead.

Hussein perspired, even though the air-conditioner blew cold air. He scoped out the area. "We have to move."

"And go where? The forest?"

He reached over and pushed the button on her seatbelt, releasing it. "Push your seat back as far as it will go."

Ellie did as he demanded.

"I will open my door and pull you out behind me. Don't make a sound, just do as I say. And don't slow me down. We will go through the field. There is traffic past those trees."

Before she could protest, he was out of the car, dragging her across the console.

"*Ow.*" He banged her head on the door frame.

Hussein jabbed the gun into her ribs. "Quiet." He jerked her away from the car and slammed the door. Rushing behind an eighteen-wheeler in the next lane, Hussein paused to look around the truck. "Stay beside me. Understand?"

"Yeah. I understand."

———

Tactical forces have a certain look, a certain stance about them. Beau recognized them immediately. The man leading the charge answered his phone and looked up. "Who is Beau?"

Stepping forward, he said, "That's me."

"My name's Paxton. McCabe wants to have a word." He handed Beau his phone.

"Hello, sir." Beau punched the phone, putting him on speaker.

"Men, the escaped prisoner and his hostage have left the car and are on the run. I have eyes in the sky to follow. Paxton, position a marksman on top of an eighteen-wheeler. Beau, you and Bendale wait until they reach the wooded area before you give chase, so he won't shoot his hostage. Parker, can you get some men on the other side of the woods?"

"Yes, sir." Paxton sent two men with a wrecker driver to the next exit to double back and get eyes on their target.

"Men, we want Hussein alive if possible, but we will not risk Ms. Bendale's life, if it comes to that." He ended the call.

Moving down the road to a cement truck, Beau got down on all fours to see where Hussein and Ellie were. She stumbled as Hussein dragged her along. Beau's blood boiled as he stood and stomped back to where Austin debriefed his officer friend.

"When this debris is cleared, I'll move her car up here with mine," Joe said. "You two be careful. If I can do anything else, just call."

"Thanks, Joe. I'm glad you were on duty." Austin turned to Beau. "Are you ready to go get her?"

Hussein and Ellie neared the forested area.

"More than."

"Lead the way. I've got your back." Austin waited for Beau's signal.

When they disappeared into the woods, Beau took off with Austin on his heels. Keeping Ellie's blonde hair in sight, he plowed forward in stealth mode, keeping noise to a minimum. Beau motioned Austin to the left as he took a path to the right. With Ellie slowing Hussein down, they could flank them.

"Ouch." Ellie rubbed her cheek where a limb scratched her. It was bleeding, but forced to keep up, she trudged on. Trekking through the forest wasn't on her agenda when she chose heels this morning. Running on her toes kept the spikes from sinking, but her calves burned. Her poor shoes. They'd be ruined.

"Faster." He jerked her forward as he risked a look behind them. Apparently not seeing anyone, he kept moving, deeper into the wooded area.

Hussein moved some poison ivy aside, and Ellie bit her tongue to keep from laughing. Accustomed to desert living, he was unprepared for this terrain, giving her an advantage. Hearing passing vehicles, she knew they were near the clearing. If she was to try to slow him down, she had to make a move.

Stopping, he scanned the area behind them, then the path ahead while wiping sweat out of his eyes.

In that split second, Ellie grabbed the gun as she hit him in the ribs with her elbow. He fought her off, keeping the gun in his grip. She rammed his body, knocking him into a tree. He grunted and grabbed her hair. Yelling, she reached for the gun again and almost had it out of his sweaty hand when it went off

—hitting her in the left shoulder. She screamed and hit the ground.

Arabic cuss words spewed from his mouth as he kicked Ellie in the side with his steel-toed boot. She heard the sound of her bones breaking. Ellie gasped, unable to scream.

Hussein aimed his gun at her head. A bullet hit Hussein's arm. As he howled, Beau sprang out of nowhere and slammed him to the ground. The gun landed three feet away and slid under a bush. Hussein came up fighting as he reached for the weapon. Beau slammed him against a tree grabbing his wounded arm. The military peronnel closed in around them with their weapons trained on the escaped prisoner.

Hussein's eyes darted from man to man. Raising his hands in surrender, he stood and huffed a breath of defeat. Beau grabbed one wrist and put it behind his back. A soldier handed him cuffs, and Beau slapped them on Hussein, who let out a shriek.

Austin rushed forward to check on Ellie as Hussein was taken into custody. Her tears flowed into her hair as she lay on the forest floor.

"Now you show up." As Austin knelt beside her in the dirt, she gripped his shirt. "I tried to stop him."

"You did great. I'm proud of you, Sis." Slipping his hand under her shoulder, he examined the wound. "You've got a bullet in your shoulder." He put pressure on her wound to stop the bleeding.

"*Ouch.* Easy there."

"I've got to stop the blood flow. We'll get you out of here in a few minutes." With his left hand, he touched her bloody cheek. "That may need a stitch or two. What about your ribs? I saw him kick you." Austin placed his free hand on her side, moving his fingers along her ribs. "At least two of them are broken. Does it hurt?"

Ellie scrunched her eyes. "Only when I breathe."

"Then stop it at once, Elliana." He teased.

"Yes, Mother." She laughed.

"Be still."

"Gladly." She closed her eyes. "Where's Beau?"

"He's with Hussein. The police are taking custody of him as we speak. He won't get away again."

"Was Beau wounded? I heard a gunshot."

"No. A sniper grazed Hussein. Your hero is still in one piece."

Two men approached carrying a gurney. They sat it on the ground next to Ellie and got to work, assessing her condition. Austin stepped back, giving them access.

Yellow crime scene tape stretched around the perimeter as police swarmed. With Hussein secure and the threat over, Beau hurried to Ellie.

They lifted Ellie onto the gurney when he reached her.

"Are you okay?"

A tear escaped from her eye. He caught it with his finger.

"I will be. Is he gone?"

"Yes, he's gone." He held her hand as the EMTs carried the gurney out of the forest.

When they reached the road, the techs released the wheels and loaded her into the ambulance.

"The shot is lodged in her shoulder, she has broken ribs, a possible concussion, and a cut on her face, but nothing life-threatening." Austin stopped next to Beau and gripped his shoulder.

"Thanks for your help, Bendale."

"You're welcome. Actually, it was good to see you in action." Austin stepped closer to the ambulance. "Ellie, did you leave your keys in your car?"

"Yeah. I don't normally do that, but I was a little busy being kidnapped."

Beau laughed. "She hasn't lost her sense of humor." He stepped around an EMT and into the ambulance. "I'm so glad you're okay. The Lord was with us."

"Yes, He was."

"Is this a habit—this getting kidnapped gig? You've got to quit scaring me."

She attempted a smile, but it obviously hurt too much.

"The EMTs are wanting in here. Austin and I will follow the ambulance to the hospital." He reached down and kissed her softly.

"Are you catching your flight tonight?" She grabbed his arm.

"No. I'm not leaving you like this. Rest now. Let's get you to the hospital." He kissed her again and went to find her Mustang.

While Ellie was in surgery, her parents paced the waiting room. Debriefing from today's incident, Austin and Beau gave the details of the kidnapping through to the apprehension of Hussein with Paxton, Joe, and McCabe via a video call in a hospital conference room.

"Gentlemen, I applaud your quick actions today that put Dhakir Hussein back behind bars where he belongs. I'm sorry Ms. Bendale was wounded but glad she survived another face-to-face with this dangerous man. She has grit, I'll give you that. Hang on to her, de La Croix."

"That's my plan, sir."

"I'm sending a report of today's incident to your superior officers. You worked as a team and accomplished your mission. Thank you." With that, he ended the call.

The men rose to leave the room. Austin walked out with, Joe, his detective friend.

"Paxton, I have to say, I was really glad to see the military on the scene when Ellie was in danger." Beau shook his hand. "Hussein's purpose today was to kill me. That sniper's shot turned the tables and gave me the opportunity I needed to neutralize the threat. Thanks. When you get back to base, tell the guys I appreciate their help today."

"Will do." Joe saluted and Beau returned the gesture before the man exited the hospital doors.

A few minutes later, a physician came through double doors. "Bendale family?"

Joining Anne and Bruce Bendale, Beau stood at attention awaiting the report.

"How is she, Dr. Wilson?" Anne wrung her hands as Bruce put his arm around her shoulders.

"Your daughter is a strong young lady. We removed the bullet from her left shoulder and had to set two ribs on her right side. One more is fractured but didn't need to be set. She has a mild concussion, and I called in a plastic surgeon to attend to the laceration on her face. Her wounds will cause pain for a while, but she'll make a complete recovery."

Bruce thanked the doctor and asked more questions.

"Austin said you put yourself in harm's way today for Ellie." Anne put her hand on Beau's arm. "Thank you."

"I'd die for your daughter, ma'am."

Austin hurried into the waiting room and straight to his mom. "Any news?"

Anne gave the doctor's report to her son, adding some drama to the details.

"Why don't we get something to eat?" Bruce said as he

joined them. "She'll be in recovery until she wakes up, then moved to a room in a couple of hours. We can see her then."

"You're staying here, aren't you?" Austin looked at Beau.

"Can you bring me something when you come back?"

"Sure, but I don't know what you like to eat, so you'll have to eat what I bring you." Austin laughed.

With a smirk on his face, Beau replied, "I don't get mad, I get even." He smiled.

The hint of a new day sent tones of pink and orange through the blinds. It took Ellie a few minutes to realize where she was. Looking around the room, she spied her mother sleeping on a couch. On the other side, her hunky hero snoozed in a chair with his hand on her bed. She slipped her fingers into his, and his eyes opened slowly.

"Hi, beautiful." He sat forward, leaning closer he ran his finger down her cheek.

"Hi, yourself." She licked her lips.

"You thirsty?" He reached for a small pitcher of iced water and poured her a glass. After putting a straw in it, he held it to her mouth.

"Thanks. So, am I going to live? I like this pain medicine."

Beau laughed, kissed her hand, and gave her the doctor's report. "Your left shoulder and your right side will both give you pain for a few weeks. I'm sorry."

"What about my face?" She narrowed her eyes.

"Your doctor called in a plastic surgeon. After another procedure, you'll be fine. Your face will be perfect again."

"Okay." Her brow furrowed. "Hussein is in custody, right?"

"That's right. He can't hurt you again." He leaned close and kissed her softly. "Don't worry. He won't escape this time."

"It was scary being in his clutches again." Her eyes filled. "How did you find me?"

"With your help. That was smart leaving your phone on. I called Austin, and we followed your cues."

"So, do you like my brother?"

"Yes, I do. He's a good man."

A nurse entered. "Oh, you're awake. How are we feeling this morning?"

"Fine, as long as I don't move."

"I need to check your incisions."

Beau stood. "I'm going to find some coffee. I'll be back." He squeezed her toes, not the ones he'd broken, before leaving the room.

Punching a number into his phone, he put it to his ear and pressed the elevator button.

"de La Croix, how's that pretty blonde of yours?" McCabe asked.

"I hope I didn't wake you, sir. I wanted to give you an update before your meeting this morning. She is in a lot of pain, but will make a full recovery."

"I'm glad to hear it. About the meeting, I was able to move it to Thursday morning. Can you fly in on Wednesday night?"

"Sure, I'll get my flight rescheduled and see you Thursday." Beau stepped into the elevator.

"It's already done. Check your email. Hussein is in shackles. Give my best to Ms. Bendale. Buy the girl some flowers." McCabe ended the call.

Following the smell of dark roast, he stepped off the elevator and stopped at Starbucks. Taking a seat, he surveyed the area. A worker unlocked a flower shop and flipped the sign to *OPEN*. His boss was a wise man—a wise man indeed.

"Can I go home? I only have a little time before my boyfriend has to catch a plane." Ellie pleaded with the doctor.

"Not until after your physical therapy session. You must have some training so you can navigate these next three weeks while your ribs heel." Dr. Wilson checked her monitors and wrote on her chart.

"But I'm feeling much better. I'll be fine on my own. My mother's maid can assist me, and I have a roommate at my beck and call." *With Beau delivering cuisine on a regular basis, I'll be fine.*

"How about I ask if the therapists can do your session in your room, and we can get you out of here before dinner this evening?"

Trying to clap her hands brought pain shooting through her left shoulder and right side. She put her hand on the bandage on her face. "*Ouch.*"

The doctor put the rail down on the side of her bed. "Can you sit up for me and hang your feet over the side?"

Her eyes widened as she pushed the sheet down and pulled her right arm back, propping herself up a bit. Gritting her teeth, she stilled, willing the pain to subside. When she started trembling with weakness, she eased herself back onto her pillow. "Doc, I think I'll need that therapy." She blew out a breath.

Smiling, he hung her chart on the end of her bed. "I'll order that session." He left the room as Beau entered.

"I'm back." He placed a bouquet of pink roses on her tray.

"Thanks, McGarrett. Those are beautiful."

He grabbed her hand, weaving their fingers together. "What did your doctor have to say?"

"After a physical therapy session, I'll get released—probably before dinner."

"Great. You want Italian or Mexican for your celebratory dinner at home?"

"Italian, please. I love lasagna."

"Is she ordering dinner?" Austin entered and handed Beau his coffee. "Don't let her wrap you around her little finger."

Ellie held the bandage on her face and laughed.

"It's too late." Beau smiled. "Hey, can I trade vehicles with you, Austin?"

"Is something wrong with my car?"

"Nothing. Your car is great, but it would be easier to let you step out of his Jeep instead of pulling you out of your 'Stang."

"Wow, You're handsome *and* smart." Ellie winked at Beau.

"Yep, I was right. You're putty in her hands, de La Croix." Austin laughed. "Get me some chicken alfredo, and I'll meet you there to help get her into the house."

But all Ellie could think about was Beau leaving. Even if it wasn't for long.

"Hey, why the tears?" Jocelyn hurried to Ellie's bed and sat beside her.

"He's gone back to D.C. I missed so much time with him by being on pain meds."

"But he'll be back as soon as he can."

"It could be weeks. They're sending him to France for some meetings."

"That will give you time to recover. I heard you cry out in the night. Back-to-back kidnappings have taken a toll." She handed Ellie a tissue. "I'll get you a Coke to drink during your counseling session with Jessica."

"Hey, aren't you supposed to fly this afternoon?"

"I traded with Alicia. I fly on Saturday. I wanted to keep playing nursemaid for a few more days."

"You're worried about me, aren't you?"

"Yeah. You were kidnapped and shot. Leaving you alone

wasn't an option, and your mother wanted to move in, which is out of the question." She stood. "I'll get that Coke."

Her friend returned, then left her alone again.

Ellie took a drink of her favorite beverage, then snuggled down in her covers and dialed Jessica's number. Within thirty minutes the counselor had her reliving the trauma she'd suffered through. She was patient with Ellie's crying jags and walked her through the pain and intense fear pointing her to the ultimate source of peace. Healing came slowly. It felt good for the grip of the trauma to loosen its hold on her emotions.

———

Hurrying through an airport took Beau back to the first time he laid eyes on the beautiful blonde who captured his heart. He couldn't wait to have her in his arms again. Three weeks was too long to be so far away. Grabbing his duffle from the carousel, he hurried to the curb in hopes of grabbing a cab to get him to Kingwood, to Ellie.

He shouldered his backpack, picked up his duffle, then turned to look for the proper exit—but halted. Ellie stood waiting for him, her blonde hair glistened under the lights, her dress fit her curves perfectly, and her smile was radiant. She walked toward him but stopped a few feet away.

Dropping his bags, he kept her gaze. "Afraid to come closer?"

She shook her head. "As a matter of fact, I am. You see, I have a history of getting my toes broken by handsome Frenchmen in airports."

"Is that so? Maybe you need a bodyguard."

"Oh, I had one of those too. It ended with me losing."

"Losing what?" He eased closer.

"My heart."

"That sounds serious." And closer.

"Yes, I'm very serious."

"About what?" He cupped her face in his hands.

"You." She leaned in and met his lips.

He lengthened the kiss before pulling back to see her face. "I missed you."

"I missed you, too, Macho Man. My Mustang is by the curb."

"Not afraid of getting towed?"

"No. The officer on duty knows my dad. Ready to go?"

"More than ready." He kept his arm around her, and she nestled into his side as they exited.

He put his bags in the trunk. "Are you okay to be driving?"

"Yeah." She didn't meet his gaze.

He slipped into her Mustang. "Ellie, do you have a doctor's release yet?"

"Not yet, but I didn't want anyone to come with me to the airport."

Reaching over, he cut the engine. "Let's switch drivers."

After sliding in, Ellie kept him talking as he drove. "So, did you get everything done that you needed to finish while you were in Paris?"

"Yeah. I packed and shipped some crates to D.C., signed my flat over to my brother, visited my foster parents, and completed the paperwork ending my assignment."

"You accomplished a lot in a short time."

"Missing you made me hurry." He squeezed her hand.

Once at her condo, he followed as Ellie unlocked the front door and disarmed the security. "Welcome back, Beau."

When the door clicked behind him, Beau wrapped his arms around her and kissed her with the pent-up passion building in his heart.

Putting her hands on his chest, she pushed back a little. "Careful there, Rambo. I'm still sore."

"Oh, I'm sorry. Did I hurt you?"

"No. Just don't squeeze me too hard." She leaned close and kissed him tenderly. "I love you, de La Croix."

"And I love you."

Motioning toward the living room, she pulled away. "I'll get us something to drink. It's time for my medicine. Then we can talk."

"No, you sit, and I'll get us some Cokes."

After taking her meds, she faced him and folded her leg under her on the white leather sofa. "You look like you have something you want to talk about, your new assignment, our future, my tendency to get kidnapped—so, shoot." She slapped her hand over her mouth. "Maybe I shouldn't say shoot to a military hero."

He laughed and kissed the back of her hand, then laced their fingers together. "Seriously, E, what is the doctor saying about how you're healing?"

"He says I'm doing good. Right on schedule. I might be released on my next therapy visit. Then, I'll go see the plastic surgeon to schedule a procedure to fix the scar on my face. The tenderness in the shoulder and the soreness of my ribs slow me down." She took a drink of her soda.

"You scared me." He moved closer. "Can I make a request? Could you curtail your life-and-death scenarios, please?"

"I'll try. But you're such a handsome hero."

"And you're a beautiful damsel in distress and a joy to rescue, but I'd like to discuss a long-term relationship—a happily ever after." Beau moved her hair away from her forehead in a tender move.

"Okay, no more getting kidnapped, I promise."

"I have a question."

"Ask away."

"Can I use your keys?" Beau held out his hand.

"They're on the table in the foyer. Are you going somewhere?"

"No. I picked up something for you in Paris." He winked and went out the front door. After returning, he stood by the fireplace with his hands behind his back. "I racked my brain to try to find a perfect gift for you. It wasn't easy, but when I saw this, I knew you would love it and would understand my meaning behind it."

Taking a moment to stand, Ellie took in a nervous breath. "If you bought it for me—I know I'll love it."

With a long package in his grasp, he stepped closer and placed his gift in her hands.

She gingerly tore the wrapping paper at one end and gripped the handle of an umbrella. "An umbrella? Are you expecting rain?" She met his gaze.

"Keep going." His lip hitched in a smile.

She pulled the umbrella out of the wrapping. "It's red!" She saw the tag and looked at Beau. "It's a red heart-shaped umbrella." Tears welled up in her eyes. *Does this mean what I think it means?*

"I want to grant your wish of a honeymoon in Paris. I knew you'd need a red umbrella—"

Planting her hands on his muscular chest, she blurted out her answer. "Yes! Yes! Yes! I'll marry you!"

"But I haven't asked you the question yet!" He knelt on one knee and held up an oval solitaire engagement ring that sparkled in the glow of sunset streaming through the front windows. "Elliana Bendale, will you marry me?"

Hesitating, she tapped her finger on her chin as if in thought, drawing out the moment, obviously enjoying the magic.

"I want to be the guy kissing you behind the red umbrella in front of the Eiffel Tower."

"Yes, Beau, I will marry you." Ellie grinned as Beau slipped the ring on her finger. "It's gorgeous."

He kissed her hand and stood. She leaned forward for another kiss—Beau stopped her progress.

"Wait, we need the full effect." He opened the umbrella and carefully pulled her close. "Now, where were we?"

She slowly eased her arms up around his neck and grinned. "I was kissing my fiancé."

"Well, please continue." Beau smiled as he captured her lips for a lingering kiss that would take them into their happily ever after ... and it was *perfect*.

THE END

ACKNOWLEDGMENTS

I love this story, and I'm so excited to bring you the second novel in the African Skies Series. So many wonderful people helped on this novel's journey.

Learning to write Christian Fiction under the amazing Susan May Warren at Novel Academy has given me the tools to get words onto the page. Her team of talented authors/teachers, Rachel Hauck, Lisa Jordan, Tari Farris, Alena Tauriainen, and Beth Vogt are truly wonderful. I'm forever grateful for all their expertise.

Donna Yarborough has walked this writing journey with me for several years. Together we have braved writing conferences, entered writing contests, and kept each other encouraged to create prose to please the masses. Thanks, my friend.

To my tribe, Shelayne, Sharee, Shontel, Sheri, Johnnie, Jana, Judi, Karen, Darlene, Ramona, Carol, and Nina. You ladies have prodded me to keep writing. I appreciate each of you so much. To Lisa, you give the best book signing events. My MBT huddles have encouraged me during this writing process. Every prayer is appreciated. I love you, ladies.

Having great parents has given me an amazing advantage. Thanks, Mom, & Dad. The work ethic you taught us girls set me on a path of personal success. The Christian foundation you built our family on has remained with me. I'm so blessed.

I have the best family. Their encouragement has been invaluable and much appreciated. My sons-in-law have supported me, each in their own way. My girls are talented women who have made me so proud. And my magnificent seven who put joy in my heart and a spring in my steps. I love you Madi, Jake, Finley, Charlotte, Judah, Blakely, and Lyda.

I'm so grateful for Shannon Vannatter, a friend as well as an author extraordinaire. She has read this manuscript several times and her editing expertise has taken my work to a new level. She introduced me to Scrivenings Press, my new home in the Publishing world. I owe you, Shannon.

I'm so grateful for my friend, Linda Fulkerson. She's an author, an editor, she's my publisher, and the owner of Scrivenings Press. I love the book covers she creates, the encouragement she offers, and the constant support she gives her authors. Her line edit polished my prose. I am thankful to be part of her publishing family.

To my Lord, thank You for the call You placed on my life so many years ago. I'm humbled to share the Good News through speaking, singing, and written words using the power of story. You have led my path and been with me every step of my journey. I'm eternally grateful.

AUTHOR'S NOTE

In Escape From Timbuktu, Ellie reaches for her dreams of becoming a photojournalist with a popular magazine. A handsome French-speaking interpreter helps her get the story and the photos she needs until terrorists wreak havoc and have them running for their lives.

The enemy of our souls is constantly looking for opportunities to thwart the Lord's plans for our lives. We must take the scripture found in Proverbs 3:5-6 as a word to stand upon. "Trust in the Lord with all thine heart and lean not on thine own understanding. In all thy ways acknowledge Him, and He will direct thy paths." KJV

I've tried to fix things on my own, leaning on my abilities, and have failed. Dear friend, I want to encourage you. When you're faced with fiery trials, trust the Lord and allow Him to direct your path. You will see the Hand of the Lord in your situation every time.

Thank you for reading my second novel.

Blessings,
Shirley

Four Ways to Support Your Favorite Author

1. TELL OTHERS ABOUT THE BOOK

Word of mouth is still the best way that readers to discover new authors.

2. WRITE REVIEWS

Please go to Amazon, Goodreads, or BookBub and leave a review. It encourages others to buy my novel.

3. ASK YOUR LIBRARY TO CARRY MY BOOK

Many libraries will purchase books at their patron's request.

4. GIVE MY NOVEL AS A GIFT

ABOUT THE AUTHOR

Shirley Gould is an inspirational speaker, an African missionary, and the author of The Sahar of Zanzibar. She's the founder of Kenya's Kids Home for Street Children, an orphanage in Kenya. Shirley has written nonfiction for thirty years and is presently writing Christian fiction novels. She lives in the Nashville, Tennessee area. Follow her writing journey and watch for the sequel's release at shirleygould.org.

Shirley Praying

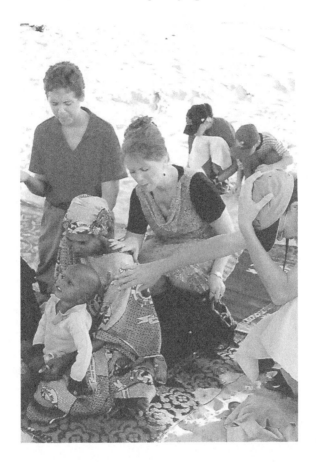

This is Shirley praying for a direct descendant of Mohammed. The Lord healed her and she went home smiling and thankful to be introduced to the God that heals!

J.R. Gould

This is JR standing by the completed roof of the only church and Christian school in Timbuktu where Muslim children are taught to read using the Bible as a textbook.

MORE FROM THE AFRICAN SKIES SERIES

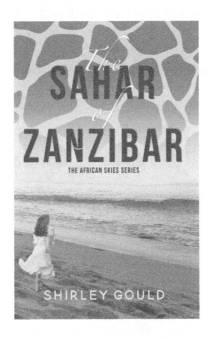

The Sahar of Zanzibar

The African Skies Series - Book One

In a scary case of mistaken identity, Olivia Stone is threatened by Aga Kahn, a powerful Indian ruler, because she could pass as the twin of the missionary's deceased wife. Kahn calls her the Sahar of Zanzibar, who has returned from the grave to torment him and demands that she leave the island or face his wrath. She'd come to exotic Zanzibar in search of adventure, but she experiences much more.

A handsome widower, Missionary Eli Deckland, steps between Olivia and the angry Indian, rescuing her. There's an instant connection between Olivia and Eli that escalates when he comes to her rescue again and again. Amid the chaos, Eli tries to prove Kahn murdered his late wife. After several attempts on Olivia's life, she's kidnapped. Eli joins the police to find her before it's too late.

As every moment passes, Olivia's life is in more danger. Will she be saved in time? If she is rescued, would it work between her and Eli? With an ocean keeping them apart, will their feelings fade? The answer is in the African skies ...

https://scrivenings.link/thesaharofzanzibar

YOU MAY ALSO LIKE ...

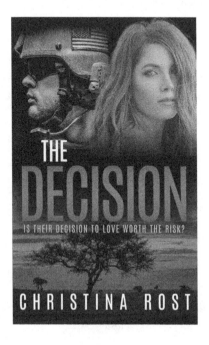

The Decision

by Christina Rost

Running from her grief, interior designer Ava Stewart makes a hasty decision to join a missionary group heading to Uganda. She's in the country only a few days before tragedy strikes, and a mistaken identity leaves her with an uncertain outcome.

Special Operator Blake Martin is assigned to a humanitarian mission when he's captured by a group of armed men. Wounded and miles away from his team, Blake's brought to Ava, and she's ordered to care for him.

Thrown together in chaos, with the threat of danger pressing in from all sides, Ava and Blake are forced to rely on each other—and God— to escape. An undeniable bond is formed during their flight to safety, but opening their hearts to love carries its own risk. A risk they aren't sure they're willing to take.

Now, miles apart and living separate lives, they need to decide if the connection they shared in the untamed, wilds of Uganda is strong enough to confront the future. A future where Ava's fragile heart and Blake's hazardous job collide, and only God knows the outcome.

Get your copy here:

https://scrivenings.link/thedecision

Scrivenings
PRESS
Quench your thirst for story.
www.ScriveningsPress.com

Stay up-to-date on your favorite books and authors with our free e-newsletters.

ScriveningsPress.com

Made in United States
Orlando, FL
03 November 2023

38559962R00166